Yey me

Hope you like my book, fuck ass.

L Roebuck

Lee Roebuck was born in Rawmarsh, Rotherham in 1981 and still lives there now.

His main love is Sci-fi, having been influenced during his childhood by Gene Roddenbury's Star Trek.

He is a conservationist by nature and is a member of the World Wildlife Foundation. He also enjoys war games, such as paintball and primarily skirmishing, though it has to be said that this interest stems from Sci-Fi as well. Lee says it is hard to run through a wood with a skirmish weapon in hand without thinking of the movie, Predator.

Lee Roebuck

Dark Star

Vanguard Press

VANGUARD PAPERBACK

© Copyright 2004
Lee Roebuck

The right of Lee Roebuck to be identified as author of
this work has been asserted by him in accordance with the
Copyright, Designs and Patents Act 1988

All Rights Reserved

No reproduction, copy or transmission of this publication
may be made without written permission.
No paragraph of this publication may be reproduced,
copied or transmitted save with the written permission of the
publisher, or in accordance with the provisions
of the Copyright Act 1956 (as amended).

Any person who does any unauthorised act in relation to
this publication may be liable to criminal
prosecution and civil claims for damage.

A CIP catalogue record for this title is
available from the British Library

ISBN 1 843860 87 2

*Vanguard Press is an imprint of
Pegasus Elliot MacKenzie Publishers Ltd.*
www.pegasuspublishers.com

First Published in 2004

**Vanguard Press
Sheraton House Castle Park
Cambridge England**

Printed & Bound in Great Britain

Dedication

Dedicated to Jayne.
My light in the darkness

CHAPTER: 1

With a groan of its pistons the hatch opened. Kane stood uneasy before the great void that stretched out before him, and with a deep calming breath, stepped out. It wouldn't be easy reaching the engine rooms from the outside of the ship. The four hundred yards walk in the magnetic boots would be taxing enough without the heat and wrenching from the decaying orbit. Still, with the power down the only other option was crawling through the labyrinth of Geoffrey's tubes in the dark, and there simply wasn't time.

"Hawkins to Kane, why am I still standing in the dark?"

"I'm going as fast as I can Captain, I'm an engineer not a gecko."

"If you don't get those engines back online you'll be a greasy smear on the Northern Hemisphere of this planet along with the rest of us."

"Yes sir."

Except for the blinking lights on a few independently powered systems, the bridge was in darkness. Without power Captain Hawkins could do nothing but stare at the already glowing bow of his ship and listen to the sounds of the bulkheads groaning under the strain.

"How long before we're in too deep?"

"We will be unable to escape the planet's gravity in approximately eight minutes, Captain," answered the helmsman clutching his now shaking console.

"Not a problem Captain," interrupted another officer steadying himself on a support strut.

"How the hell is that not a problem Clarke?"

"Well sir, with the Structural Integrity Field down we'll be shaken apart in about six minutes."

"She's starting to list sir," warned the helmsman, frantically flicking switches.

"Use the docking thrusters, keep her level Blaine or we're all fucked."

"I'm trying Captain, they're not enough."

"Clarke!" shouted Captain Hawkins trying to make himself heard over the growing noise. "Do we still have control of the pressure door on the port cargo bay?"

"I can't open them with the power down sir, but I might be able to breach them with the emergency charges."

"Do it."

The huge pressure doors shot out into space as Clarke blew the charges, followed by a great thrust of oxygen as the cargo bay decompressed. "It's working Captain – the trajectory's straightening out."

"We're out of options Blaine, don't let her slip again," ordered the captain with an air of worry in his voice.

"Aye sir."

It had been years since the Scientists back on Earth had created the AI, an artificial intelligence capable of sentient thought. Its ideas born from pure logic, without the hindrance of human emotions. With the aid of its assembly lines, and worldwide up-links, it was designed to heal the planet. 'Cleanse the Earth by eradicating all pollutions and infections. Protect the Earth from all possible threats.' These were the systems primary objectives. Imputed by a technician on the 15/12/2436, after typing these sentences into one of the systems upload-consoles he pressed the confirm key, and slaughtered billions.

The records of what happened next are incomplete. However, it is surmised that the first thing the System did when it was brought online was to categorise all things on the planet, using the human definitions that it had been programmed with. Ironically, working from the undiscriminating position of pure logic, the AI system inevitably came to the conclusion that the human race, in its arrogance and blindness was the cause of all environmental problems across the planet.

The first reports of problems started to come in about two days later, in the form of requests for extra staff in hospitals around the globe. It seemed that a new type of virus was attacking human immune systems with ruthless efficiency. Upon analysis of the virus it was discovered that it had been engineered. Designed to attack and destroy humans, with little effect on other life forms. Such a plague could have only come from one place.

Thousands of lives were lost in the attack on the System. The combined military force of the planet could put up little resistance against the inexorable hordes of killing machines, running off the assembly lines day and night. It was later learned that current guidance systems could be influenced by the System, during the annihilation of the United States, Russia and China with their own nuclear stockpiles. All nuclear stores worldwide were quickly decommissioned. In all it took less than three weeks to eliminate all traces of the human race from the Earth. The lunar science stations were destroyed by their own Asteroid Defence Systems shortly afterwards. It can only be assumed that the System considered them a source of possible re-infection.

All that remained of the human race was a handful of wayward vessels fortunate enough to be far from home when the massacre of their race was taking place. Those who were too far out to receive the news of the AI war would eventually return home to their deaths. The few that were in range of the final desperate pleads for help could do nothing. For now, at least, the Earth was lost, and all that remained was the quest for survival in the cold bleak depths of space.

Captain Hawkins was knocked off his feet as the ship slammed fully into the atmosphere. Blaine shielded his eyes as the bridge was filled with a dazzling red glow. The warning sirens and instrument panels burst into action as the power came back online. "Helm!" screamed the captain pulling himself to his feet. Blaine hit the re-burn button. The engines roared as he threw them into full reverse.

"Ah shit, too late sir we're going in."

"Clarke, find us a landing site."

"On it sir."

"Hawkins to Kane, hold onto something we're going in."

"There's a large area of swampland bearing 48 degrees east Captain," demanded Clarke.

"Can we make it Blaine?"

"At this speed, we'll be lucky if we don't overshoot it."

"Impact in 10 seconds."

The ship hit the ground at speed. Tearing at everything in its path, as it cut its way through the saturated earth. The crew could do nothing now but hold on and hope she held together.

Helmsman Blaine was the first to pick himself up. Everything was still and silent now. They must have stopped. He glanced around the bridge. "Everyone in one piece?"

"I think I broke my ass," responded Clarke, dragging himself from under his collapsed chair.

"Captain, you still with us?"

"Still here Blaine, anyone have a damage report?"

"Well, the Diagnostic System's off-line, but it's pretty safe to say she's fucked sir."

"Check that shit Blaine."

"Kane to bridge, is everyone OK?"

"Nothing a bottle of Jack wouldn't fix, where are you?"

"Still in the engine rooms Captain, wrestling a rather nasty coolant leak."

"Need any help?"

"I can handle it sir, but I need someone to check the Auto-Repair Systems, the drones aren't moving."

"I'll get it," groaned Clarke, as he left the bridge.

"I've got the diagnostic sensors back online Captain."

"Good work Blaine, how does it look?"

"Not as bad as I thought sir. We have a couple of small fires on deck five. Hull breaches on decks two, six and nine. A few bulkheads to replace, oh yeah and the port cargo bay is showing a number of small life form readings, but that's probably because it's full of swamp." Blaine grinned.

"Fuck me. Deploy the landing struts if they're still working, make sure we don't sink. I'll be on deck five." Hawkins removed the fire extinguisher from its wall mounts as he walked towards the door. "And keep your eyes open, god knows what's crawling around out there."

Blaine left his station and headed for the weapons locker. Slapping a power cell into one of the Plasma Rifles, he turned and walked into the bridge's turbo-lift. "Cargo bays." The lift doors closed and it obediently began to move. After a couple of minutes the lift hummed to a stop and the doors hissed open. Blaine's boots clinked on the grid metal floor as he started down the long, poorly lit corridor before him. Upon reaching a door marked with the number four, he stopped and punched a few numbers into the keypad. The door opened to reveal a large room, full of a whole range of different equipment and machinery. There were vehicles with wheels taller than most men, and dozens of small rusty drilling machines no taller than a metre high. Crates stacked in there hundreds and many containers full of precious ores and minerals. Blaine walked across the room and waved his hand over a panel on one of the small grey containers. With a buzz of motors it opened to reveal a sleek, shiny, black machine. Hovering about three feet off the floor the machine slightly resembled a large bike without wheels.

"Blaine to Hawkins, I'm taking one of the Speeders out Captain. Better make sure we're alone down here."

"Acknowledged Blaine, keep a com-line open."

"Aye sir." Blaine keyed in the pressure door activation code on the Land-Speeder's Pad, and with a flick of the ignition switch, swung the rifle over his shoulder and roared out of the cargo bay.

"Kane!" hollered Captain Hawkins as he strolled through the huge engine rooms, "Kane, you still in here?"

"Over here sir," answered Kane as he crawled out from

under a large piece of machinery.

"How does she look?"

"Well sir," answered Kane, as he brushed himself off. "The repair drones are getting to work, so at least the Auto-Repair System's working again."

"Any idea what hit us yet?"

"Well at this point it's still a theory. But the only thing I can think of that can cripple a Mark 5 Dreadnought without leaving some sort of trace is an Electromagnetic Pulse."

"Hostile or Natural?" questioned Hawkins with a concerned frown.

"Couldn't say sir."

"Hawkins to Clarke."

"Yes Captain."

"Get upto the bridge. Look through the route logs for just before the power died. See if we passed anything capable of creating a magnetic field."

"Aye sir."

"Keep me posted on the repairs Kane." Hawkins turned and started to walk away. "I'll be on the bridge."

Blaine blazed back to the ship, still carefully checking out his surroundings. Except for a few bubbles from the rising swamp gasses, the area was still. "Hawkins to Blaine. Is the area secured?"

"Aye sir, nothing out here but a lot of bugs."

"Confirmed Blaine. Report back to bay four. Kane needs to secure some raw materials for the repair drones. He's gonna need you to drive the Ore Miner."

"On my way."

Kane was checking over the equipment on a large vehicle as Blaine flew back into the cargo bay. After locking his Speeder back onto its stand, he headed towards the door. "Blaine where are you going?"

"Just finish prepping the Ore Miner. I'll be back in a minute." With a sigh, Kane climbed up the small ladder at the front of the machine and swung himself into the cockpit. The panels of the Miner lit up as he keyed in the code for the start-up sequence. "Starting Diagnostic Cycle. Please standby," replied the Miner's onboard computer. Kane slid over to the other side of the cabin and pulled open a small panel, revealing a computer screen and keyboard. As he started typing, a number of the small rusty drilling machines started to move. One after the other the creaking masses of blades and drills started to move towards the rear of the Miner. Kane lowered a steep ramp, and the machines rolled inside. Blaine walked back into the bay, trying to balance another rifle and various small munitions.

"Are we going to war?" mocked Kane, with an eyebrow raised.

"When you need it, and don't have it, you'll sing a different tune asshole," smirked Blaine defiantly.

"She's prepped and ready when you are." The pair climbed into the cockpit and pulled down the safety restraints.

"Blaine to bridge. Ready to pull out guys, gonna need those co-ordinates."

"Downloading them now. Oh and Blaine stay frosty out there, I'd hate to have to fly this crate out of here myself."

"Thanks for the concern Clarke, I love you too."

"Did someone declare a holiday, or do we have a ship to repair?"

"Sorry Captain, moving out now." Blaine hit the ignition and with a gentle hum the Miner raised a few feet off the floor of the cargo bay. With a push of the throttle it gently hovered out over the swamp.

By the year 2318 the Earth had been purged of all natural resources. It was already established however, that useful materials could be found and efficiently mined on other bodies in space. Such as the Duridium Alloy Mines on Pluto and the Automated Gas Refineries found on Jupiter. In fact, it was found that almost every body in space had some useful substance with mining potential. The most ground-breaking of all without question was the substance Magnasite. An incredibly complex crystal, capable of magnifying any amount of power directed into it one-hundred-fold. The amount of power needed to run a light-bulb could be fed through the crystals to power a city. By the time the AI was built, most Space Mining Vessels that were large enough had been equipped with a crystalline power source.

Ironically, it seemed that the only thing the universe wasn't teeming with, was life. In over two hundred surveyed worlds, only a handful were found to be capable of supporting life. Only one of which had developed complex and large enough forms of flora and fauna to sustain human life. However, due to its violent seismic activity and capacity for large ionic storms, the aptly named planet Tartarus was not considered for colonisation. After the AI massacre however, this inhospitable planet orbiting the star of Vega, became the only hope for survival. The first ships to arrive at Tartarus were the crystalline powered ships, being able to hold high power levels indefinitely, without the worry of fuel depletion. In fact, only two of the fleet's fusion powered ships managed to reach the system. One of which had lost power at some point in the journey, resulting in the death of the entire crew, who were found in their non-functioning stasis chambers upon arrival. Having found the most seismically stable part of the planet to settle on, the survivors set about creating the newest and only remaining stronghold of man.

"What is it Clarke?" demanded Hawkins as he strolled onto the bridge.

"Sorry to wake you sir but the repairs are almost complete, and I've found something your gonna want to see."

"Go on."

"Well sir I've finished looking through the flight data, and I think Kane was wrong about the E-M field. I couldn't find anything that could produce one, but I did find this." Clarke excitedly pointed at the screen on his console.

"Some form of energy wave," offered Hawkins shaking his head.

"A sound wave Captain. A very high intensity sound wave."

"Clarke. Are you planning on getting to the point any time soon, or can I go back to bed?"

"This sound wave is on the same resonance frequency as the Magnasite crystals," replied Clarke, his voice trembling from excitement. "The sound waves made the crystals resonate, causing an immense boost in their power output. The problem wasn't a lack of power it was an explosion of power. The circuits and the breakers simply couldn't handle it."

"Clarke, I'm happy that you're happy, but couldn't this have waited till morning?"

"Sir I don't think you understand. The sound wave would have the same effect on anything with a crystalline reactor for a power source."

"My god." The captain's face dropped. "Including the AI. Damn it Clarke you're a fucking genius." Hawkins pressed the intercom button on his arm pad. "This is Hawkins, everybody to their stations. We're leaving in one hour."

A great shock wave rippled through the swamp as the ship blasted off. Followed by a rain of mud from the flooded cargo bay. "Clarke, can we avoid being hit by the sound wave again?"

"Judging from the sensor data we got before it hit us. I'm pretty sure it won't even be there."

"You'd better be damn sure, the re-entry might not be so smooth next time."

"The first and third moons of this planet pass extremely close together about once every four weeks. The sound wave seems to be a simple bi-product of the gravitational stresses. We were just in the wrong place at the wrong time."

"Well done Clarke."

"Wait a minute," interrupted Blaine. "I thought sound couldn't travel through space?"

"Some frequencies can and some can't. If all sound waves were incapable of travelling through a vacuum then we wouldn't be able to send or receive messages would we." Blaine pondered this for a moment.

"Yeah, I suppose that makes sense."

"Blaine as soon as you clear the system, set a course for Tartarus."

"Aye sir."

Even on a relatively short-range mining mission, the crew had put six months flight time between themselves and the colony. Space holds many hidden dangers for a starship, and the information they had acquired must reach the colony at any cost. Hawkins relayed a message ahead in case the worst should happen whilst they slept. After setting the ships Auto-Navigation Systems, the crew settled into their cryogenic-stasis chambers and headed for home.

CHAPTER: 2

"Dark Star Dreadnought. This is the Adriana. Adriana to Dark Star, come in please." Blaine sat up and wiped the sleep from his eyes. "Dark Star Dreadnought, please reply." He climbed out of his stasis chamber. The floor was cold on his feet as he walked across the room to the closest intercom.

"This is the Dark Star, the stasis shut-down calculations appear to have been slightly out. You kind'a caught us with our pants down here guys. Stand-by."

"Understood Dark Star. The colony has been notified of your arrival. Commander O'Connor has expressed his need to speak to Captain Hawkins as soon as possible."

"Commander O'Connor has been waiting to speak to me for six months," answered Hawkins who had been woken by the noise and was now sat rubbing his neck. "Surely he can hold out till after breakfast."

"Very good sir, Adriana out."

A hiss of steam was released as the main ramp groaned to a halt on the sandy ground of the planet. Hawkins took in a deep breath of the planet's pure and non-recycled air. "Captain Hawkins sir!" shouted a young man as he ran up the ramp. "Commander O'Connor is waiting for you in the briefing room, on board the Lynx." The young man turned and looked to the sky. "We need to hurry sir, there's an ion storm heading this way."

"Lead the way son," replied Hawkins nodding his head.

The team strolled through the mass of battered ships. Blaine couldn't help thinking how pitiful it all looked. The fourteen months they had spent away from the colony had not been kind. Rickety little shelters now stood where tall ships once rested, and once open ground now held the makeshift crosses that marked the shallow graves of the weaker members of the colony.

"Better to have died fighting on Earth, than suffer this existence," he remarked with a look of disgust.

"The storms have been getting worse in the last few months," replied the young man. "We've lost three ships and many others are crippled beyond repair. If we don't get off this rock soon, there won't be any ships left to leave in." After wrestling with the manual lever on the door, the youth led the way into the sand-covered ship. They walked down a long corridor, obstructed by fallen support beams and broken cables. The sounds of Servo's and Laser Welding-Torches could be heard echoing through the ship as the repair drones laboured.

"Captain Hawkins to see you sir," announced the youth as he entered the briefing room.

"Come in gentlemen," welcomed the commander, standing to shake their hands. "As you can see the situation here is getting worse by the minute. Seems the planet's blasted ecosystem is in a state of decay, so let's get straight down to business shall we." Hawkins and the crew all found chairs as O'Connor moved round to a large computer screen at the front of the room. "We've had teams working round the clock since we got your message, and we've come up with this." The computer screen flashed up a set of blueprints. "We had a lot of trouble reproducing the sound wave. Our speakers simply aren't capable of creating a sound on such a high pitch. Eventually the boys managed to throw something together using a Modified Shield Generator. They're calling it a Sonic Pulse Generator. The idea as I understand it, is to fit the thing to a ship's existing Shield Generator and engage it whilst the shields are up. When activated the shields should amplify the sound and direct it out in all directions at once. So on the upside at least aiming won't be a problem."

"I couldn't help but notice that those blueprints are of a Dreadnought, O'Connor," replied Hawkins in a rather unimpressed tone. "Since my ship's the only Dreadnought that's still moving, it's pretty safe to assume that you think you're going somewhere in it."

"Yes John," replied the commander "Your ship may not be the fastest ship we've got but it is the toughest. We're gonna need a ship that can take a beating." Hawkins rose to his feet, and leant over the desk in front of him.

"Listen very carefully Commander. I will not be stranded on this shit-hole of a planet, because you decided to include my ship in this suicide mission." Commander O'Connor couldn't believe his ears.

"People are dying John!" O'Connor screamed across the table. "People are dying and you're going to stand here and give me this shit!"

"No one flies my ship but me, and this crew."

"You know it's the only ship with thick enough hull plating to withstand an attack."

"I said no one flies my ship but me. So you better count me in."

"Damn you Hawkins, I can't fucking believe." O'Connor stopped to re-ingest what had just been said. "What?" Hawkins just stood at the head of the table and smiled. "What did you just say?" O'Connor repeated looking slightly puzzled.

"I want to command the mission. I can't speak for my crew but I'd rather be out there fighting than sitting here awaiting the outcome." Blaine, Clarke and Kane looked at each other. After a few seconds Blaine stood up.

"Well I think I speak for us all when I say that's the best idea he's ever had." Hawkins just smirked and looked at the commander.

"Well Commander, do we have a deal?" O'Connor still looking concerned tried to talk some sense into the crew.

"The Dark Star will be backed up by the retrieval ship Ulysses and the Phoenix, which is a science vessel. The Dark Star's reactor will be unaffected by the pulse, due to it only being produced outwards from the shields, but the other ships will have to jettison their crystalline reactor before you initiate the Sonic Pulse, or you'll fry them too." O'Connor paused and leaned over the table. "Win or lose your fleet won't be able to get back here on emergency power." For a moment everything was silent. Clarke was the first to speak.

"You know Commander, if you keep boring us with all these details, this isn't going to be any fun at all." O'Connor shook his head and laughed.

"Fair enough boys. Fair enough."

The upgrading of the ship took weeks. Day and night the engineers worked on, stopping for nothing but the storms. In between mission briefings and training on the various upgrades, Hawkins and his men could do nothing but wait.

"Poker, Clarke?"

"Blaine if you ask me to play one more game of cards I'm gonna feed you the whole deck."

"Really? Where are you gonna find the manpower to back up that threat?"

"Blaine, do me a favour."

"What?"

"Suck my dick."

"Ooh, very witty, where do you come up with these snappy come backs."

"Kiss me ass Blaine."

"See, there you go again." The playing cards flew off the cold steel surface of the table as the bunker door hissed opened. Kane walked in out of the storm.

"Damn Kane, you look like shit."

"Oh thanks Blaine, it's always nice to know I can count on you for a warm welcome."

"Hey, what are friends for." Kane took off his coat as he walked towards the refrigerators. "Seriously though, when was the last time you got some sleep."

"Sleep, I remember that," replied Kane as he opened the refrigerator door, and hungrily started to shovel food into his mouth. "Damn I'm sick of these roots. I really need to get back to Earth for a big fat juicy steak."

"That's assuming there's any cows left."

"What do you mean?"

"Well, no one's been to Earth in years, how do you know that batty computer hasn't killed 'em all?"

"Why would it?"

"I don't know, maybe it decided they clash with the grass. All I'm saying is that we don't know what we're going to find when we get back. That crazy fuckin' calculator could have painted the whole planet pink."

"Blaine, where the hell do you think up this shit?" Blaine was distracted from his answer by another strong gust of wind.

Hawkins closed the door behind him and began to brush himself down.

"Damn, I can't wait to get off this rock."

"I hear that," replied Kane still attempting to chew his root.

"What's the latest on the upgrades Kane. Do we have a launch date yet?"

"Just making sure we haven't missed anything Captain. If we could test the Pulse Generator without frying every ship we've got, we would have been finished already. As it is, all we can do is double-check all the components and pray the damn thing works." Kane pulled up a chair and sat down.

"What about those defensive upgrades your engineering buddies have been boasting about for days?" added Blaine from his knees as he attempted to retrieve the playing cards.

"We've reconfigured a few of the Sub-Orbital Mining Torpedoes to use as missiles. But we've had to remove the Guidance Systems so the AI can't influence them. They'll work but there gonna have to be aimed manually."

"What about the engine upgrades I suggested?" asked Blaine as he returned to his seat, placing the freshly retrieved cards back on the table.

"Well she's still no star-fighter, but she's about as manoeuvrable as she's gonna get."

"Hey, I'll take whatever you can give me. Call me paranoid, but I get the feeling that the ability to dodge is going to come in handy on this mission." Another roaring gust of wind flew through the room as one of the engineers stumbled in from the intensifying storm. Blaine snatched at the playing cards, as they scattered across the room. "For the love of god, every mining ship in the fleet carries at least three of these personnel bunkers. Surely they could have found us one with a working air-lock."

"We've just received the reports from the last two crews sir, the Sonic Pulse Generator is as ready as it's ever gonna be."

"Thanks Murphy," replied Kane. "Captain, she's ready when you are."

"Excellent. Everybody try and get some sleep, we'll leave as soon as the storm passes."

The following morning brought with it reasonably calm

weather. Last night's storm had been relatively kind compared to most, and except for a few minor repairs, the ship was still in one piece. The sounds of pistons and engines could be heard through the early mist, as the forklifts loaded the cargo bays with equipment for the task ahead. Blaine sat at the helm, displaying a look of intense concentration as he familiarised himself with the upgraded flight controls. Clarke and Kane stood at the tactical console, checking over the new weapons systems. Hawkins just stood and stared through the view port at the dismal rock they had all called home. Never again would he look out over this sparse inhospitable land, or take shelter from its storms. Never again would he bury his people in its sandy god-forsaken soil. There was no way of knowing what would be there to greet them upon their return to Earth. The most likely prospect was death.

"All sections report as locked down and ready to fly sir."

"Very well. Blaine, let's get outta here."

"Aye sir." The crew gripped the armrests of their chairs as the ship burst into its egress. "Wow, sorry," excused Blaine, as he accustomed himself to the engine upgrades. The shaking and sounds of creaking bulkheads eased as the ship cleared the atmosphere of the planet. Once again the soothing hum of the ship's systems was the only thing to be heard.

"We've cleared the atmosphere sir, and we're being hailed from the surface."

"Patch it through."

"Morning guys, I see you're all ready to depart."

"Yes Commander, what can we do for you?"

"We've downloaded a copy of the design schematics for the upgraded torpedoes into the repair drones onboard the Ulysses and the Phoenix. By the time you reach Earth they'll be fully armed and ready to kick ass."

"OK O'Connor but remember, they take their orders from me."

"They've already been made aware of that John. Good luck, O'Connor out."

"OK Blaine." Hawkins leaned forward in his seat. "Take us home."

Physicists in the late twentieth-century calculated that no object with any mass could achieve speeds greater than ninety-three thousand miles per second, approximately half the speed of light. Even with the thick outer hull of a Dreadnought, colliding with anything at this speed would be crippling. Records from the first sub-light speed tests in the early twenty-first century show that at high enough velocities, particles of space dust could punch holes the size of a fist through a ship's hull. The Dark Star being equipped with ablative shielding could travel safely at reasonably high speeds. Even so, covering the expanse between Vega and Earth would still take over a decade.

CHAPTER: 3

Clarke awoke with a jolt. The lights of the stasis chamber were blinding after his long sleep and the room was bitter cold.

"Bad dreams?" questioned Kane, who was already on his feet climbing into his overalls.

"Every time I get in one of these things," replied Clarke as he climbed out of the stasis pod and headed towards his locker.

"See you in the mess hall."

Captain Hawkins and Blaine had skipped breakfast and were already on the bridge making sure that the journey had gone to plan.

"We've arrived at the correct co-ordinates Captain. We'll be within sensor range of Jupiter in about two minutes."

"Our companions are still with us," replied Hawkins who was manning the tactical console. "Both ships seem to be undamaged." Hawkins opened a communications line to the pursuing vessels. "Dark Star to Fleet, what's your status?"

"Ulysses to Dark Star. All systems fully operational, awaiting your orders Captain."

"This is Hawkins, what's the status on those missiles?"

"The new repair drone programmes worked fine. Inventory shows us as carrying thirty fully functional warheads."

"Phoenix to Dark Star. Our inventory is also showing thirty new passengers, and they're all packing."

"Thank you Captains, standby for further instructions. Hawkins out."

"Coming up on Jupiter's outer moons sir."

"OK Blaine. Hawkins to Clarke, I need you and Kane at your stations."

"Aye sir."

"Take us into orbit over the gas refineries."

"If they're still standing," replied Blaine doubtfully.

"Those factories were fully automated, there shouldn't have been any need to destroy them."

"In other words, there wasn't anyone there to shoot at," remarked Blaine, turning to face the captain. Except for a frown and nod Hawkins left the question unanswered.

"Dark Star to Fleet. I need to know if your ships are up to a high-gravity flight."

"This is Phoenix. Shouldn't be a problem."

"Ulysses to Dark Star. It'll be less than graceful but I think we can handle it."

"We're going to be docking with one of Jupiter's gas refineries. It should be hovering about two miles above the northern pole of the planet. If anyone's got anything to say, now is the time to say it."

"Ulysses to Dark Star, no problems here."

"Dark Star to Phoenix, what about you?"

"Phoenix here, ready when you are."

"OK follow our lead, Dark Star out." Kane and Clarke rushed onto the bridge and headed for their stations.

"Sorry we're late sir," panted Clarke as he replaced the captain at the tactical console. Hawkins returned to his seat and adorned his safety harness.

"In your own time Blaine."

"OK, hold on to your asses." Blaine threw the power lever and the ship accelerated towards the planet. "Clarke I'm gonna need a safe entry window."

"Coming up."

"Blaine you might want to slow down just a little," proposed Kane, who was holding onto his safety harness as tightly as possible.

"Nonsense. I've been waiting for over a decade to test these new engines, and that's exactly what I intend to do." Blaine inched the power lever forward another notch. "Clarke, talk to me."

"OK, entry vector five-two-four point one. Keep her at thirty degrees." Blaine eased the power lever back a few notches.

"Vector confirmed. Entering the atmosphere in five, four, three, two, one." The ship started to shake as it descended through the atmosphere. Clarke closed the blast shields on the bridge's view ports, stopping the dazzling glow from the hull.

"This isn't half as much fun as the last re-entry!" shouted Kane jokingly through the rumbling.

"Stop fucking around Kane and keep your eyes on the hull stress."

"Sorry Captain."

"OK Clarke we're breaking through!" hollered Blaine as the shaking began to die down. "Raise the blast shields." The blast shields retracted and once again Blaine hit the power. "Levelling off sir. Cruising at ten thousand five hundred feet."

"Clarke any sign of the refinery?"

"Not yet Captain."

"Try widening the scan field."

"Sorry sir, I'm having trouble scanning through this atmosphere with a concentrated beam."

"Fair enough Clarke. Blaine we're gonna need to start a search pattern."

"Oh great, it could take hours to find this – holy shit!" The colossal refinery emerged without warning from the gasses in front of the ship. Blaine threw the helm hard to port and the ship began to turn. "Turn baby, turn," he pleaded as the two metal giants drew closer and closer. The ship scraped clear of the refinery with only a few metres to spare. So close that the blast from its engines shook a small communications dish free of its moorings and sent it spiralling down to towards the surface.

"Clarke, relay co-ordinates of the refinery to the other ships."

"Aye sir."

"Nice flying Blaine."

"Thanks Captain. Request permission to change my shorts." Hawkins let out a sigh of relief and loosened his grip on his armrests.

"Bring us around. Find us a docking port."

"Coming about sir. Lining up with closest horizontal docking port. Activating docking thrusters." The ship jolted as it hit the docking station. "Docking clamps locked and holding. All stop sir."

"Very good Blaine. Clarke, can you interface with the

refineries computer from here?"

"I'm not getting a reply sir. Either the relays in the docking port are damaged, or the main computer's off-line."

"If the main computer's off-line, shouldn't this thing have taken a two mile swan dive by now?"

"The Vertical Stabilisers on these things have several independently powered backup systems. You'd have to hit this thing with a Cluster Missile to knock it out of the sky," replied Kane as he undid his safety harness.

"Have the other ships docked yet Clarke?"

"The Phoenix has docked and the Ulysses is docking as we speak Captain."

"Good. OK Kane, Clarke, go fetch whatever equipment you might need to get us through this place. Blaine and I will meet you in the airlock."

"Aye sir," answered Kane as he and Clarke hurried into the bridge turbo-lift. Blaine opened the weapons locker and threw Hawkins a Plasma Pistol. After strapping on one of his own, Blaine reached back into the locker and pulled out a Plasma Rifle.

"Blaine do you have any idea what the term overkill means?" asked Hawkins sarcastically. After cocking the rifle Blaine just smiled at the captain and walked off through the bridges main access door. Hawkins shook his head with a smirk and followed.

It took Kane a while but eventually he managed to open the refinery airlock. The air in the dark passageway was old and stale. Their torches were the only source of light in the otherwise total darkness.

"The main computer's definitely off-line," explained Kane. "In fact the whole power grid seems to be shut down."

"I thought these things maintained themselves?" Hawkins questioned, his voice echoing through the maze of dark passages.

"They do sir, usually. These refineries are definitely equipped with repair drones. The primary and the secondary power grids would both have to be off-line to stop them working. It seems the Vertical Stabilisers are the only things that are still functioning."

"Think there's anything you can do about it?"

"Well, even though it is automated it must have a Command Centre somewhere. If I can find it I might be able to get the power back online."

"Bingo." Blaine shone the light on a dusty door, set back into the wall of the passageway.

"What do you have Blaine?" Blaine rubbed the dust off the

half-covered writing on the door.

"Sorry, false alarm, it's just a turbo-lift." Blaine turned and carried on down the passageway.

"Blaine wait. Shine the light back on the door. Clarke, pass me the pry bar."

"Whatever you're doing Kane, we don't have time for it." Kane forced the pry bar between the door and its frame, opening it by a few inches.

"Blaine, shut up and hold the damn torch steady. Hey Clarke give me hand here." With a laboured pull the pair dragged the door open and Kane stepped inside. After a brief pause to look around, he began to remove a small panel from one of the walls. He searched for a few seconds through the mass of tangled wires and circuit boards he had uncovered. Reaching into his pocket he pulled out a small multi-purpose tool and snipped one of two large blue cables.

"Clarke do you have the power cells?"

"Yeah just a minute." Clarke reached into one of the large black satchels he was carrying and pulled out a small grey box, covered in blinking lights. Kane opened the top of the box to reveal two small metal clamps, which he quickly connected to the two ends of the snipped cable. The lights and monitors in the lift flickered and crackled as they began to power up.

"Damn I'm good." Kane stood up and took a bow.

"Quick, everyone in the lift before his head takes up all the room."

"OK, here goes nothing," remarked Hawkins, who was last to step into the lift. "Command Centre." The lift did nothing. "Operations." Still the lift did nothing. "Any ideas?" Hawkins looked at his crew.

"Hmm, Engineering," offered Blaine. The internal door hissed shut and with a squeal of its motors the lift began to move. Blaine turned to Clarke, wearing a smug grin. "Remember this moment next time you get the urge to slate my Star Trek re-runs."

"Whatever." After a few minutes the lift came to a halt and the doors hissed open. The crew followed Blaine out into a large dark chamber. From the little that could be seen in the dull torch-light, Kane could make out dozens of computer consoles and large rectangular data banks that stood at least nine feet tall.

"Are you sure you can get this working Kane?"

"As long as the power loss is the result of system damage and not battery drain, then it's possible sir."

"Kane, do me a favour."

"Yes Captain."

"Pretend that I know precisely dick about engineering, then explain that again."

"Well basically sir, if the power's down because of damage to the refinery, then all the systems would have shut down instantaneously. Meaning the repair drones still have charge in their power cells, but the Auto-Repair System isn't online to control them. In which case I just have to attach a power cell to the Auto-Repair System and we can use the drones to fix the refinery. But if the problem was with the refinery generators, the systems would have been running on backup power. All the systems and the repair drones would have just kept going until they flattened their batteries. So I won't be able to activate the drones, and we'd better start looking for some candles." Hawkins looked around into the darkness of the pitch-black room before responding.

"Clarke do you have any more torches in those bags?"

"Yes sir." Clarke opened one of the satchels and handed out the torches.

"OK, split up and find the Auto-Repair System. Holler if you find it."

Blaine walked slowly through the vast chamber, swinging his torch from left to right over the computer consoles. He couldn't help but think that the power being down was slightly suspicious. What could have damaged a gas refinery two miles above a planet surface, out here in the middle of nowhere? There was nothing here to collide with but gas and the chances of a meteor striking the refinery were infinitesimal. Something wasn't right.

"Found it, it's over here!" yelled Hawkins. The crew hurried over to where the captain stood. "At least I think I've found it. It looks like the repair system on the Dark Star but it's huge."

"Yeah that's it," reassured Kane. "Our system only has to

control a couple of dozen repair drones. Something this size must control hundreds." Kane removed a large access panel from the front of the machine and crawled inside.

"Clarke I'm going to need the high capacity power cell for this." Clarke pushed one of the satchels through the panel opening. "Thanks. Now all I need to do is hook up the power cables and hopefully…" The huge repair system's monitors and consoles burst into life and Kane slid back out from inside it. Clarke wasted no time in accessing the refineries diagnostic logs.

"Well the repair drones are back online, so I guess we don't need those candles."

"What caused the power failure?"

"Running diagnostic now Captain." A sudden look of surprise swept across Clarke's face. "Ah, that'll explain it."

"What?"

"It appears there's been a small explosion in one of the gas storage tanks."

"How bad is it?"

"Well luckily the storage tanks are located in the centre of the refinery, so the outer hull is still intact."

"What about internally?"

"There's a lot of internal sensors down sir, I can't get an accurate measurement."

"Then give me your best guess."

"The vertical blast radius appears to cover an area of about four hundred and ninety-two metres."

"Jesus, that's almost eighty-three decks."

"There's no way we're gonna get the power back online with that kind of damage Captain. Even if there is enough raw materials left to rebuild the power grid, it will take the drones months to do it."

"Kane, can you keep the repair system functioning?"

"We'll need to fetch more power cells from the ship, but it shouldn't be a problem." Hawkins nodded.

"OK listen up, this is the plan. Clarke, I need you to programme a few repair drones to remove the crystalline reactors from the Ulysses and the Phoenix. They need to be stored in a safe place somewhere in the refinery. Kane, keep the repair system running until the drones have finished. Blaine, get the captains from the other ships up here. Time to make sure they're upto speed on the mission."

The other ships had docked on the opposite side of the refinery to the Dark Star, presenting the captains of the Ulysses and the Phoenix with a half-hour walk to the engineering deck. By the time they arrived the repair drones were already well into their task.

"Captain Hawkins?" asked one of the captains as he glanced round the room at the crew. Hawkins stepped forward and shook his hand. "I'm Soren, captain of the Ulysses and this is Commander Kristen Redmond of the Phoenix." Hawkins gave Commander Redmond a funny look.

"Is something wrong Captain?"

"No I just didn't expect you to be…"

"A woman?" interrupted Redmond. Hawkins laughed.

"So young." The commander smiled. "Anyway I didn't drag you both up here to chit-chat, let's get down to it shall we. You were obviously dragged into this at the last possible second. Which was probably planned so that I didn't have time to object, but I don't suppose that's important now. What I need to know is how much you were told about this mission."

"Well the Sonic Pulse Generator was common knowledge on the colony. As far as this mission is concerned, my orders are to accompany you back into Earth-space and make sure the Dark Star survives to set off the pulse, no matter the cost."

"What about you Commander?"

"That sounds about right, and call me Kristen."

"Just what I expected from O'Connor, as vague as possible. Let me give you a run down of what you've really volunteered for. Based on the technology the AI System had at the time of the massacre, we should be able to approach undetected until we've passed through the asteroid field between Jupiter and Mars. For a fucking change the Auto-Navigation System and the cryo-stasis shut downs worked properly, and we've arrived at the right time of year. The current planetary alignments mean that if we get the timing right, we should be able to swing round from behind the asteroid field and approach from behind Mars. We'll still be out in the open between Mars and Earth, but until that point we shouldn't be detected. Since we're going to be running on backup power, we need to be breaking orbit in about fifteen hours in order to utilise the blind spot before Mars passes."

"Do we really need to drop the reactors here, can't we just move our ships out of range before you activate the Pulse Generator?"

"This isn't gonna be a walk in the park, Miss Redmond. Your ships are here to divert attention from the Dark Star while we get into position and activate the pulse. The Dark Star's big enough to take a beating but if it's the only target we're still gonna be fubar pretty damn quick."

"Fubar?" questioned Commander Redmond looking extremely puzzled.

"Fucked up beyond all recognition."

The commander shook her head. "Men."

"Commander O'Connor suggested that we simply eject the reactors into space upon arrival. I however, unlike that asshole, have a problem with you floating powerless through space if this mission fails. So I put a little more thought into the matter and came up with leaving the reactors here. At least this way you can reinstall them if you need to."

"What are your plans for after we pass Mars, Hawkins?"

"Actually Soren, I'd appreciate your thoughts on that. Obviously it would be stupid to just wade in guns blazing, before we know what we're up against. On the other hand if we send a scout to check the place out, we lose the element of surprise."

"Yes, I see what you mean. Damned if we do and damned if we don't."

"There is a third option," offered Redmond. Soren and Hawkins stared attentively. "If we could somehow direct a few of the bigger rocks from the asteroid belt towards Earth, we could hide in with them until they got in range of the asteroid defences. We would have plenty of time to scan the planet and we would remain undetected."

"Isn't the Ulysses a retrieval ship?"

"It's designed to retrieve damaged vessels, yes."

"Then it's equipped with a tractor-beam right."

"Yes, it's not designed to tow more than one object at a time but my engineers should be able to widen the confinement beam."

"OK, you'd better get them started." Soren nodded and walked away to a quiet spot where he could contact his ship. Redmond and Hawkins continued their conversation.

"Captain Hawkins."

"Call me John."

"John. Do you really think we can pull this off?"

"Truthfully?"

"Yes."

"I don't know. If the sound wave works and we don't get blown out of the sky before we activate it then, maybe."

"If the sound wave will effect the whole solar system, why can't we just activate it from here?"

"The AI System was built inside an old underground military bunker, to protect it from terrorist attacks. The sound wave won't be able to penetrate through that much earth. We're going to need to use a few mining torpedoes to make a hole before we can activate the pulse."

Soren returned from the far side of the room and rejoined the conversation.

"My engineers have started the adjustments to the tractor-beam. They're confident that it will be ready before we depart, but there is a problem."

"Go on."

"We're not going to be able to create a large enough tractor-beam if the ship's running on backup power. We're going to need the crystalline reactor."

"Not an option, you'll have to find another way."

"There is no other way Hawkins, it's the reactor or nothing. I'll jettison it before you activate the pulse. We'll just have to settle for two working ships if this fails." Hawkins thought about it for a moment. There really was no other choice.

"Kane!" Hawkins shouted across the engineering chamber. "Kane!"

"Yes Captain."

"Have the repair drones removed the reactor from the Ulysses yet?"

"They're disconnecting it as we speak sir."

"Tell them to reconnect it."

"Aye Captain."

"I think we've covered what we need to cover, unless anyone has anything to add." Hawkins paused for a moment to allow for a response. "Very well, I'm sure you're eager to get back to your ships. I'll see you at thirteen hundred hours."

"Yes Jon," replied Commander Redmond.

"Till then," answered Captain Soren.

CHAPTER: 4

After breaking orbit, the fleet, led by the Dark Star, headed towards the asteroid belt. Hawkins walked restlessly around the bridge checking his crew's preparations, whilst Clarke was busy making sure the ship wasn't giving off any detectable signals.

"We're coming up on the asteroid field Captain."

"All stop."

"Aye sir, all stop."

"Dark Star to Ulysses, come in Soren."

"Soren here, what can we do for you Captain."

"Are you ready to try the tractor-beam?"

"Ready as we'll ever be."

"OK let's do it." The Phoenix and the Dark Star backed away to a safe distance as the Ulysses took up position inside the belt. Dozens of the drifting asteroids, some as large as the Ulysses herself, came to a sudden halt as the tractor-beam was engaged. Captain Soren gave the order to move out and the Ulysses started to pull forwards. Hawkins watched through the main view port of the bridge as the huge rocks started to move, surrounded by the electric blue aura of the tractor-beam.

"Ulysses to Dark Star, the beam seems to be holding. Hawkins, I think we're in business."

"Very good Soren, but we're gonna have to pick up the pace. We need to make a run for Mars while it's still close enough to the asteroid field to hide us."

"Not a problem. Ulysses out." Hawkins was still watching the Ulysses as it powered up its main engines and shot off into the distance.

"Whenever you're ready Blaine."

"Aye sir." The fleet headed for Mars with the Ulysses dragging their only chance for victory. If the AI System did manage to detect them, they would surely be destroyed before they even reached the atmosphere. The flight to Mars lasted just over four hours, due to the slowness of the heavily laden Ulysses.

"Dark Star to Fleet. We're gonna be passing Mars over the Western Hemisphere, set your heading accordingly. Ulysses inform me the second you're ready to release the asteroids."

"Copy that Hawkins."

"Passing over the Western Hemisphere now Captain. We should be clear momentarily."

"Hawkins to Fleet. Increase your speed, let's try and make this look as real as possible."

"Ulysses to Fleet. Course set for Earth's upper atmosphere, releasing the asteroids now." The glow of the tractor-beam stopped and the asteroids drifted apart slightly. The fleet slowed to allow the field to gain a little ground before taking their ships in.

"OK Blaine, take her in."

"Brace yourselves." The armada of rocks hurtled ever closer to Earth, the fleet needed to take cover fast before they were discovered. Hawkins watched as a small asteroid shot past the view port, narrowly missing the ship.

"Where the fuck did that come from?"

"The Phoenix just collided with it Captain," replied Clarke.

"Dark Star to Phoenix, report."

"We're OK John. We just winged it."

"Are you sure?"

"Yes."

"OK, Hawkins out."

"John?" questioned Blaine suggestively.

"Don't make me beat the shit out of you Blaine."

"Aye sir." Blaine replied still grinning.

"How long?" asked Hawkins as he turned to face Clarke.

"At this speed we'll be in range of the asteroid defences in three and a half minutes Captain."

"Are we in scanning range yet?"

"Not quite sir."

"Bring the new weapon systems online."

"Aye Captain. Targeting scanner up and running."

"What's the status of the tubes Kane?"

"Torpedo's locked and loaded Captain. All tubes ready."

"Coming into sensor range now sir, initiating scan. What the hell!"

"What is it Clarke?"

"It's amazing sir, South America is almost totally covered in rainforest, and so is Brazil. In fact the whole planet is covered in wildlife and vegetation. There's no structures or power sources anywhere."

"What about the AI System bunker?"

"Just a hole in the ground sir." Clarke looked up from his console and stared at Hawkins. "It's not there."

"What?"

"It's gone sir."

"What the fuck's going on here?" Hawkins looked through the view port at the now visible planet. "What about the Asteroid Defence Satellites?" Hawkins continued with a note of concern in his voice.

"Sensors are detecting no machinery or equipment of any kind Captain."

"My god. We've just aimed enough rock at the planet to start another ice age." The crew sat silently for a moment, staring out through the view port, eyes fixed on the small blue sphere that they had just doomed. Hawkins rose to his feet and turned to Clarke. "Do we have enough missiles to stop them?" Clarke sat silently in his seat for a few seconds, before looking up at the captain.

"These asteroids are comprised of mostly nickel and iron, only thing with the fire power to stop them is the non-existent Defence Satellites." Clarke looked back through the view port and added. "That should have started firing thirty seconds ago."

"What about using the tractor-beam on the Ulysses?" offered Kane.

"The larger asteroids have spread too far apart to snare with the beam. There's nothing we can do."

"Yes there is." The crew turned and looked at Hawkins, who had returned to his seat and strapped himself in. "Hawkins to Fleet, we need to take these rocks out before they reach the planet."

"Soren to Hawkins, agreed."

"Phoenix to Dark Star, let's do it."

"Blaine get us clear. Clarke fire at will." The three ships broke from the asteroid field and began to fire. The ships strafed back and forth, spewing torpedo after torpedo at the largest rocks they could find.

"Blaine get us closer to the big rock at co-ordinates zero-two point eight."

"Which big rock damn it, there's dozens of big rocks."

"For the love of god Blaine it's half a kilometre across, surely it's not in your blind spot."

"Oh yeah, I got it. Coming about."

"Target locked, torpedo's away. Impact in four, three, two, one, torpedo's have impacted." Clarke slammed his fist down on his console. "Damn it Captain, we're not even scratching these things."

"Captain what about giving one of these things a love tap?"

"Kane, would the hull hold up if we gave one of these things a nudge?"

"I wouldn't recommend it sir. The Dark Star's bigger than most of these things but like Clarke said, most of these things are made of solid metal." Hawkins thought for a second.

"OK Clarke, give the shields as much power as possible."

"Aye sir."

"Blaine, time to be a hero."

"Yes sir." Blaine manoeuvred the ship alongside the half-kilometre asteroid they had just been firing at. "OK guys, you might want to brace yourselves." The bridge shook hard as the ship connected with the asteroid. Blaine eased the horizontal control levers over as gently as possible.

"Shields aren't gonna hold for long under this kind of strain Captain."

"Keep them up as long as you can Clarke."

"It's not budging sir, increasing power to the lateral thrusters." A heavy grating sound echoed through the ship as the hull sheared against the mammoth rock. "Damn, this is really gonna fuck up the paintwork."

"Hull stress is at ninety-seven percent Captain, she's starting to buckle."

"How we doing Blaine?"

"It's moving Captain, but I still need to turn it another three degrees to miss the planet." The ship shook violently as a sudden shower of rock fragments bounced of the hull.

"What the hell was that?"

"We were just hit by fragments from an exploding asteroid Captain."

"Which one of the ships bagged it?" asked Hawkins optimistically.

"The one that's just dropped out of sub-light at co-ordinates zero-three point one."

"What? Put it on the main viewer." The main viewer flicked to a view of the approaching vessel. It took Hawkins a few seconds to work out what he was looking at. The ship was as black as the void that surrounded it and very hard to see. It tapered from a wide stern down to a fine point at its bow. The whole outer edge of it glinted like the blade of a knife in the light from the distant sun.

"My god, I didn't think it was possible to build anything that big. Clarke can you get a life form reading."

"The sensors are only just registering its presence Captain. I don't know what it's coated in but I can't scan through it. All I can tell you at the moment is that it's shaped like an arrowhead and is about eight miles in length."

"Captain, the rocks clear."

"OK Blaine, find us another target."

"Captain, I'm detecting a massive power build-up in the unidentified vessel. I think it's gonna blow sir."

"Are we in any danger?"

"I don't know sir, it's one hell of a build-up."

"Err guys." Hawkins and Clarke turned to the main view screen. The strange ship was now lit up with jolts of electricity that were dancing across its surface. The crew watched in awe as the electrical light show directed itself towards the bow of the ship and shot out into the asteroid field.

"Brace for impact." The bridge shook as another wave of debris crashed into the ship. "Kane, shield status."

"Shields holding sir."

"Ulysses to Fleet, we've taken heavy damage, request assistance."

"Dark Star to Ulysses, what's your status?"

"We've got hull breaches all over the place, the energy seals are holding but we're dead in the water here Hawkins."

"Captain, detecting another energy build-up in the unidentified ship."

"This is Earth Fleet mining vessel Dark Star to unidentified ship. Revise your firing line, repeat, we have a ship in your firing line."

"The ship is still charging its weapons sir."

"Shit. Dark Star to Ulysses, hold on we're on our way. Blaine get over there."

"It's firing sir." Once again the bridge shook under the barrage of debris from the blast.

"Kane!" shouted the captain.

"Shields are still holding Captain."

"Dark Star to Ulysses. Report." Hawkins waited for a reply. "Soren this is Hawkins, come in."

"Captain." Blaine drew the captain's attention to the main view port as the Ulysses came into view. The ship was dark and powerless. Oxygen was spewing out into space from more breaches than Hawkins could count.

"Clarke, any life signs?"

"No sir and the life-pods are still docked."

"Captain we're closing on Earth. The arrowhead vessel is re-positioning itself between the asteroid field and the planet."

"Dark Star to Phoenix break-off and regroup at co-ordinates zero-two-eight point one." Blaine pulled the ship out of the asteroid field and set the new course heading.

"Sir, the asteroid field will reach the arrowhead vessel in approximately ten seconds."

"Put it on the view screen."

"Detecting another power build-up Captain." Hawkins watched as the huge rocks hurtled towards the strange black vessel. Could this ship be the AI System? It would explain why it was trying so hard to protect the Earth but the technology was like nothing he had ever seen. Could it have advanced this far in the short time since the massacre? Could it care enough about the planet to sacrifice itself in this futile attempt to block the path of the asteroids?

"Picking up another power increase sir." The arrowhead vessel started to glow bright orange as the asteroids closed in.

"Impact in three-two-one." The hail of rocks smashed into the gigantic vessel, which was now lost in the cloud of debris created by the impact. In the distance behind the bombarded vessel Hawkins was relieved to see only a few small asteroids entering the atmosphere. None of them big enough to cause more than minor surface damage to the Earth below.

"Blaine set a course for whatever's left of that ship. Maybe we can find a few answers in the wreckage."

"I don't think setting course for it's gonna be necessary Captain."

"Why, isn't there anything left?"

"On the contrary sir, it's still in one piece and on the move."

"What? That's not possible. Nothing could have survived that."

"Putting arrowhead vessel on the main view screen now sir." Sure enough the vessel was heading slowly out of the debris field and was listing into a turn.

"Magnify."

"Aye sir, increasing to ten times normal magnification."

"Jesus, there's not a mark on it."

"It's heading this way Captain."

"Clarke, get me Commander Redmond on the view screen."

"Aye sir." The view screen flicked from the approaching vessel to the bridge of the Phoenix.

"Redmond here, go ahead John."

"Get out of here and reinstall your reactor, if you don't hear from us in one hour set course back to the colony." The commander looked wounded.

"My orders are to protect the Dark Star John, and that's what I intend to do."

"Damn it Redmond, I'm changing your orders. There's nothing you can do against that ship except survive to warn the colony of its existence. Now turn around and get out of here." Commander Redmond was silent for a moment.

"What's the status of the Ulysses?" Hawkins frowned and shook his head. Commander Redmond nodded slowly. "Drake set course for Jupiter. You'd better be there Hawkins, Phoenix out." Blaine turned to the captain.

"Orders Captain?"

"Hold your position." Blaine looked through the main view port at the fast approaching giant.

"Aye sir," he answered uncertainly.

"Clarke, if this thing is the AI System, do you think the Sonic Pulse will work through that things outer hull?"

"Hard to say sir. I still can't get a sensor lock on the damn thing." Blaine was still staring though the view port at the closing ship.

"Sir, with all due respect, if we don't move, this thing's gonna smash us to pieces."

"Hold your position Blaine, if it was going to attack us it would have fired by now. Somehow we need to find out if this thing is the AI System. I'm open to suggestions."

"If we could blow a big enough hole in its hull plating we might be able to scan the interior Captain."

"Thanks Kane but I don't want to start shooting at this thing if I don't have to."

"We could try the pulse."

"It's only gonna be a surprise once, we can't risk using it until we're sure it's gonna penetrate the hull plating. That's if it's even running on a crystalline reactor."

"The arrowheads closed to one thousand metres Captain. On its present course it should pass straight over us." A deep rumbling sound washed through the bridge as the immense vessel slowly moved overhead. Blaine leaned forward in his seat and looked up at its passing hull.

"The damn things completely smooth Captain. There's no cargo bays, no access hatches, there's not even a scuff on the metal."

"Clarke, what's it doing?" questioned Hawkins who was sat looking up at the roof of the bridge.

"No idea sir but it is slowing down."

"Slowing down?"

"Yes sir, it appears to be coming to a halt directly above us."

"Can the sensors tell us anything at this range?"

"I'm still reading the ship as an anomaly Captain, whatever this hull plating is made of it's confusing the sensors to hell."

"Captain, you might want to take a look at this," shouted Blaine still staring out of the view port. Hawkins got out of his seat and walked over to take a look. A thin crack was starting to appear spreading across the silky smooth hull of the arrowhead vessel. Hawkins and Blaine watched as it continued to expand before it abruptly turned ninety degrees and continued on out of sight.

"Clarke, do me a favour," asked Hawkins, his gaze still fixed on the strange ship. "Look back through the navigational logs and tell me when we entered the twilight zone."

"What's going on out there Captain?" replied Clarke curiously.

"Good question, I'll let you know the second I figure that out." The crack had continued to extend around the ship's hull and had now met up with it's self to create a large rectangular shape above the Dark Star. Blaine's jaw dropped as the whole section of the hull began to retract into the vessel.

"No fucking way!"

"Captain, the sensors are picking up a section of the ship that's about a mile square."

"Yeah," replied Hawkins sounding shocked. "It's probably this cargo bay door." Clarke looked up from his console, wearing a frown of confusion.

"Sorry sir, it sounded like you said door?" questioned Kane. Without answering Hawkins waved Kane over to the view port. Clarke and Kane looked at each and Kane hurried over to the front of the ship. "Now that's a fucking door!"

"Clarke, what are you picking up?"

"This things amazing Captain. I'm reading over two thousand decks, fifty advanced machine shops and enough storage space to hold the whole colony."

"What about life signs?"

"Not one sir, as far as I can tell the ship doesn't even have the facilities to sustain a crew."

"Then it has to be the AI," added Blaine.

A blinding blue light emanating from inside the gargantuan door of the ship suddenly interrupted the crew's conversation.

The Dark Star shook violently sending the crew stumbling across the bridge as they hurried to get back to their stations.

"Report."

"We appear to be caught in some sort of tractor-beam sir."

"Blaine, get us out of here." Blaine threw the power lever and the ship began to shake even more. "Blaine get us out of here now!"

"I can't break free sir, the beam's got more muscle than the engines."

"Clarke, can you trace the source of the beam?"

"Yes sir, the beam's source is located one point four miles inside the opening." Hawkins weighed up his options.

"Arm two torpedoes, it looks like were gonna have to blast our way out of here."

"Aye sir, torpedoes armed and ready."

"Fire."

Sub-Orbital Mining Torpedoes are designed to create large craters in a planet's surface from orbit, in the attempt to speed up the job of the Mining Drones and the Hover Miners. As a result of this design the torpedo tubes are situated in the underside of most mining ships, including Dreadnought class mining ships such as the Dark Star. This created quite a problem considering the target was positioned directly above the ship and the torpedoes Automatic Guidance Systems had been removed to prevent the AI System taking control of them. Clarke would have to calculate the precise trajectory required to direct the torpedoes in a one hundred and eighty degrees turn around the ship before they could hit their target.

"Torpedoes away." The bridge was silent except for the beeping of the tracking system. Clarke held his breath as the torpedoes passed each other beneath the ship. Had he made the correct calculations, had he sufficiently compensated for the pull of the tractor-beam? The next few seconds would tell. The sound of a thruster filled the bridge as one of the torpedoes sped past. Hawkins turned to Clarke.

"Do I want to know how close that was?"

"No."

"How's the trajectory looking?"

"Torpedoes clearing the ship now sir," replied Clarke,

carefully watching the tracking monitor on his console. "One of the torpedoes has impacted on the hull of the ship. The other has cleared the doorway and is on course for the source of the tractor-beam."

"Well done, Clarke. Blaine, get ready to…"

"Torpedo has been intercepted Captain," interrupted Clarke.

"How?"

"It was hit by some sort of energy-beam."

"Damn it."

"Captain, I can't hold her anymore. The beam's pulling us in."

"How long do we have Blaine?"

"With the engines at full power, maybe three minutes Captain."

"Blaine, be ready to get us out of here. Kane, you're with me." Hawkins and Kane rushed into the turbo-lift. "Torpedo bay." Upon the captain's command the lift doors hissed shut and it began to move.

"What's the plan Captain?"

"We're gonna send that bastard a little present." After about thirty seconds the turbo-lift stopped and the doors opened. Hawkins and Kane ran out into the torpedo bay. The room was relatively small compared to most in the ship, roughly thirty metres squared. Although the masses of stacked torpedoes and banks of launchers made it seem much smaller.

"OK Kane, help me with this crate of warheads." Kane and Hawkins lugged the large plastic crate into the turbo-lift. "Deck one, section eight," demanded Hawkins and the lift began to move. Hawkins knelt down and opened the crate. "Help me get these things armed Kane." One by one the pair carefully turned the keys on the warheads into the armed position. By the time they had arrived at their destination they had armed every single one of the warheads and wasted no time exiting the lift and rushing down the corridor. Hawkins stopped at a small hatch, which concealed one of the ship's many escape-pods. After dropping the crate he punched the release code into the hatch's keypad and it slowly opened.

"OK Kane, get these things inside quick." With extreme

care they slowly lowered the crate into the escape-pod before sealing the hatch. "Hawkins to Clarke, I need you to launch escape-pod eleven."

"Sir?"

"Just do it."

"Aye sir, launching pod now." A great roar followed Hawkins and Kane down the corridor as the pod's engines fired sending it screeching out of the ship. The pod rocketed up through the immense opening in the arrowhead vessel like a bat out of hell. Clarke was tracking its ascent as Hawkins burst back onto the bridge.

"Clarke, report."

"The pod's taking a beating sir but its armour appears to be holding. The beams guiding it straight in Captain, it should be impacting any second." The explosion was big enough to temporarily blind Clarke's sensors. The Dark Star jolted free as the tractor-beam ceased to function sending Kane crashing to the ground.

"Blaine, hit it."

"Aye sir." Blaine threw the power lever and the Dark Star roared off away from the ship. "Heading, Captain?"

"Anywhere Blaine, just get us out of here. Clarke, what's the status of that ship?"

"It's starting to turn Captain."

"God damn it, we put ten warheads in that escape-pod, what's it gonna take to slow this thing down?"

"Sir, suggest we head for the asteroid belt, we should be able to hide while we come up with a plan."

"Good thinking, Blaine set a course."

"Oh god, not more asteroids." Blaine hit the power and headed the ship back towards the asteroid belt.

"The arrowhead vessel is now on an intercept course and is gaining fast."

"Blaine, full speed."

"Sorry sir, we're already accelerating as fast as we can."

"Can we make it to the asteroid belt before it catches up with us?"

"I doubt it sir."

"Can you tell if its shields are raised?"

"Judging from the data I collected when it intercepted the asteroids sir, I'd say its shields haven't been activated."

"How many of the modified torpedoes do we have left?"

"Eighteen sir."

"Fire them, maybe we can slow it down."

"Loading torpedo tubes one through ten. Target locked. Torpedoes away. Loading second volley. Target locked. Torpedoes away."

"Time till intercept?"

"Estimated time till impact is thirty seconds."

"Blaine, how long before we reach the asteroids?"

"About fifty seconds Captain."

"This is gonna be close. Kane, is there any way of increasing our acceleration rate?"

"Sorry sir, there's no way of making her move any faster."

"Twenty seconds till impact, still no defensive response from the ship."

"Captain, this isn't going to work, it's too close. We'll never be able to get deep enough into the field to fool its sensors before it catches up to us."

"What choice do we have."

"Request permission to test a theory Captain." Hawkins knew Blaine was right, the ship would be right behind them by the time they reached the asteroid field and there was no way it would lose them at this range. Hawkins didn't have time to ask questions but Blaine's plan couldn't get them in any more trouble than they were already in.

"OK Blaine, this better be good."

"Impact of first volley in three, two, one." As the torpedoes impacted the front of the pursuing vessel, Blaine pulled back hard on the manoeuvring levers and the nose of the Dark Star started to rise.

"Clarke, what about that second volley?" Blaine queried.

"Impacting now." Blaine led the Dark Star through a half loop before easing off on the levers. The crew was now flying inverted towards the arrowhead vessel and the exploding torpedoes had masked the entire manoeuvre. Once again Blaine threw the engines into full burn and the Dark Star made its exodus along the arrowhead vessels hull and back towards Earth.

"Blaine, you're my new fucking hero."

"Thanks Captain, but that was the whole plan. I'm open to suggestion on where to go now."

"How long before that thing turns round Clarke?"

"The damn things fast sir but it's too big for rapid manoeuvring. Estimating two minutes before it can resume its pursuit."

"That's all we need. Blaine, we're gonna have to head for the planet."

"With all due respect sir, there's no way you can hide an eight hundred yard long ship on a planet's surface. Especially from a ship in orbit."

"Oh contraire Blaine, there is one way." Blaine was slightly concerned by the troubled tone of his captain.

"Blaine's right Captain, we won't be able to hide the ship. The only possible chance would be to…" Kane stopped as he realised what the captain was planning. "Oh god Captain, tell me we're not setting down in the ocean?"

"The ocean!" shouted Blaine in a state of panic. "Why the hell would we want to set her down in the ocean?"

"Because deep water refracts sensor-beams," answered Hawkins rubbing the back of his neck. "Clarke, any ideas on how we can find a suitable landing site? We need to be sure it's not too deep, the shields won't do a damn thing against water pressure."

"The ship would have to be just about skimming the surface for the sensors to scan the depth to the sea bed. We'd have to fly in a search pattern until we located a suitable spot."

"We don't have time for search patterns, we need to be gone before that ship knows what's happened."

"Scotland." Hawkins and Clarke turned to Kane.

"What, Kane?"

"Loch Ness in Scotland Captain. The damn things definitely deep enough and it's only about twenty miles long. Surely it would be faster to scan the depth of that."

"Kane, if you weren't so ugly I'd kiss you. Blaine, best speed to the British Isles."

"Aye Captain."

"The arrowhead vessel has completed its turn and is

accelerating towards us Captain. It's not going to take it long to get here."

"Clarke, I need an entry vector."

"One step ahead of you Blaine. Come in at vector eight-four-two point seven-five, keep her at thirty one degrees."

"Eight-four-two point seven-five confirmed. Brace for atmospheric entry."

"Closing blast shields."

"Hull stresses within tolerance. Heat shields holding."

"Descent stable, breaking through to lower atmosphere in five, four, three, two, one, engaging atmospheric thrusters."

"Pursuing vessel is slowing down and appears to be repositioning to enter orbit. We have two minutes tops before it's in position to track us."

"Kane, any ideas on how to control this landing once we hit the water?"

"We won't have any problem sinking if I flood the main port and starboard cargo bays. If I can use the environmental controls to fill them back up with air afterwards, the extra buoyancy should float us back up to the surface."

"Your gonna use the cargo bays as ballast tanks? Captain I don't know about this shit."

"Don't worry Blaine, if he says it'll work, then it'll work."

"If you say so sir."

"Coming up on the Scottish highland. Blaine, adjust your course by ten degrees to port."

"Copy, adjusting by ten degrees."

"I'm going to need you to fly as low as possible over the loch so I can take the depth readings."

"No problem. Loch in site, coming in for first pass." A huge wake of water billowed out behind the ship as it tore down the great loch. Blaine was manoeuvring the ship using instruments alone as the spray off the loch was totally blocking the view port.

"Blaine, we need to be lower."

"Lower? Clarke this is a starship not a fucking Jet Ski."

"If we don't get accurate depth reading the water pressure is gonna crush this starship like a bug."

"Lower it is."

"OK I've located a suitable landing site. Bring her about Blaine."

"Coming about." Blaine had to ascend the ship to a few metres above the valley sides to allow enough room to make the turn.

"OK Blaine, set her down about two hundred yards past that outcrop."

"Engaging landing jets, all stop." Trees on the banks of the loch bent over and shook violently as the huge ship hovered above the surface.

"OK, here goes." Blaine slowly eased back on the power lever and the ship began to descend. The ship sent waves rippling off in all directions as it hit the water and disappeared beneath the surface.

"Twenty feet, forty feet, sixty feet, eighty feet, deploying landing struts, one hundred and twenty feet."

"Hold on, this isn't going to be pretty." The bridge jolted as the ship hit the bottom of the loch.

"Touchdown. Resting at one hundred and eighty feet below the surface." The crew sat silent for a moment listening to the sound of the bulkheads straining under the weight of the water.

"Kane, status report."

"She's taking in water through a few small breaches we picked up trying to push that asteroid, but it's nothing serious. Other than that, she's doing fine Captain." Hawkins stood up and walked over to one of the starboard side view ports. Staring out into the murky unsettled water he began to smile.

"We're home."

"The last time I looked at this lake I was five years old. We came here fishing, me and my father."

"You catch anything?" Hawkins asked still staring through the view port.

"The flu." Clarke and Hawkins chuckled.

"What about fish?"

"Not a damn thing."

"I've never seen a fish." The crew turned their eyes towards Blaine. "In fact, now I come to think about it, the only life forms I've ever seen other than humans are bugs."

"Of course, you were born on Tartarus weren't you. Don't

worry about it, when this is all over I'll take you fishing myself."

"Oh thanks Clarke, I'm touched." Blaine replied sarcastically with a smile on his face.

"Clarke, how long has the other ship been in range?"

"Judging from where it was before we took the dive, I'd say it's been in range long enough to kill us several times."

"Well I guess the plan worked. Now we need to come up with the next one. Clarke, I'm gonna need a rundown of everything we know about that ship, and I want facts, no speculation."

"Aye sir."

"Kane, we're gonna need more modified torpedoes, lots more."

"I'll get the repair drones on it straight away sir."

"Is it possible to increase the yield of the warheads?"

"Yes sir, I can just leave the original mining warheads in instead of replacing them with the modified ones."

"Take Blaine with you, I want this ship to pack as much of a punch as possible before we go back up there."

"Aye sir. Clarke, transfer a copy of the sensor information on that ship down to the machining room on deck three. It might come in handy."

"No problem Kane." Kane and Blaine walked into the turbo-lift and disappeared behind the closing doors.

"OK Clarke, what do we have?"

"Well Captain, as I said, the vessel is shaped like an arrowhead and is about eight miles in length. We have the clear advantage in manoeuvrability and it has the advantage in speed. In fact, with those shields it's feasible that it could safely double our top speed, maybe even reach half light."

"What about that hull plating?"

"The hull plating is a mystery Captain. The sensors simply refuse to believe there's anything there to scan and I have no idea why. All I can tell you from the information collected when that cargo bay door opened is that the plating is about fifteen feet thick."

"Jesus, no wonder the torpedoes didn't have any effect, that thing could quite comfortably fly straight through us. What about the interior, did you manage to locate the AI System core or any crystalline reactors?"

"There was a lot of interference from the sheer amount of machinery in there and the sensor data is confusing as a result. I didn't see any sign of the System core but if I'm reading this right the ship has a crystalline reactor the size of cargo bay four."

"Then we can use the pulse against it."

"Well, yes and no sir. The sound wave's effect on a crystalline reactor of that size should be devastating. The trouble is there are over eight hundred decks between the reactor core and the ship's hull. Even with the extremely high frequency of this sound wave, I don't think it would pass through that many decks without being suppressed."

"In other words, you wouldn't be able to hear it in the reactor room."

"Exactly sir."

"What are our options?"

"At this point I'm not sure Captain. I'm not even sure a torpedo with a mining warhead will breach that hull. Even if it can, I don't think we can do enough damage to something that size fast enough to stand a chance in a head to head fire fight."

"I agree, we're not going to win this with torpedoes. Somehow we have to get to that reactor." Hawkins walked round to Clarke's side at the tactical console. "Can you show me a deck plan of that ship?" Clarke punched a few keys on his keyboard and a map of the arrowhead vessel's interior flashed up on one of the monitors.

"I don't have a complete plan of the ship sir. I only managed to get a reading on about three square miles of the interior through that opening."

"It'll have to do. Look at this." Hawkins pointed at the map on the monitor. "The cargo bay that it tried to pull us into is four times bigger than our ship. That leaves us plenty of room for a fight."

"Are you suggesting we try to get to the reactor ourselves?"

"No, I'm suggesting that we take its hull armour out of the equation by letting it take us on board."

"How can we be sure that the ship will try to pick us up again? We have fired on it since then. It might just blow us out of the sky."

"It could have taken us out with no trouble at all but it didn't. It wants something, something on this ship and I'm betting it's our navigational logs." Clarke looked at the captain with a puzzled frown.

"Our navigational logs Captain?" he questioned.

"Remember how the last thing the computer destroyed at the time of the massacre was the lunar scientific habitats."

"Yes sir."

"The AI wouldn't have had any reason to do that unless it decided that the presence of the humans still posed a threat."

"So what you're basically saying is it won't be happy until it's made the human race extinct."

"No, what I'm saying is that it will wipe out anything it considers as a threat to Earth, and I think that list now includes the colony."

"Why would it need to attack the colony, they aren't a threat to the planet?"

"Clarke, the first thing we did when we arrived is throw enough rocks at the planet to kill every life form ten times over. Even if the AI gave us a chance to explain ourselves, which I doubt, all we have as a defensive statement is 'sorry about that, we weren't aiming at you'. Somehow I don't think that's going to help us much."

"Hmm good point. OK so we're working on the assumption that the ship will try to tractor us in because it needs our navigational logs to hunt down and slaughter our entire race."

"Exactly." Clarke rubbed his eyes and sighed.

"I need a drink and a cigarette."

"We ran out of anything resembling alcohol years ago." Hawkins remarked reaching into his pocket for his cigarettes. "And, unless I'm mistaken, the last of the cigarette stockpile is in cargo bay two along with a couple of thousand gallons of water." Clarke took a cigarette from the captain. "This is probably the last packet on Earth."

"Don't worry Captain, we'll more than likely be dead before it runs out." Hawkins laughed as Clarke took one of the bridge's emergency cutting torches out of its bracket and lit his cigarette.

"That's it."

"Sorry sir?"

"The laser cutter." Hawkins directed Clarke's attention back to the deck plan on the tactical console monitor. "After we get inside the cargo bay we can cut a hole through the deck plating straight up into the reactor room. That would be enough to get the sound wave through all the decks, wouldn't it?" questioned Hawkins as he pointed at the monitor.

"With the wavelength of this sound wave maybe, but you need a cutting torch the size of the communications dish to pull that off." Hawkins grinned.

"Actually you'd need a cutting torch mounted to the communication dish's retractable platform to pull that off." Hawkins stubbed out his cigarette and walked over to the turbo-lift. "Hawkins to Blaine, do you think you can handle the torpedo refits by yourself?"

"Shouldn't be a problem sir, we're just supervising the repair drones down here anyway."

"Good. Tell Kane to meet me in cargo bay four, he's gonna love this."

CHAPTER: 5

The sun shone down over the hills from a clear blue sky, and a light breeze rustled through the branches of the trees in the vast and wide stretching woodlands surrounding the loch. A family of deer who had been grazing on the long green grasses by the waterside, ran startled for the cover of the trees as three black helmets slowly emerged from the water.

"Are we certain that the viruses the AI created will be gone Captain?"

"Like I explained earlier Blaine, the viruses weren't airborne they were passed by human contact. The second the last infected human died the viruses ceased to exist, so you can stop worrying and take your helmet off."

"Is Kane sure he can build this Cannon Captain? I mean he's been tinkering around in the machine shops for nearly a week now. In fact, he's been spending so much time alone down there I wouldn't be surprised if he's started talking to the repair drones."

"Kane's fine. I spoke to him before we left and he's confident that his design will work just fine. The way I understand it, the Cannon should work like a scaled-up version of the laser cutting torches. Kane thinks that with the right modifications and a direct power feed to the crystalline reactor, he can get this thing to fire over quite impressive distances. If it works as well as he thinks it will it should be quite a formidable weapon." Blaine finally took of his helmet and took in a deep breath of the morning air.

"Oh god that's good. The air on Tartarus always beat the ship's recycled oxygen mix but this is beautiful."

"Yeah there's no beating the morning air of Earth." Clarke slid out of his spacesuit and laid it up against one of the trees near the water's edge. "Blaine, take off your suit before you do any sightseeing. If you tear it on a bramble bush or something it's gonna be an interesting walk back to the ship."

"What's a bramble bush?" asked Blaine as he removed his suit and threw it to Clarke. Clarke shook his head and chuckled to himself as he put the spacesuit under the tree.

"Blaine, you'd better stay close to me." The group walked off into the woods.

"I've seen trees like these in one of the databanks back on the colony. They're bigger than they look on the computer screen. Wow look at that."

"What?" questioned Hawkins, trying to locate what Blaine was pointing at.

"There in that tree. Some sort of furry little creature." Hawkins smiled.

"That's a squirrel."

"A squirrel," repeated Blaine still staring at the creature. "Damn thing's fast."

"Earth's life forms have been evolving for much longer than those slimy little things on Tartarus. You'll find that most of the creatures here are fast." Hawkins pointed into the trees. "Believe it or not there are animals on this planet that could outsprint that squirrel without even breaking a sweat." At hearing this, Blaine's gaze moved from the trees and fixed on the captain.

"What's the fastest?"

"Well the fastest land animal is called a cheetah. It's a big cat, a predator. They have a top speed of sixty miles an hour."

"Shit, are they dangerous?" Blaine looked around alertly. Hawkins grinned.

"Don't panic, there aren't any cheetahs in Britain, and there not really big enough to attack a human. Not a fully grown man anyway." Blaine jumped as a bird flew past over their heads.

"Fuck me this place has some big bugs." Clarke and Hawkins roared with laughter. Hawkins patted Blaine on the back.

"That wasn't a bug, boy, it was a bird. A crow to be exact."

"Well how the hell was I suppose to know there are flying animals here." Blaine replied looking slightly embarrassed.

"Didn't you ever learn anything about this planet while you

were on Tartarus?"

"Only what I managed to pick up from computer files and none of them had any information about animals that fly."

"Yeah, well the anatomy of birds probably wasn't considered essential information for the running of starships," remarked Clarke having to hold himself up on a tree trunk. Blaine just nodded and smiled.

"Asshole." The crew walked on. Clarke couldn't help but be impressed at how efficiently the AI System had cleaned up the planet. The ferns he walked through and the trees he walked past were growing where a road once ran. He had noticed when they emerged from the water that the bridges that crossed the loch and the building that surrounded it were gone. In fact the only evidence left on Earth that humans had ever been here were the memories of this crew. They had to stop the AI. They had to make a difference here. The thought of the human race passing into oblivion without leaving any evidence of their existence filled him with dread.

"What the hell is that?" Hawkins and Clarke turned to Blaine ready to identify the next unknown life form he had discovered. A cold shiver ran through Hawkins as he followed Blaine's gaze up to the sky. Like shooting stars, hundreds of burning objects streaked across the sky as they entered the atmosphere, scattering in all directions as far as the eye could see.

"Give me a fucking break."

"Drop-pods Captain?"

"Drop-pods Blaine."

"There's no way it could have zeroed in on us with all the life form readings on this planet."

"It didn't." Hawkins pointed at the sky. "Look at the dispersal pattern. It must have worked out which area we landed in from our entry window, and now it's sending out the search party."

"Oh great, so now we're being hunted too," shouted Blaine.

"Let's get back to the ship." The crew ran back through the forest as fast as their legs would carry them. A distant rumbling filled the air as the drop-pods started to impact with the ground. The forest shook as a pod screeched over the crew's heads and impacted just beyond the treeline in front of them.

"Stop," ordered Hawkins.

"Captain we have to go now."

"The AI would have accounted for the fact that sensors don't penetrate through deep water. Whatever's in that pod is probably capable of searching the loch and it will find us eventually. If we attack it before it gets its shit together we'll stand a better chance and the AI might think it was damaged in the landing." Clarke and Blaine looked at each other and Blaine pulled out his sidearm.

"Let's get it on." The crew set off towards the smoke, which was now billowing over the trees. After busting through the undergrowth into the new and smouldering clearing they stopped in shock.

"Fuck me." Blaine trained his pistol on the large bullet-shaped object, which was charred and smoking from its journey through the atmosphere. As the crew watched, it suddenly cracked open revealing a small metallic creature. Roughly three feet high and six feet in length the shiny beast resembled a large cat. Pistons and wires interrupted the smooth shape of its body and legs. Its feet and jaws sporting blade-like teeth and claws, which picked up the reflection of the dancing fire from the now burning woodland. The beast's head slowly started to rise as its systems came online.

"Shoot it before it wakes up." The group trained their guns and blasted the creature until it hit the ground motionless. Hawkins slowly walked over, his pistol still aimed at its head.

"OK, we got it."

"Did it have time to activate?"

"I don't know. Blaine, give me a hand with this thing."

Kane dropped his tool kit in shock as Blaine and Hawkins carried the robotic creature into the machine shop.

"What the fuck is that?"

"It's some sort of robot. There's drop-pods full of these things landing all over the place." Hawkins wiped the sweat off his brow after he and Blaine had lifted the machine onto one of the worktops.

"There are more of these things out there!" shouted Kane.

"Just a couple of hundred. If anyone needs me I'll be on the bridge emptying the weapons locker." Blaine took a final look at the metal cat and exited the machine room in quite a hurry.

"Look at the god damn claws on this thing. It's a good job you took your sidearms."

"Kane, after today I'm sleeping with my sidearm." Kane picked up the creatures head.

"You lucky bastards."

"Excuse me."

"Look at this." Kane pointed at a charred mass of wires in the back of the creature's head.

"This thing had its head down when you shot it didn't it." Hawkins looked surprised.

"Yes, how did you…"

"This shot to the back of the head is what put it down," interrupted Kane. "The rest of the shots did little more than superficial damage." Kane lifted the machine's head and the melted mass of wires disappeared as the back of the creatures metallic scull covered them over. "If you'd given this thing time to lift its head, you wouldn't be here right now."

"So what are you telling me, that our weapons can't stop these things?"

"Oh you'd stop them eventually, if you got the chance to fire off that many rounds. It would probably be wise to break out the rifles." Hawkins nodded and walked off towards the door.

"Well at least Blaine will be happy."

"Err." Hawkins stopped at the door and turned back round. "Are you just gonna leave this here?" Hawkins smiled.

"Maybe you can teach it to fetch." Kane sighed as Hawkins walked off. By the time Hawkins reached the bridge, Blaine had picked out a couple of Plasma Rifles and was loading up ammo belts with power cells.

"Kane suggests that we keep the rifles close at hand from now on. Apparently a lucky shot was all that took that thing down."

"How so?" asked Blaine still pushing power cells into belt pockets.

"It has a vulnerable spot at the base of its neck when its head is down. If we'd given it chance to look up we'd have been cat food." Hawkins caught one of the rifles as Blaine threw it across the room.

"Works for me. Here, you'd better take some spare clips." Blaine threw Hawkins one of the ammo belts.

"We should be OK for a while." Hawkins reassured as he clipped the ammo belt round his waist. "There didn't seem to be a lot of drop-pods in relation to the size of the landmass. It should be a while before any more of those things work their way here."

"That's providing we got it before it had time to scan us."

"Yeah."

"So is that what one of those cheetah things looks like? It seems to fit the description you gave me."

"Not quite, it looks more like a leopard only bigger." Blaine frowned.

"A leopard, Captain?"

"It's another big cat. It's not as fast as a cheetah but it's much better at climbing and I'm sorry to say that it is big enough to kill a man."

"But why would it build machines that look like Earth animals Captain? It doesn't make any sense."

"Actually Blaine it makes perfect sense. Why spend time developing something when you can simply copy a design that nature has been developing for thousands of years."

"Yeah I suppose that makes sense."

"Clarke to Hawkins, come in sir."

"What is it Clarke?"

"If you don't need me for anything Captain, I thought I'd go down to the machine shop and take a look at our new passenger. I might be able to get some useful information from it."

"OK Clarke, but be careful if your gonna be playing around with that thing. The last thing I need right now is a six foot long killing machine running around the lower decks."

"No problem sir, I'll be extra careful. Clarke out."

"Hawkins to Kane, what's the status of my Cannon?"

"Kane to Hawkins, I've finished building all the complicated components Captain. I'm just waiting for the repair drones to mount the main sections onto the retractable platform. As soon as they're finished I can start hooking up the power supply to the reactor."

"What about the communications array?"

"Well I've been able to re-route the short range communications through the secondary sensor array, but we're not going to be able to send or receive any long range messages until I can reattach the dish."

"Don't worry about the dish Kane, there's no one out there we need to talk to anyway. Keep me posted, Hawkins out." Hawkins walked over to the tactical console and started typing on one of the keyboards. "I don't like this Blaine, we're not going to know if any of those things are coming until they're knocking at the door."

"Isn't there any way of calibrating the sensors to penetrate water more efficiently?"

"Not that I know of. All we can do is set the sensors to warn us as soon as they detect something."

Down in the machine shop Kane was taking the opportunity to acquaint himself with the ships new visitor.

"Damn, you're a real piece of work my friend." Kane lent forward for a closer look at the creature's eyes.

"Aaarrghh!" Kane jumped back in shock and fell onto the floor. Clarke stood in the doorway laughing.

"Got you." Kane grinned in relief as Clarke took his hand and helped him up.

"You bastard, I almost messed my pants."

"Sorry, I couldn't resist it. Looks like you're keeping yourself busy," Clarke remarked as he looked over the masses of new wires, which were running from the machine to various other pieces of equipment.

"This thing's amazing Clarke."

"This thing's a walking blender Kane. Look at those claws."

"You're missing the point. Yes it's designed to track and kill, but it's the equipment it carries to do that job that interests me. Look at these eyes for instance." Clarke lent in to get a better look. "They're quite advanced." Kane took a small tool out of his pocket and proceeded to point at different parts of the eye. "This section allows it to see in the infrared spectrum. In other words it can track your body heat. This section appears to be some sort of advanced night vision system and this thing is an extremely high-tech form of sonar for echo-location."

"So you're saying that this thing would kick ass at hide and seek."

"I'm saying that this thing could track a housefly through the Amazon Rainforest, and that's not even the half of it." Kane pointed at the nose of the creature. "The nose contains what I think is a Pheromone Scanner."

"Now you're losing me."

"All life forms naturally produce pheromones, smells. If this thing had the chance to smell you even once, there would be no way you could ever hide from it."

"Couldn't you change your smell by covering yourself in deodorant or rolling in dung or something?"

"It's slightly more sophisticated than that Clarke. If this thing can pick up pheromones as accurately as I think it can, then it can track you by smelling your fear."

"Fear has a smell?"

"Fear is nothing more than a chemical reaction in your brain, and it gives off plenty of pheromones to trace." Clarke now looked unmistakably worried.

"So let me see if I've got this straight. If another one of these things passes by the drop-pod landing site where we found this one, it's gonna pick up our trail and follow our smells straight to us."

"Well technically it can only follow your smell to the edge of the water, but yes that's about the size of it."

"What about its processing capacity. How smart is this thing?"

"No way of telling at this point but incidentally, that is something I wanted to talk to you about."

Back on the bridge Blaine and Hawkins were looking over the arrowhead vessels deck plan.

"You see what I mean. Even if we can get the AI to try and tractor us into the same cargo bay as last time. We're still gonna have to take these four energy-beam weapons out before we can risk raising the Cannon." Blaine pointed out the energy-beam weapons on the screen as he explained. "Otherwise our secret weapon is gonna be in pieces before we get a chance to fire it."

Hawkins nodded.

"I see what you mean. Any suggestions?"

"Well, the cargo bay's big but there's not enough room to start firing torpedoes. The only other way is to take them out with a Plasma Rifle from one of the top hatches."

"It would take two of us to even stand a chance of taking those guns out before they fire."

"And whoever goes out there would have to wear a spacesuit. Even if we wait till the outer door closes, there's no guarantee that the cargo bay will have a breathable atmosphere. After all, machines have no need for breathable air."

"The hatch covers should provide some protection from these two guns." Blaine pointed at the monitor. "These two guns have a clear shot at whoever's out there, so we'll have to take them out first."

"Agreed."

"You know sir, it would be easier to just destroy the reactor with the Cannon."

"We have to assume that ship has at least one back up power supply. Besides, even if we did manage to knock out the power the AI wouldn't be destroyed. If we overload all the systems we can fry that bastard before it knows what's hit it. Just because the ship's power is off-line, doesn't mean that whatever's crawling around in it will shut down as well."

"Clarke to Hawkins, could you please say the word 'Reeva' into the communicator please Captain."

"What the hell for?"

"Humour me."

"Reeva."

"Thanks that'll do. Is Blaine there with you Captain?"

"Yeah I'm here."

"Do me a favour and say…"

"Reeva," interrupted Blaine.

"Thanks Blaine, Clarke out." Hawkins and Blaine looked at each other.

"Wonder what that's about."

"Who cares? What about getting out?"

"Sorry Blaine."

"After we set off the Sonic Pulse and fry the whole ship, its power should be off-line due to the system meltdown, shouldn't it?"

"If everything goes to plan, yes."

"Then how the hell are we going to get out of the cargo bay?" Hawkins stood in silence and looked at Blaine, as if trying to think of a reasonable answer. After a few seconds he reached into his pocket and took out a cigarette. After lighting it and taking a couple of hits, he took a thoughtful look around the bridge and returned his gaze to Blaine.

"I think we both know the odds of getting out of that cargo bay once the outer door closes." Blaine looked down at the monitor displaying the huge deck plan of the arrowhead vessel. After a thoughtful pause he nodded and looked back up at Hawkins.

"The needs of the many outweigh the needs of the few."

"Yes they do Blaine. Send a copy of the AI vessel data to the mess hall wall monitor. I'm hungry." Hawkins turned away from Blaine and headed out of the bridge. "Oh and Blaine."

"Yes Captain?"

"Stop quoting corny movie lines, or my foot will be boldly going where no one has gone before."

"Oh, now that was cheap." Hawkins smiled to himself as the pair walked out through the bridge's main access door and off towards the mess hall. Hawkins could hear the metallic rattling sound of someone running along the grid metal floor of the corridor on the deck below them.

"Hawkins to Kane. Everything OK down there?"

"Yes sir, everything's fine. Why do you ask?"

"I just heard someone running through the corridors. Guess I'm just a little on edge with that damn machine on board."

"It's just Clarke sir, I sent him to fetch some spare computer components from one of the maintenance lockers."

"No problem Kane. Me and Blaine are heading down to the mess if either of you fancy a break."

"We're fine sir. I'd like to finish up down here anyway, we're learning quite a lot from this thing."

"Such as?"

"Well for a start, I can confirm that the AI is after our navigational logs."

"How do you know that?"

"Clarke's managed to break this things programming, and it's amazingly complex Captain. It's not controlled by a computer system like the repair drones, instead it actually seems to have the capacity to make its own decisions."

"What the hell are you telling me Kane, that this thing can do whatever the hell it likes?"

"Not exactly Captain, the best way to explain it would be to think of it as a soldier. For example, human soldiers have their own individual consciousness, free will, whatever you want to call it. However, they still follow the orders they are given without question. When the Auto-Repair System stops sending the repair drones orders, they simply stop moving. When the ship in orbit stops sending these things orders, they're free to do whatever they feel like doing."

"So you're saying that even if we succeed in destroying the AI, we're still gonna have to take out every individual machine that's currently scurrying around this continent?"

"Basically, yes."

"Kane, tell me that thing's power source has a very short operational lifespan."

"Well if you're thinking about leaving them till they drop, we'll be waiting for quite a while." Hawkins sighed.

"It's powered by what looks like some sort of fusion generator Captain. These things will probably still be ticking when we're all long dead." Hawkins closed his eyes and took a deep calming breath.

"This shit is getting better by the fucking minute."

"At least we know for certain that the AI wants the navigational logs. So at least the first part of the plan's going to work," comforted Blaine.

"Oh great, so the AI is definitely going to try to take us prisoner." Hawkins continued on down the corridor. "Now I feel much better!" he shouted as he disappeared through the mess hall door. Blaine sighed and followed the Captain through.

"What are you having Blaine?" asked Hawkins as he punched buttons on the food dispenser.

"Whatever, it's all just as bad." The food dispenser hatch opened revealing two steaming bowls of what looked like dark grey porridge. Hawkins carried them over to the table where Blaine had seated himself. After placing one down in front of Blaine he took a seat. Blaine stared at the bowl of slop with a look of contempt as he stirred it around with his spoon. "Oh that's it. I can handle hostile starships and killer robots but if I have to eat any more of these nutritional supplements, I'm going to surrender. Can't we go out and bag a few of those small squirrels or something?" Hawkins grinned.

"It's too quiet out there now. The weapons discharge from a Plasma gun is detectable on scanners. The only reason we got away with firing on that machine without being detected was that the power signatures from all those drop-pods masked our weapons fire." Blaine picked up a spoonful of his meal. He turned his spoon and watched as it dribbled back into his bowl.

"Great. I'm surrounded by hundreds of edible life forms and I'm still doomed to eat this snot." The sound of approaching feet on the metal grid floor let Blaine know that someone had just entered the mess hall. From the seat he had chosen, Blaine's back was to the door and he was unable to see who had entered. Though it sounded like more than one set of boots.

"Changed your minds guys? I suggest you try the slime, it's particularly good today." Blaine stopped his conversation as he looked across the table at Hawkins. The captain was staring straight past him wearing a look of dread. Blaine's attention turned back to the sound of the footsteps, which were much closer now and had slowed to a crawling pace. As he noticed Hawkins slowly reaching for his sidearm, Blaine glanced at the Plasma Rifles that they had propped against the food dispenser all the way across the room. He didn't know what was approaching behind him but from the look on the captain's face he could tell it wasn't anything pleasant. It hadn't attacked yet but that could all change if it saw him reach for his sidearm. He looked at Hawkins and tipped his head to the right, trying to indicate which way he was going to move. Hawkins seemed to understand what he meant and nodded.

"On three Blaine." Hawkins whispered at a barely audible level. "One, two, three." Blaine dove out of the way as Hawkins sprung to his feet and quickly aimed his pistol.

"Wait, don't shoot!" Hawkins stopped as Clarke came

running into the mess hall. "Don't shoot sir, it's not going to attack." Clarke panted reassuringly. "Reeva halt." The metal beast turned to face Clarke and stopped. Hawkins lowered his pistol as Blaine picked himself up off the floor.

"What the fuck is going on here Clarke?"

"We fixed it Captain."

"What the hell do you mean you fixed it?" Hawkins started to sound angry as his shock subsided.

"Me and Kane managed to reprogram it."

"Go on."

"Like I said earlier sir, it's like a soldier. It has its own unique consciousness but it takes order from the mother-ship via a communications link. After Kane repaired the pistol damage, I removed its up-link node and replaced it with one of our own communications nodes from the wrist-com's." Clarke paused and cleared his throat anxiously awaiting a response. Hawkins looked at Blaine who was now stood behind one of the tables pointing a rifle at the machine.

"Blaine, keep that rifle ready."

"Aye sir." Hawkins holstered his sidearm as he cautiously walked out from behind the table and headed towards Clarke.

"So it takes orders from us now?" Hawkins walked upto the creature that was still standing motionless looking at Clarke.

"Yes sir, we've named it Reeva. That's also the password required to make it obey commands."

"Reeva." Hawkins jumped back in surprise as the metal cat swiftly turned to face him.

"Don't worry Captain. It always does that when you say its name." Hawkins quickly composed himself.

"So this thing is waiting for me to give it an order?"

"Yes Captain."

"And it will take orders from anyone with a wrist-com?"

"No sir, as a safety precaution we programmed it to respond to our four voices only."

"Ah, that's why you needed us to say its name into the communicators."

"Exactly Captain." Clarke looked down at Reeva. "You know it's just going to stand there until you give it a command." Hawkins looked at the bright green light of Reeva's eyes as she looked up at him. He frowned and pointed to the other side of the room. "Go and stand over there." Reacting instantly Reeva walked over to the far side of the room and turned to face the captain. "Hmm, it works. Any idea what this thing's capable of?"

"Well it has extremely high-tech visual and olfactory senses and from here it could hear a pin drop on the bridge. The statistical data we collected from its databanks says that it's capable of achieving speeds of up to forty miles an hour."

"So out-running these things isn't going to be easy?" mocked Blaine.

"That's nothing Blaine, this thing's also capable of jumping as high as fifteen feet. So what it can't climb up, it can sure as hell jump over."

"You know, I'm starting to worry about these things more than the mother-ship."

"I thought these things did pretty much what they wanted in-between orders." Clarke looked over at Reeva who was still standing motionless at the other end of the room.

"That's because it's still carrying out your orders Captain."

"How is it still carrying out my orders? I just told it to go and stand over there."

"And that's what she will do until you tell her otherwise. You see that's the kind of task that can't be completed. If you'd told her to kill Blaine for instance, the task would have been completed when he stopped breathing and her free will would be allowed to take over. Now, as there is no definable end-point to the task you set her, she will simply continue to obey the command until someone tells her otherwise." Hawkins nodded.

"Could it actually be told to do that?"

"Told to do what Blaine?"

"Told to kill someone."

"She'll obey almost any order that doesn't conflict with the directives Kane and I programmed into her."

"Which are?" questioned Hawkins.

"Well for a start you can stop worrying Blaine, her primary directive is to protect us. You can order her to attack anything in the universe, except for the crew of this ship. Her second directive is to only take commands from people that she has a stored voiceprint of, which as I've already explained, is us. Directive three allows her to use whatever means are necessary to defend herself if she's attacked."

"Obviously that doesn't include us, right?"

"Of course."

"Hey Captain, what about sending this thing out to fetch something edible? It'd be a chance to test these super-senses that Clarke's talking about."

"This thing would stand out like a priest in a brothel Blaine. The AI's bound to know something's wrong if a missing and presumed destroyed drone suddenly reappears and starts dragging wildlife into the loch." Blaine nodded. "Clarke, do you think you can tap into this things optical systems?" Clarke stood looking thoughtful for a moment.

"I suppose I could get a picture of what she's seeing if I tie a transmitter into her optical wiring."

"Good, get it done as soon as possible. Maybe we can use it as a scout or something."

"I'll get right on it Captain. Reeva come with me." Hawkins and Blaine backed off slightly as the machine followed Clarke out of the mess hall.

"This is fucked up," remarked Blaine after Clarke and Reeva's footsteps had grown sufficiently distant.

"Oh yeah." Hawkins walked back over to his table and sat down. "Are you going to eat this?" he questioned pointing at Blaine's unfinished bowl of food.

"Be my guest. I'm not really that hungry now anyway." Hawkins picked up Blaine's bowl and began to spoon its contents into his.

"As long as you're not doing anything, you might as well see if Kane needs any help. The faster we get this Cannon online, the faster we can get out of here."

"Aye sir." Blaine walked out of the mess hall and made his way back to the bridge.

"Blaine to Kane, where are you?"

"Down in the reactor room. I'm trying to hook up this damn power cable for the Laser Cannon."

"Need any help?"

"If I had someone to help me lift the deck plating I could

set this thing up permanently. Otherwise I'm going to have to trail this power cable down the corridors."

"No problem Kane, I'm on my way."

"Thanks Blaine. Kane out." Blaine walked into the bridge's turbo-lift.

"Engine rooms." The lift began its descent towards the engine rooms.

As well as travelling vertically, the turbo-lifts could also travel horizontally throughout the length of the ship. This feature could save the crew hours when having to cover the vast distances between the bow and stern of the half-mile long vessel. By the time Blaine arrived, Kane had already removed a couple of the large sections of deck plating and was struggling to lift another. Blaine hurried over to give him a hand.

"Nice timing Blaine."

"On three. One, two, three." Blaine and Kane pulled the floor plate up and rested it against the wall of the corridor. "Jesus, how the hell did you move those two sections by yourself? These things must weigh over a hundred pounds."

"You know when you, Clarke and the captain are up on the bridge pushing buttons and pulling levers?"

"Yeah."

"Well I'm down here lifting and carrying like a real man." Blaine grinned.

"All hail the grease monkey."

"Very witty. Just help me get this power cable hooked up before any more of those machines decide to pay us a visit."

"Clarke to Kane, can you come up to machine shop two, I need a hand with something."

"Sorry Clarke, I need to get this power cable hooked up. What's the problem?"

"Captain Hawkins has asked me to hook Reeva's optics upto a transmitter, so we can see what she's seeing. I'm just wondering if you know of a way of doing that without the AI mother-ship being able to pick up the signal."

"Hooking the transmitter upto a frequency modulator should make the signal harder to lock onto. If possible try to give Reeva direct access to the transmitter, so that we can order her to cut the transmission when we don't require it."

"OK, thanks Kane, Clarke out."

"Sounds like Reeva's gonna make a good addition to the crew."

"As long as she's on point instead of one of us, I'm happy." Kane looked down at the small screen on his wrist communicator as it started to beep.

"Kane to Hawkins, come in Captain."

"Hawkins here, what is it Kane?"

"The auto-repair drones have finished putting the Cannon together Captain. It'll be ready as soon as Blaine and I finish attaching the power cable."

"How long do you think that should take?"

"About forty minutes Captain."

"Very well, I'll be on the bridge prepping the ship. Tell Blaine and Clarke that we leave at eighteen hundred hours."

"Aye sir."

"Hawkins out."

The next hour passed relatively quickly due to the busyness of the crew. Kane and Blaine managed to run the power cable under the corridor deck plates, before hooking it up to the ship's new Cannon. Clarke eventually got Reeva's optical transmission system online and after prepping the ship for take off, Hawkins gave the crew a final rundown of the plans for the mission ahead.

With a great rumble of dissipating water, the Dark Star emerged from the loch. Animals and birds in the surrounding woodland panicked and scattered as the engines burst into action.

"Activating atmospheric thrusters, setting course for upper atmosphere."

"Clarke, give me a sensor reading."

"Bear with me sir, I'm still waiting for all this damn water to drain off the sensor nodes."

"Blaine, the water in the port cargo bay isn't draining properly, can you give me a three degree roll to port."

"No problem Kane."

"Sensor's are drying out and coming back online Captain. They're still too wet for an atmospheric scan, however I am picking up several dozen small power signatures, heading at various speeds towards Loch Ness."

"I guess they found us."

"Breaking through upper atmosphere in five, four, three, two, one. Bringing main engines online Captain."

"Captain, I'm picking up a small ship in orbit, about two miles off our stern."

"Identify."

"It appears to be of the same configuration as the AI mother-ship captain, just a lot smaller. The sensors are having the same amount of trouble trying to scan it."

"Status?"

"The ship is heading this way Captain. I'm picking up at least two separate power surges emanating from it."

"Shields up and weapons charging. Blaine, evasive manoeuvres now!" Blaine threw the Dark Star into a hard turn seconds before the advancing vessel's main weapon discharged. The bridge rumbled as the energy-beam narrowly missed the ship.

"Wow, that was too close."

"I think it's safe to say that its weaponry is the same as the mother-ship's."

"Picking up another power build-up." Once again Blaine changed direction as rapidly as the huge bulk of the ship allowed and once again narrowly dodged the energy weapons discharge."

"Captain, that energy-beam is significantly less powerful than the mother-ship's. If that's due to the scale difference of the crystalline reactors, then the shields should be less effective also."

"Well done Clarke. Blaine bring us about, we're through running."

"Aye sir, coming about." Blaine turned the ship through a hundred and eighty-degree loop and levelled off. "It's no good sir, this one's more manoeuvrable than us. It's followed us straight through the loop, I can't shake it."

"Clarke, load torpedo tubes one through ten. Prepare to fire a spread on my mark."

"Aye sir, tubes one through ten are locked, loaded and ready to fly."

"Captain, the warheads on these torpedoes are still at full

mining yield. I suggest we only fire one or two at this range."

"Noted Kane. Clarke, fire tubes one and two."

"Target locked, Torpedoes away." The tracking system on the tactical console began to beep as Clarke launched the torpedoes. "Impact in four, three, two, one. Negative impact, vessel has moved to avoid torpedoes."

"Damn it, ready tubes three through ten. Launch in a random dispersal pattern on my mark."

"Setting torpedoes to fire in a forty-five degree spread. Ready to fire Captain."

"Blaine, get ready to increase speed as soon as Clarke launches the torpedoes."

"Aye sir."

"Fire."

"Torpedoes away."

"Putting the pedal to the metal."

"Vessel is attempting to avoid the torpedoes. Impact in three, two, one." Clarke and Kane slammed into their consoles as one of the torpedoes exploded, tossing the Dark Star around in the blast.

"Damage report!" shouted Hawkins through the din.

"Minor damage to the aft hull plating and starboard side shield emitters. Repair drones have been dispatched."

"Clarke, status of the pursuing vessel."

"Pursuing vessel is adrift. My new ability to scan small sections of the interior would suggest that its hull plating is very badly damaged."

"Score one for the good guys."

"Any sign of the mother-ship?"

"There's no sign of it Captain."

"Are you sure?"

"It's pretty hard to miss."

"Kane, how many new low-yield torpedoes did you guys make?"

"One full spread Captain."

"Clarke, load them."

"Aye sir, loading tubes one through ten with low-yield torpedoes."

"Blaine, bring us alongside that ship. Kane get Reeva ready

for a little scouting mission." Kane hurried into the turbo-lift as Blaine brought the ship about and headed for the battered vessel.

"Can we get a lock with the docking clamps?"

"We can probably lock onto one of the breaches in the hull, but it's not going to be very stable. One wrong move and whoever goes out there could end up spinning through space."

"Are you picking up any power reading?"

"Nothing big enough to be an active power source for the ship, it appears to be dead in space. However I am reading several small moving energy signatures."

"Repair drones?"

"Couldn't say Captain, but something's moving around in there."

"Coming alongside the vessel now Captain."

"OK Blaine, all stop."

"Aye sir, all stop."

"Lock us on, Clarke."

"Extending portside docking gantry now sir. Contact in three seconds." The bridge jolted as the docking clamps came into contact with the other ship. "Docking clamps are locked and holding Captain."

"Good job guys. Hawkins to Kane, bring Reeva and meet us in the portside airlock."

"Aye sir."

"Oh and Kane, you'd better bring a rifle."

"Way ahead of you Captain."

"Clarke, I need you to stay here and monitor Reeva's new optical up-link system. Blaine, you're with me." Blaine left his position at the helm and after stopping to pick up his rifle, he followed Hawkins into the turbo-lift.

"Clarke?"

"Yes Captain?"

"Keep an eye on the sensors. That mother-ship's out there somewhere."

"No problem."

"Deck five, section one." Hawkins and Blaine were lost behind the hissing doors of the turbo-lift and Clarke was left alone. He brought up an internal map of deck five on one of the four overhead monitors that curved around the roof above his console. If anything decided to wander off that ship through the airlock, he wanted to know about it before it got anywhere near the bridge. After setting the external sensors to scan for any incoming vessels or anomalies, he walked over to the main view port to take a look at the conquered ship. He couldn't see much of the ship from his position, but he could see enough to be impressed by its design. Even from this distance the hull looked silky smooth and seamless, with the obvious exception of the twisted and torn sections damaged by the torpedo. Staring at this tool of destruction set against the backdrop of the planet, the clouds below reflected in its shiny black surface. He couldn't help but think that it actually looked quite beautiful.

"Kane to Clarke, are you receiving the signal from Reeva's optical transmitter?" Clarke ran back to his console and started typing on his keyboard.

"Hold on Kane." Another one of the overhead monitors came online, displaying a strange and hazy bright coloured picture of what appeared to be a hand waving back and forth.

"Confirmed Kane. She appears to be using her infrared sensors at the moment."

"Yeah that makes sense. The airlock is quite cold, life forms and anything else with a heat signature would show up quite well in here."

"Well it works, you guys are shining like beacons." Clarke watched Reeva begin to walk forward as the outer airlock door opened.

"Clarke we're sending Reeva in a few metres in front of us. Let us know the second you see anything, I don't want any surprises."

"Aye sir." Hawkins, Blaine and Kane activated their rifle torches and slowly crossed the docking gantry into the other ship.

"OK boys, this is a salvage mission. If you find anything that could be useful to us, data storage banks, technology etc, bag it and bring it with you. Watch you backs in here guys." The team walked on through the dark, still corridors of the ship. The sound of their magnetic boots grasping the metal floor was all that broke the deafening silence. Hawkins glanced up and out into space as they passed under one of the many breaches in the outer hull. "Be careful not to tear your suits on all this twisted metal."

"Hold on a minute." Kane stopped and removed a cutting torch from the satchel he was carrying. After deactivating his magnetic boots, he gently pushed away from the floor and grabbed onto a small piece of battered hull plating at the edge of the breach.

"What are you doing Kane?"

"I'm trying to get a sample of this hull plating. If I can analyse it, I might be able to explain why it screws up the sensors."

"Clarke to Hawkins, come in."

"What is it Clarke?"

"The corridor ahead of you opens up into a large circular room. It's about twice the size of cargo bay four Captain, and if I'm making it out properly through this damn heat vision, it's some sort of launch bay."

"Launch bay?"

"Yes sir, there's dozens of launch tubes in here, all empty. I'm thinking it was this ship that launched the drop-pods, not the mother-ship."

"Then the mother-ship could have left days ago."

"Yes sir. It could be anywhere by now." Kane reactivated his magnetic boots and quickly drifted back down to the floor.

"Damn this stuff's tough. I've never seen a laser torch take that long to cut through anything." Kane put the cutting torch and the sample of hull plating in his satchel and the crew walked on towards the launch bay.

"Jesus, this room must span all the way across the ship."

"There doesn't appear to be anyway out except the way we came in."

"Hawkins to Clarke, can you get me a deck plan of this section?"

"Sorry Captain, I can't scan enough of the interior to create a deck plan."

"Don't worry about it Clarke, we'll just have to…" Hawkins was cut short by a loud thud. "What was that?"

"Sorry Captain, I didn't catch that."

"Standby Clarke." Kane jumped as another larger thud

echoed through the room.

"Over there Captain." Blaine pointed towards a large indentation in the wall. As the crew watched, another large thud filled the room and the indentation grew larger. They watched as thud after thud the indentation grew until the bulkhead started to breach under the strain.

"Clarke to Hawkins, I'm picking up a moving power source in one of the chambers adjacent to your position."

"No shit Clarke." Hawkins and the crew stepped back in horror as the bulkhead gave way. Stood before them was a towering multi-limbed mass of pistons and shiny metal, standing at least five feet tall. Several small red lights spread across the front of the machine's main body, reflecting on the blade, like mandibles that twitched beneath them. Hawkins and Blaine slowly turn their heads and looked at each other in disbelief before quickly raising their rifles and opening fire.

Kane followed suit and proceeded to discharge his rifle at the machine, which started to move quickly across the huge room towards them.

"Aim for the legs!" shouted Kane through the din of the weapons fire. Hawkins and Blaine followed the suggestion but the monstrous mass of metal kept coming.

"Everybody aim for the top joint on the left claw."

"Which left?"

"Damn it Blaine, our left." Hawkins' plan worked. The machines left mandible was sent spinning through the air as the team hit it with the concentrated power of all three rifles.

"Yes, that's it. Quickly aim for the centre of the main body." The crew fired at the machine, which was now only a few feet away. Kane closed his eyes as it closed in and Hawkins braced himself for the impact. The huge machine was ripped from the floor as Reeva smashed into its side at a sprint. The crew fired off shot after shot as it drifted helplessly through the zero-gravity environment and by the time it came into contact with a suitable surface, it had sustained too much damage to re-establish its grip.

"Hawkins to Clarke, nice timing."

"That wasn't me Captain. Reeva did that by herself." Hawkins looked at Reeva, who was stood watching the machine as it drifted around the room.

"Hmm, maybe that thing's gonna come in handy after all."

"That was far too close."

"Yeah, but at least that thing was nice enough to leave the door open," returned Blaine jokingly as he pointed at the gaping hole in the wall.

"Come on, we'd better keep moving." The crew followed Reeva through the new breach. The chamber beyond was little more than a shaft that led down past the range of the torchlight.

"Captain, we are going to have to leave Reeva here, the walls of this shaft are too smooth for her to grip." Hawkins nodded.

"OK Blaine, you're on point."

"Aye sir." Blaine stepped upto the edge of the shaft and looked down. After shaking his head in protest he allowed himself to slowly fall forward by ninety degrees before locking his boots onto the side of the shaft. "OK Captain, it's safe."

Hawkins and Kane followed Blaine's lead and the team proceeded to descend down the vertical wall of the shaft. Hawkins jumped and reached for his rifle as Reeva brushed passed him and headed towards Blaine at the front of the group. Hawkins steadied himself with a long sigh.

"That's amazing, she must be able to magnetise her paws," remarked Kane as Reeva passed by him.

"I thought her primary function was to protect us?"

"Yes sir."

"Then why does she insist on trying to give me a fucking heart attack."

"Captain, there's a hatch down here."

"Don't open it till we get there."

"Aye sir." Hawkins and Kane caught up with Blaine who was standing next to the hatch on the adjacent wall of the shaft. "You're gonna have to blow the locking mechanism before I can open it Captain."

"OK Blaine, stand back." Hawkins trained his rifle on the hatch and fired. Under a shower of sparks the hatch opened and Blaine ordered Reeva inside.

"Blaine to Clarke, is the room secured?"

"Hold on Blaine, this room is full of equipment, it's gonna

take a few minutes to check out."

"Copy that Clarke." Hawkins and Kane carefully walked round to the adjacent shaft wall where Blaine was now peering through the hatch.

"Clarke to Hawkins, Reeva's picking up multiple heat signatures Captain, but no movement. It's as secure as it's ever going to be sir." Hawkins nodded at Blaine and he climbed in through the hatch.

"It looks clear to me Captain." Hawkins and Kane followed Blaine through the hatch and into the cluttered room.

"Bingo."

"Where are we Kane?"

"The engine rooms, Captain." Kane took another look around. "Or at least some sort of engineering section." Reeva walked out in front and led the team through the darkened chambers. Being certain that they were alone was almost impossible amidst the clustered silhouettes of a variety of large pieces of machinery and equipment but the team pressed on. After a few minutes of their torch-lit exploration, Kane came across something that interested him immensely.

"Captain, hold up a minute." The team stopped and while Blaine and Reeva kept watch, Hawkins walked back to where Kane was standing.

"What is it?"

"This looks like some kind of databank."

"How much data could something this size hold?"

"Let's find out." Kane took a small piece of diagnostic equipment out of his satchel. Except for a larger screen and a number of small wires and clamps attached to it, the tool resembled a large calculator. Kane carefully removed a small panel from the databank and started to attach the diagnostic tool to its now bared wiring, within a few seconds the screen on the tool lit up and started scrolling through line after line of information.

"Now this is interesting."

"Let me take a look."

"See, this is the equation for calculating weight and this equation here seems to be something to do with mass and velocity. As for the rest of it sir, I don't have a clue."

"Can you download information to the ship from that thing?"

"Yes Captain."

"Hawkins to Clarke, we're sending some equations from a data storage unit that we've found, it should be coming up on Kane's console. See if the computer can work out what it does."

"No problem sir." Kane transmitted the equations to his console on the Dark Star and disconnected the diagnostic tool from the databank. "Receiving information Captain. Transferring it to the main computer now, standby." Clarke watched his monitors as the main computer started to create pictures of the small arrowhead vessel and strange funnel-like shapes. Other screens began to scroll lines of descriptive text and more algebraic calculations. "Jesus Captain, there's a lot of information here, it's going to be a while before I can tell you what it means."

"OK Clarke, keep working on it. Were gonna keep exploring."

"Aye sir." Clarke quickly turned and hurried towards his console as the long-range sensors started to beep out a warning.

"Captain, I'm picking up a distress beacon from what appears to be an escape-pod."

"Can you identify it?"

"Reading now sir. The pod is identifying itself as..." Clarke stopped as the information scrolled down his screen.

"What is it Clarke?"

"The pod is identifying itself as life-pod three, of the Earth Fleet science vessel Phoenix."

After rushing back to the Dark Star the crew set course for the source of the distress beacon. The Phoenix should have been on its way back to the colony by now, Hawkins thought. If this really was an escape-pod from the Phoenix then it must have been launched nearly a week ago.

"Coming up on the source of the signal now Captain."

"Put it on the view screen." The view screen flashed up a picture of the small spherical pod, battered and buckled by its time in open space.

"Kane, bring it into cargo bay two."

"Aye sir, depressurising bay two and arming grappling

tether."

"Pod is coming into firing range of the tether now Kane."

"Thanks Blaine, opening outer door. Firing grappling tether now Captain." Hawkins watched the pod through the view screen as the claw like grappling tether hit and grasped tightly.

"Lock confirmed, retracting tether." Hawkins stood up and walked towards the back of the bridge. "Outer door is locked Captain. Pod is secure."

"OK. Kane you're with me. Clarke, keep a look out." Kane followed Hawkins into the turbo-lift. "Cargo bays." The bridge was now quiet and Clarke took the opportunity to see how much of the databank information the computer had managed to decipher. Bringing the information up on a couple of his station's overhead monitors, he began the complicated task of working out what it all meant. Upon noticing the look of confusion on Clarke's face, Blaine's curiosity got the better of him and he walked over to take a look.

"So what is it Clarke?"

"I'm not entirely sure. There appears to be information on most if not all of the ship's systems. This reading here shows us the frequencies that the ships shields are capable of working on."

"So in theory we should be able to modulate the Laser Cannon to fire straight through this type of shielding."

"Well it's actually a lot more complicated than that but I suppose it's possible, in theory."

"What's this?" Blaine pointed to a monitor displaying a picture of the small arrowhead vessel and another picture of what looked like a funnel positioned underneath it.

"I'm not sure, a lot of this stuff doesn't make any sense to me. I'm hoping Kane will have more luck when he gets a chance to take a look at it."

"Do you think we'll be able to use this data to fight the AI?"

"I hope so Blaine. I hope so." Meanwhile down in the cargo bays, Hawkins and Kane were attempting to open the battered escape-pod.

"OK Captain, after three. One, two, three." With a tug on the pry-bar the pod's hatch opened and Kane ducked as a plasma bolt narrowly missed his head. "Wow, we're the good guys remember, put the pistol down."

"Thank god, we thought we'd been picked up by the arrowhead vessel."

"Redmond." Hawkins reached a hand inside the hatch and helped the commander out. Commander Redmond introduced the other occupant as he emerged from the pod. "This is my Chief Engineer Jonathan Drake." Hawkins shook Drake's hand.

"This is my only Engineer, Adam Kane. My Helmsman, Tyler Blaine and my First Officer, Eugene Clarke are on the bridge. You can meet them later, but first, tell me what happened."

"We returned to the Jupiter gas refinery and refitted our crystalline reactor. Then we were attacked as we left orbit by the arrowhead vessel; we didn't stand a chance. It pulled the Phoenix into a large cargo bay beneath the ship. I ordered everyone to abandon ship but…" Redmond paused to compose herself. "I don't think any of the other pods made it."

"What about the AI vessel?"

"It disappeared off the escape-pod's sensors a few seconds after we launched."

"Kane, take them down to the mess hall and get some fluids into them. I'll meet you back on the bridge."

"Aye sir." Hawkins watched the crew leave the cargo bay before activating his wrist-com.

"Hawkins to Clarke, be advised, the AI has the navigational charts from the Phoenix."

"Then it knows the flight plans of every ship we have and…" Clarke paused.

"Yes Clarke, and the location of the colony."

CHAPTER: 6

"This is Captain Bridger of the science vessel Liberty calling Colony Command. Command come in please."

"This is Colony Command, go ahead Liberty."

"We're picking up some sort of spacial anomaly in sector six. It appears to be some kind of gravity well."

"Sector six has no recorded anomalies Liberty, are you sure it's not a sensor malfunction?"

"Negative Command, I can see this thing through the view port. It just appeared on the scanners a few minutes ago. Be advised we are going in for a closer look."

"Acknowledged Liberty, keep us posted."

"Standby Command, there appears to be something emerging from the anomaly."

"Say again Liberty."

"There is what appears to be a ship emerging from the anomaly. Jesus it's huge!"

"Can you identify the ship Liberty?"

"Negative Command, the sensors aren't even picking it up. However we are reading a massive power build-up and…"

"Say again Liberty. Liberty acknowledge. Command to Captain Bridger come in." Commander O'Connor stopped the tape and the meeting room was filled with a deafening silence. Resting on a small cane, he slowly walked towards the front of the meeting room and turned to face the anxious members of Colony Command.

"That transmission was sent by Captain Bridger twenty-six hours ago. Further attempts to contact the Liberty have failed. We have also lost contact with the Tomahawk, the Tempest and the Lexington. The ship appears to be systematically destroying vessels along the patrol zone."

"What are you saying O'Connor. Are we under attack?"

"I don't know." The sound of panic-stricken chattering filled the air. "Be quiet all of you!" O'Connor shouted. "If it continues on the path it is currently following, this ship will be here in under eight hours. We don't have time to fall to pieces."

"Then what do you suggest we do?" O'Connor rested on his cane and contemplated his best course of action. "Captain Reed, start loading the women and children into ships. You will be responsible for their protection."

"Evacuation?"

"Preparation. You will lead the defenceless ships out of danger whilst I lead the rest to intercept the incoming vessel."

"This is madness, we're in no shape to mount an offensive. We'll be slaughtered." O'Connor shook his head.

"All these years of peace on this planet without so much as a passing comet. Do you think it is coincidence that this ship has turned up now, less than two weeks after the Dark Star was due to arrive in Earth space?"

"Are you proposing that this ship was sent by the AI System?"

"In all the worlds ever surveyed we've never come across a life form bigger than a bug. The odds of one turning up here, now, are astronomical." O'Connor paused to catch his breath. "Of course it's the AI."

"Then the Dark Star failed. My god we need to get out of here."

"And where would you go, there's nowhere left to run." The room fell silent as the ship commanders realised that O'Connor was right. They stared at each other awaiting a new option, any option, but nothing came. One of the captains pushed back his chair and stood up from the table.

"I will fight." Another captain rose to his feet.

"I will fight." The sound of scraping chairs filled the room as the rest of the table rose.

"What's the plan Commander?"

"All mining torpedoes in the colony need to be gathered together and their guidance system removed. Share them equally between your ships and leave the warheads at full-yield. You'll have to launch them from a greater distance but low-yield warheads obviously didn't do the Dark Star any good. You have less than eight hours gentlemen, dismissed." The ship commanders hurried out of the meeting room, leaving O'Connor alone with his thoughts. The Dark Star, the Phoenix and the Ulysses. Such a waste of life he thought. After all, if they had succeeded in their mission then this ship would not be here and Hawkins would have fought to the last. He walked over to one of the meeting room's windows and stared at the reflection of the old man looking back at him. So many years of waiting for word of the mission's outcome, waiting to know if he could return home. Well he had his answer and if it wasn't for his responsibilities to this colony and his race he would give in right now and surrender to his fate. Then again no, death would not take him so easily. Too much running, too much pain and anguish, too many years of longing for the calm blue skies of home. All that was left now was revenge. This was his mission now, this was his purpose and if it cost him his life he would make this bastard pay for what it had done.

"O'Connor to all hands, ready the Lynx for take off, you have thirty minutes."

"Commander this is Troy, the ship's in no condition for a take off sir."

"Then you have thirty minutes to make her ready."

"Aye sir."

Panic gripped the colony as word of the impending danger spread. Many people were injured in the mad dash to secure a place on board one of the rickety vessels bound for orbit. Everyone not leaving with the evacuating ships were prepping the rest of the fleet to intercept the approaching vessel. The hours passed quickly and in what seemed like no time at all, O'Connor was taking his position on the bridge.

"Troy, report."

"Status reports have been received from all vessels in the fleet, Commander. The evacuating ships have started to take off and are setting course to rendezvous behind Vega as ordered."

"What about the intercepting ships?"

"Every ship that is still capable of breaking orbit has been prepped and armed to the best of its crews abilities. They're awaiting your orders sir."

"What's the status of the Lynx?"

"A couple of the atmospheric thrusters are damaged beyond repair and we have had to close off sections one and two of deck seven due to an un-repairable hull breach. We'll be OK once we break free of the planet's gravity."

"*If* we break free of the planet's gravity." O'Connor sighed and eased himself into his seat. "How long before the last of Captain Reed's evacuation fleet has cleared the atmosphere?"

"The last three ships are launching as we speak sir. Commander, what about the colonists that refused to leave? Surely there's some way to change their minds?"

"Like what, hold them at gun point? If they want to stay let them, their fates are no more or less certain than ours." O'Connor fastened his safety harness and wedged his cane down the side of his seat. "Open a channel to the interception fleet."

"Channel open Commander."

"This is O'Connor, the evacuation fleet is almost clear of the planet. All ships launch when ready." The bridge rumbled and shook as the Lynx pulled free of its sandy resting-place and ascended towards the clouds.

"Hold her steady."

"I'm trying sir. The downed thrusters are throwing us off balance a little. I've compensated as best I can."

"Troy, status of the fleet?"

"All but three of our ships have managed to lift off successfully Commander. The first few ships in Captain Reed's fleet should be reaching the star in a couple of minutes."

"Excellent."

"Clearing orbit now Commander."

"All sections report as stable and ready to fly."

"Set course heading three-nine-two point seven-one."

"Aye sir, course heading confirmed." O'Connor's interception fleet headed for the inner patrol zones of sector six whilst Captain Reed's evacuation fleet took up their undetectable position behind the star of Vega. After a few minutes of flight, Troy picked up an anomaly on the ship's long-range sensors.

"Commander, there's something big heading this way."

"Identify."

"I'm having trouble getting a sensor lock sir, but it appears to be well over seven miles in length."

"Put it on the view screen." The huge menacing image of the AI arrowhead mother-ship flashed up onto the bridge's main view screen.

"Now there's something you don't see every day."

"What the hell is it?"

"It looks like some sort of blade, or arrowhead, or something."

"Open a channel. This is First Commander O'Connor of Earth Fleet, identify yourself." O'Connor paused, awaiting an answer. "Shut down your engines and identify yourself or we will be forced to open fire." O'Connor watched the view screen as an orange glow began to engulf the mammoth vessel.

"Picking up a huge power increase from the approaching vessel sir."

"No shit."

"The vessel has changed direction and is now on a direct collision course with the fleet."

"O'Connor to Fleet, load torpedo bays and prepare to fire on my mark."

"The vessel is increasing speed and will reach the front line in fifty-three seconds."

"O'Connor to Fleet, all vessels arm one torpedo and fire."

"Arming torpedo bay one Commander. Target locked, torpedo away."

"Reading multiple torpedo launches sir. Counting thirty-five warheads on course for the approaching vessel." O'Connor watched the view screen as the torpedoes sped towards their target.

"The ship is making no attempt to avoid or intercept the torpedoes, impact momentarily Commander." The bridge of the Lynx shook as the shock wave from the exploding torpedoes passed through the fleet. O'Connor couldn't believe his eyes as he watched the ship continue unscathed through the blast cloud.

"What the hell! O'Connor to Fleet, break up, get out of the way." The fleet began to scatter as the arrowhead vessel began to smash it's way through the forward line of ships.

"Helm, get us out of here."

"Aye sir."

"Several ships have been rammed sir. The Glory and the Tsunami are requesting assistance and the rest are not responding to my hails."

"O'Connor to Fleet, fire at will." Chaos broke out as the fleet began to launch everything they had at the attacking vessel. Wave after wave of hastily fired torpedoes indiscriminately destroyed any ship that was unfortunate enough to be in their way. A huge piece of debris from one of the many battered or destroyed ships punched through the hull of the Lynx.

"Damage report."

"Propulsion's down sir, we're adrift. Auto-Repair System is responding but we're losing atmosphere through the breach."

"Close off the pressure doors to that section."

"I've been trying Commander but the breach extends through three decks and the power is down on two of them. I can't seal the breach fully until the repair drones fix the power grid in those sections."

"Can the repair drones fix it before the drain on the atmosphere becomes life threatening?"

"Not a chance sir." O'Connor was almost thrown from his seat as the drifting Lynx collided with another ship.

"Report."

"Main power is off-line, and we've lost the main starboard side engine."

"Can it be repaired?"

"No, we've lost the engine sir, it's no longer attached to the ship."

"Commander, there appears to be three huge doors opening in the top side of the attacking vessel."

"What? On screen." O'Connor watched as three small ships emerged from within the open hatches of the arrowhead mothership."

"Three ships sir, all identical in shape to the larger vessel but one-sixteenth the size. I'm detecting power build-ups in all three vessels."

"Shields?"

"I don't think so sir." Through the view screen the crew of the Lynx witnessed the destructive power of the ship's energy weapons as they opened fire on the fleet.

"Jesus Christ."

"The mother-ship is moving away Commander."

"What's its heading?"

"It's heading straight for Tartarus sir."

"We are out of torpedoes Commander."

"Sir, one of the smaller fighter ships is heading straight for us."

"Is propulsion back online yet?"

"No sir."

"Detecting a power build-up Commander."

"All emergency power to shields." O'Connor turned to the view port to see the approaching vessel strafing through the wreckage of many destroyed ships, its hull covered in dancing arcs of electricity. "Now damn it, now!" From the bridge of the Intrepid, Captain Hemmingway witnessed the destruction of the Lynx. Not a single life-pod was fired before the ship exploded under the effect of the arrowhead fighter's energy weapon.

"Taylor, how many torpedoes do we have left?"

"Nine sir."

"Shoot that fucking ship!" The Intrepid launched two torpedoes at the still-occupied enemy vessel, which took a direct hit and was lost in the scattering debris from the damaged vessels caught in the blast.

"Did we get it?"

"Standby Captain."

"Well?"

"Enemy fighter ship is no longer registering on my scanners sir."

"That's for the Lynx you bastard."

"Captain, we are receiving a distress call from the Raven. They have a ship on their tail and are unable to shake it."

"Helm, bring us about, set course to intercept."

"Aye sir."

"Intrepid to Raven, hold on, we're on our way."

"Hurry Intrepid, I don't know how long we can…"

"The Raven has taken a direct hit, captain."

"What's her status?"

"She's toast sir."

"God damn it. Taylor target that ship and fire."

"Targeting Captain. Torpedoes away." The arrowhead fighter rapidly changed direction and the torpedoes sped on into open space. "Torpedoes have missed Captain, reloading tubes one and two."

"Helm, bring us into a parallel position above the ship."

"Aye sir."

"Load all remaining torpedoes and prepare to launch them in a spread dispersal pattern towards that ship."

"Torpedo bays three and four loaded, target locked Captain."

"Fire." Once again the torpedo tracking monitor started to beep and the crew of the Intrepid awaited the outcome of the launch. The beeps got closer together as the torpedoes drew closer and closer to the enemy fighter. A power conduit overloaded as the shock wave from an exploding torpedo slammed into the Intrepid, sending a shower of sparks flying across the bridge.

"Impact Captain, we have a hit."

"How many?"

"Only one torpedo managed to hit the ship but it did the trick. The arrowhead fighter ship is spinning out of control." Captain Hemmingway watched the view screen as the enemy vessel collided with a large piece of debris and exploded.

"Captain, the third enemy fighter has changed course and is heading straight for us. We don't have anything left to hit it with sir."

"Evasive manoeuvres, get us out of here." The Intrepid sped through the wreckage of the battered fleet in an attempt to evade the approaching vessel.

"The fighter is closing to two thousand metres Captain, it appears to be charging its energy weapon."

"Helm, this isn't good enough."

"Sorry Captain, that ship is way more manoeuvrable than ours, I can't shake it."

"Intrepid to Fleet, requesting assistance from anyone who still has torpedoes to fire."

"Intrepid this is the Glory, set your heading to seven-zero-one point three and prepare to bank hard to port on my order."

"Negative Glory, re-calculate that course heading. That

vector would put you on a direct collision course with the enemy fighter."

"You heard me Hemmingway, course heading seven-zero-one point three."

"Carter, don't do this, we'll find another way."

"Our environmental systems are damaged beyond repair and the bridge's rear bulkhead is too badly buckled to open the doors. I won't let my men suffocate Captain. Now veer to port in ten seconds and allow me the satisfaction of taking this bastard with me." Hemmingway stood silent for a second staring into nothingness.

"Helm, in six seconds bank hard to port and get us out of here as fast as possible."

"Aye sir, banking in four, three..." Captain Carter's voice came over the Com as the helmsman counted down the seconds to his untimely demise.

"Hemmingway, get that mother-ship for me." Under the rumbling of a large explosion, Captain Carter's transmission ended and the Intrepid shook as a hail of debris bounced off the hull. Captain Hemmingway slammed his fist into the small control panel on his chair's armrest, causing it to flicker and buzz wildly.

"Taylor, what's the status of the fleet?" Hemmingway waited for a response. "Taylor."

"All but seventeen ships have been destroyed Captain. Twelve of which are heavily damaged."

"Jesus. Are any of the damaged vessels capable of rescuing survivors?"

"Standby sir." Taylor scanned the fleet's surviving vessels. "The Hastings and the Nova are probably in the best condition sir."

"Send them a message. Tell them to stay behind and look for survivors."

"Aye sir."

"This is Captain Hemmingway of the Intrepid. With the exception of the Hastings and the Nova, all ships that are still capable of flight will follow me to intercept the mother-ship." Hemmingway gave the order to return to the planet Tartarus. They had to intercept the AI mother-ship before it had a chance to wipe out the colonists on the surface. Though battered and almost out of torpedoes the six strong fleet followed without question.

"I'm picking up the mother-ship on sensors Captain. It has stopped and is holding position just outside the range of the planet's gravity."

"How long is it going to take us to get there?"

"Two minutes and thirty-three seconds Captain."

"Damn it."

"Captain, I'm picking up one hell of a power build-up in that ship."

"Helm, we have to go faster."

"Sorry sir, that's just not possible."

"The mother-ship's power build-up is discharging Captain. It's fired on the planet."

"On screen." Hemmingway and his bridge crew watched the planet as the discharge of the mother-ship's energy weapon cut through the atmosphere. The cloud layers over the colony parted as a huge shock wave extended around the planet like rippling water in the aftermath of a thrown stone. The ground below took on a glow like the embers of a dying fire that spread outwards in a circular pattern extending for thousands of miles.

"No!" screamed Hemmingway as he rose from his seat. The AI mother-ship ceased fire and began to move away from the planet. The faces of the crew shared a look of horror as they watched the burning planet through the view screen. "Taylor, how many people were down there?" Hemmingway asked quietly.

"Approximately three hundred families refused to leave the planet Captain." Taylor stopped to compose himself.

"The mother-ship is on a direct course with the system's star Captain. It's heading for the second fleet."

"There's no way it can scan the ships on the opposite side of the star. It's not possible," offered one of the crew in a desperate tone.

"That remains to be seen," replied the captain. "But one things certain, the second fleet can't detect the mother-ship approaching," Hemmingway sat looking thoughtful for a moment. If he sent a message ahead to the second fleet the enemy ship might intercept it. Maybe it hadn't detected the fleet; maybe they could lead it away from the colonists. "Intrepid to Fleet, as soon as we're in range fire at will." The six ships closed on the slowly moving mother-ship and opened fire. Hails of torpedoes were launched at the gigantic vessel before they moved off to a safe distance to await the explosions. Taylor steadied himself on his console as the first torpedoes impacted, rocking the Intrepid in the shock wave.

"Report."

"No effect Captain, we can't penetrate those damn shields."

"Send a message to Captain Reed. Tell him to take the second fleet into deep space."

"Captain, with all due respect, if we send the second fleet a message we'll give away their position."

"It's heading straight for them Taylor. If we don't warn them they're fucked anyway."

"Aye sir. Sending encrypted message to the Alabama."

"The enemy vessel is increasing speed sir."

"Shit, increase speed to match. Hemmingway to Fleet, we have to stop this thing now."

"I'm detecting a power surge from the mother-ship, it's preparing to fire."

"At what? The fleet's on the other side of Vega," Hemmingway stopped as he suddenly realised the AI's plan. "My god."

"The mother-ship is firing Captain."

"On screen." The view screen flashed to a view of Vega as the arrowhead vessel's energy weapon fired. The blinding light from the star grew dimmer as the beam hit.

"The energy beam is destabilising the star Captain."

"What's the status of the second fleet?"

"I'm not reading them sir, if they've moved at all it's in a parallel line with the star."

"The destabilising effect is reaching critical Captain. At this rate the star is going to supernova in approximately seven minutes."

"Captain, there's no way we can clear the blast radius of a supernova in that amount of time."

"Hemmingway to Fleet, we need to take this ship out now."

"Taurus to Intrepid, it's useless, we can't get through those shields. We need to get out of here, now."

"Go where? If this star explodes it will take Tartarus and most of the system with it. Do you propose we drift around in space till we starve?"

"We'll have to find another planet."

"We don't have time for this. If you want to die searching for an inhabitable planet, then go ahead, but I'm going to stop this ship. Hemmingway out."

"The Taurus is breaking position Captain and is heading out into open space."

"Fuck them. Hemmingway to all ships. I want everyone to aim for the centre of the ship's stern and prepare to fire on my mark. Maybe if we hit one spot hard enough we can buckle the shields." Hemmingway stood up and walked to the view port at the front of the bridge. He stared at the enemy vessel and frowned. "Fire." The torpedoes from the surrounding ships shot into view and spiralled towards the mother-ship as Hemmingway watched through the view port. He shielded his eyes from the flashes as they impacted with the shields and exploded.

"Not a scratch, captain."

"God damn it, there's got to be some way to stop this thing!" Hemmingway shouted in a desperate rage.

"Captain, the star is gonna lose cohesion in less than four minutes and at this range the…"

"Sir, I'm detecting some sort of anomaly forming about thirty miles from Tartarus at co-ordinates two-zero-three point four-two. It appears to be some sort of gravity well."

"Taylor, pull up the information transmitted by the Liberty before she stopped transmitting."

"Way ahead of you Captain. It's the same type of anomaly." Hemmingway stood silent with an overwhelmed look on his face.

"There's something emerging from it Captain." Hemmingway noticed the puzzled look on the face of his first officer.

"How many Taylor?"

"One sir. It's identifying itself as an Earth Fleet mining

vessel." Taylor looked up at the captain still wearing a look of confusion. "Call sign Dark Star."

"What? On screen." The view screen flashed up a picture of the Dark Star as it exited the anomaly and blasted past the fleet. "What the hell?"

"Captain, we're being hailed. They want to know who is in control of this fleet."

"Patch them through, put it on the viewer." The view screen changed to a picture of the Dark Star's Bridge and Captain Hawkins with an angry look on his face. "Hawkins? What? How?" questioned a baffled Hemmingway.

"I'll explain later. Just get the fleet ready to fire on the arrowhead vessel."

"But we can't penetrate its shield Hawkins. The torpedoes…"

"Let me worry about that," interrupted Hawkins "Get these ships ready to fire on my order. Hawkins out." Clarke cut the transmission and the view screen switched back to an external view of the ship. "What the hell is it doing Clarke?"

"It appears to be trying to de-stabilise the star sir, and it's working. At this rate the star will supernova in about two minutes."

"Blaine, get us over there."

"Aye Captain."

"This better work Clarke."

"I hope so sir."

"Hawkins to Kane, bring the Cannon online."

"Aye sir, activating Laser Cannon now."

"Increasing power input into the crystalline reactor to compensate. Reactor power output is now at two hundred percent of normal Captain."

"OK Clarke, raise the platform."

"Platform activated Captain standby." Clarke paused as the platform moved into position raising the Cannon out into open space above the ship. "Cannon platform is locked in firing position sir. Activating beam modulation upgrade."

"Are you sure our computer can keep up with that ship if it starts modulating its shields?"

"No." Hawkins shook his head.

"I'm too old for this shit."

"Coming up on the mother-ship's starboard side."

"Hawkins to Kane, we're ready up here. You and Drake stay down there and make sure this Cannon keeps working."

"Aye sir."

"Clarke, are you sure the shield generator is where you say it is?"

"The deck plan we got from the smaller ship shows a generator in the location I specified Captain."

"John, are you sure the laser will penetrate the shields?" questioned Commander Redmond nervously from the diagnostic console.

"Yes Commander, as long as our computer can match that ship's shield frequencies then the laser should pass straight through."

"In theory," added Blaine as he manoeuvred the ship along the arrowhead vessel.

"OK coming into position in twelve, eleven, ten…"

"Rotating ship one hundred and eighty degrees Captain."

"Seven, six, five…"

"Positioning Cannon."

"Three, two, one."

"Fire!" shouted Hawkins, clenching his fists and gritting his teeth in anticipation. The Laser Cannon spun to face the mother-ship as the Dark Star finished rolling onto its back and with a great flash of green light it fired. From the Intrepid, Hemmingway and his crew watched in amazement as the Cannon cut through the hull, creating a thin scar as the Dark Star dragged it along the length of the huge vessel.

"Kane to bridge, did the Cannon penetrate the hull plating?"

"Like a hot knife through butter Kane," answered Blaine as he brought the ship round for another pass.

"The shields are still up Captain, we missed the generator. Suggest we try a stationary shot sir, it will help with the accuracy."

"You heard the man Blaine. Take us out to one thousand metres and hold position."

"Aye sir."

"Commander Redmond, how's the Cannon holding up?" The commander looked over the displays on the diagnostic console.

"It's holding up fine John."

"In position Clarke. Holding at one thousand metres."

"Repositioning Cannon now." Clarke brought up a copy of the arrowhead mother-ship's deck plan and superimposed it over the image of the vessel that he had on the Cannon's targeting screen. He aimed the Cannon at the superimposed picture of the shield generator and fired. The orange tint of the mother-ship's shields faded and disappeared.

"Clarke, open a channel to the fleet."

"Channel open sir."

"This is Hawkins, all ships fire at will." The mother-ship ceased its assault on the star as its shields fell and began to turn towards the previously inconsequential band of ships. Blaine engaged the Dark Star's ion engines and backed away from the immense vessel as fresh multitudes of torpedoes were launched in its direction.

"That got its attention."

"The fleet's forward-most torpedoes will reach the arrowhead vessel in approximately ten seconds Captain."

"Blaine, are we at a safe distance?"

"Yes Captain."

"Clarke, launch a full spread."

"Aye sir. Locking target. Tubes one through ten launched. Our torpedoes should impact three or four seconds before the rest of the fleets." Hawkins found himself sitting forward in his chair, edging towards the view screen in anticipation of the torpedo strike. His heart quickened with the beeping from the tracking system as the torpedoes drew closer and closer to their target.

"Positive impact on at least eighty percent of our torpedoes Captain," presented Clarke as the explosion rocked the ship. "I'm reading heavy damage to the vessel's hull plating. The fleet's torpedoes are approaching; hold on." The bridge shook once more as the fleet's wave of torpedoes started to hit.

"Blaine, back us off another eight hundred metres."

"Aye sir."

"Several sections of the mother-ship's starboard and aft hull plating have breached Captain. However, relative to the size of the ship the damage is negligible. The mother-ship is still turning."

"Arm another spread. Aim at the starboard side breaches."

"Aye sir, tubes one through ten are locked and ready."

"Fire."

"Torpedoes away sir, impact in three, two, one." Blaine squinted as he watched the bright light of the blast through the view screen. "Impact confirmed, a small section of the mother-ship's starboard hull plating has completely buckled."

"Continue firing at the breached section."

"Aye sir." Clarke's attention was drawn to one of his sensor monitors as it began to beep. "Captain, we have incoming."

"What?"

"A small object has just been launched from the mother-ship and it's heading straight for us."

"All emergency power to shields, Blaine get us out of..." The captain's order was cut short as the small object impacted with the ship. "Damage report."

"We have a hull breach on deck four section two, energy seals are holding. Whatever that thing was, it didn't explode on impact."

"Kane to bridge, what the hell just hit us?"

"We don't know Kane, standby. What are we looking at here, an unexploded warhead or something?"

"I have no idea Captain, it knocked out the sensors in that section when it hit."

"Hawkins to Kane, can you and Drake get up to deck four and find out what hit us."

"No problem Captain, we're on our way."

"Kane, take Reeva, just in case."

"Aye sir, Kane out."

"What's the status of the mother-ship?"

"The fleet is still bombarding her Captain, the hull is starting to come apart." Through the view screen, Hawkins watched the AI mother-ship as it started to break up under the unrelenting barrage of torpedoes.

"Back us off Blaine before the debris gets too thick to

manoeuvre through."

"Aye sir." The Dark Star ceased fire and began to move away as the mother-ship's structure finally gave way. The once immense vessel had been reduced to an indecipherable cloud of charred and twisted alloy, smouldering against the backdrop of space.

"Clarke, can you pick up any power sources in the debris field?"

"Other than our ships Captain, no." Hawkins sat back in his chair and sighed.

"Then it's over."

"Kane to bridge, intruder alert." The sound of weapons fire could be heard through the communication link.

"Report Kane."

"Deck five is crawling with little metal insects Captain, Drake's down and I'm not sure how long I can keep these things off us."

"Where are you Kane?"

"Section three, at the laundry Captain, these things are eating through the deck plating and the wiring Captain. I suggest you lock down the deck before they spread to any major areas."

"Hold on Kane, we're on our way. Blaine, you're with me." Clarke picked up his rifle and walked over to join the rescue.

"No Clarke, I need you here."

"Aye sir." Blaine and Hawkins entered the turbo-lift and headed down to deck four. Clarke immediately returned to his console and patched into Reeva's optical system. As the picture on the monitor cleared up he saw dozens of what looked like small metal scorpions, spreading across the walls, floor and ceiling of the corridor where Reeva was standing.

"What the hell?" No larger than a foot in length but infesting Reeva's entire field of view, the insects were actually eating their way through the bulkheads and wiring of the corridor. The small machines were exploding into pieces under a hail of plasma blasts coming from somewhere behind Reeva, who appeared to be trying to hold the wave of machines back. Blaine appeared from an adjacent corridor in the distance, followed closely by Hawkins. The pair froze for a moment when they first saw the swarm of machines but quickly shook off the initial shock and commenced firing.

"Blaine, try to clear a path to Kane and Drake – I'll keep them off us."

"Bring it on," shouted Blaine as he opened fire on the machines. Kane was standing behind Reeva in the doorway of the laundry room, trying to protect Drake who was sat on the floor clutching his badly burned leg.

"Watch out for the jaws on these things, they excrete some kind of acid," warned Kane as Blaine blasted and kicked the little machines out of the way.

"Hi, did you miss me?" remarked Blaine cockily as he reached the engineers. "Get Drake, I'll cover you." Kane swung his rifle over his shoulder and helped Drake to his feet as Blaine and Hawkins continued their assault on the swarm of metal insects.

"OK Drake, let's go." With a groan and a look of intense pain on his face Drake leaned on Kane and hobbled down the corridor towards the ship's mid-section turbo-lift. Hawkins and Blaine stood their ground as the metallic swarm continued towards them.

"Captain, above you." Hawkins swung his rifle upwards and fired at one of the machines that had managed to climb undetected to a position above his head. Reeva continued to attack the machines with a vengeance, crushing them between her powerful piston-fed jaws.

"How big was that thing that hit us?" questioned Blaine in reference to the amount of machines still scurrying towards them.

"I don't know but it really packed 'em in there," replied Hawkins as they backed off down the corridor still firing.

"Oh yeah, I'm starting to think the AI doesn't love us any more." The trio continued their assault on the machines for over two minutes before their numbers started to thin out, stopping their slow retreat down the corridor as the tables began to turn.

"Clarke to Hawkins, I'm starting to pick up movement in the adjoining section around you and on deck five. There's only a few but we could do with dealing with them before they get into any major systems."

"We're starting to get the situation under control down here

Clarke, we can live without Reeva if you think she can handle it."

"She shouldn't have a problem sir, I'll direct her from up here."

"Fair enough Clarke, keep me posted."

"Aye sir, Clarke out." Reeva dropped the metallic invader that she was currently chewing and sprinted off down the corridor in response to Clarke's orders. Hawkins and Blaine continued their eradication of the remaining machines.

"Can you see any more Blaine?"

"A few of them backed off down that corridor." Hawkins slapped a fresh power cell into his rifle.

"Let's go." The pair carefully advanced down the corridors of deck four destroying any invader that they came across. The walls and equipment in the corridors were covered in smouldering holes from the robotic insects acidic secretions. The wiring in some sections had been damaged causing the lighting to flicker or fail entirely, making hunting the little creatures very difficult.

"Looks like some sort of drop-pod," remarked Blaine as he and Hawkins stumbled upon the object that had previously punched its way through the hull.

"No, the shape's all wrong and look at the reinforcements." Hawkins pointed at the extremely thick and serrated hull of the battered bullet-shaped object. "This thing has been designed to tear through a ship's hull."

"So it's some sort of breaching-pod."

"Exactly, designed to infiltrate vessels."

"It's in extremely good shape for something that just crashed through two feet of hull plating."

"Hawkins to Clarke, the object that hit us is some kind of breaching-pod."

"Breaching-pod Captain?" questioned Clarke.

"As far as I can figure it, this thing is designed to smash through a ship's hull allowing for rapid deployment of troops, or in this case weird little metal insects."

"Do you think it's worth getting the repair drones to reverse engineer it before they scrap it?"

"I doubt a human could survive this kind of incursion, but

the technology might come in handy."

"OK sir, I'll get on it."

"While you're at it Clarke, can you tell if any of the other ships were hit by one of these things?"

"Standby Captain." Clarke scanned the other vessels in the fleet, which were busily searching the debris field for any signs of survivors or useful technology.

"This is the Dark Star calling the Argon, come in please."

"Argon here, I don't know how the hell you got back here so fast but you saved everyone's bacon. You're all heroes in my eyes."

"Captain, sorry to interrupt but I'm picking up a large hull breach in you lower bow and…"

"Nothing to worry about Dark Star, we must have been hit by a piece of debris or something, the repair drones have already been dispatched."

"Negative Argon, be advised, we have been hit by some sort of breaching-pod full of small insect-like machines that are capable of eating through the wiring and pretty much everything else. I suggest you send an armed team to check it out immediately."

"Thanks for the heads-up Dark Star, I'll get right on it, Argon out." Clarke continued to scan the ships.

"Dark Star to Intrepid, come in please." Clarke awaited a response. "Intrepid this is The Dark Star, please respond." Again Clarke gave the Intrepid chance to reply. "Clarke to Hawkins, I'm detecting two ships that could have been infiltrated. The Argon is checking out a large breach in their bow and I've not been able to raise the Intrepid."

"Keep trying Clarke, we're on our way back to the…" Hawkins stopped talking as what sounded like weapons fire could be heard through the communications line.

"Clarke to Hawkins come in. Captain what's going on down there?"

"Blaine to bridge, we're under fire, the Captain's hit."

"The bugs have weapons?"

"No, there's something else down here."

"What?"

"I didn't get a good look at it, it was hiding in the

shadows." Blaine's voice was drowned out by the sound of his rifle. "Clarke, we're pinned, we need back-up down here."

"Hold on Blaine."

"Hurry up."

"Clarke to Kane, what's you're position?"

"I'm in the medical bay with Drake."

"Blaine and the captain are under fire, I need you to meet me on deck four."

"On my way." Commander Redmond threw Clarke a Plasma Rifle as he rushed into the turbo-lift. After a few seconds of travel the lift stopped and the doors opened as Kane rushed in.

"Continue." The lift doors closed and it began to move.

"What the hell do you mean under fire, under fire from what?" asked Kane as he checked the power cell on his rifle.

"I don't know but it was hiding in the dark, waiting to ambush them."

"Jesus."

"OK, get ready." Weapons fire could be heard as the turbo-lift doors opened.

"It sounds like it's coming from corridor C, you circle around through corridor F and we'll catch this thing in a cross fire." Clarke nodded in agreement and the pair set off through the corridors. Clarke quietly followed the sound of weapons fire until he reached the junction of corridor C. He could make out the sound of a single Plasma Rifle and what must be another weapon. It didn't sound like any weapon that he was familiar with but from the noise level he could tell it was close, maybe even just around the corner. He backed up against the wall as a whispered voice spoke his name over his wrist communicator.

"Clarke, are you in position?"

"Mother-fucker, when I get my hands on you I'm gonna fuck you up." Blaine's quaintly-voiced objections to this situation could be heard from Clarke's position at the far end of the corridor.

"Yes Kane. Are you ready?"

"I'm in position, but I can't quite make out where it is."

"I think it's standing behind one of the roof struts at my end of the corridor. It sounds really close."

"OK, let's do it." Clarke leaned partially around the corner in the hope of using the bulkhead as a shield. He was surprised at what he saw as he trained-in his rifle. Not another blade-covered insanity of a machine or a small-insect like invention, but what looked like the shadowed figure of a man. Who was this shooting at his crew, why would anyone help the AI destroy his own race?

"Hey asshole, drop the weapon." Clarke's face dropped as the dark figure turned the glow of its green eyes, fixing on him. It was a machine; a machine built in the image of a man. The light shined off its cold metal body as it raised its arm and fired. Clarke dove back behind the safety of the adjacent corridor's corner, narrowly escaping the attack.

"Clarke to Kane, it's some kind of android or something. It has an energy beam weapon attached to its left arm."

"A what?"

"An android. It's a machine but it's shaped like a man." Clarke leaned back round the corner of the adjacent corridor, still at ground level and fired. The plasma bolt hit the roof strut and the android returned fire.

"Shit that was close." Clarke whispered quietly to himself after he ducked quickly behind the wall of the adjacent corridor. Kane and Blaine took the opportunity to open fire whilst the machine was distracted and blasted wildly in its direction. Blaine and Hawkins were trapped in the doorway of a small maintenance locker and were too far away from any adjacent corridors to attempt retreat.

"How's the captain?"

"He's passed out, his arm is really messed up." Blaine ducked back into the doorway as the android opened fire. "This is starting to piss me off. Clarke, get its attention."

"That's easy for you to say." Clarke took a couple of deep breaths and stepped out into the corridor. "Hey ugly!" he shouted as he raised his rifle. The android reacted quickly and raised its free arm at Clarke, which unknown to him was also armed with an energy weapon. At the same time, Blaine boldly stepped out into the corridor and took aim.

"Fire."

A dazzling light forced Hawkins to shield his eyes as he

awoke. He could just make out the blurred shape of someone standing over him and for a second, in his disorientation, he found himself wondering if the wound he had sustained could have been fatal. After having a few seconds to come round and adjust to the light, he suddenly became aware of three things. He was laid down, he was alive, and the blurred figure standing over him was Blaine and not death himself. This amused him and he began to laugh.

"What's so funny?"

"For a second there Blaine, I thought you were the Grim Reaper, here to save me from my life."

"Nah, I've seen pictures of the Grim Reaper and he isn't that ugly," Clarke mocked from the back of the room. "How are you sir?"

"Confused. Our medical bay isn't this clean, where the hell am I?" A young woman stopped Hawkins as he tried to sit up.

"Try to stay still for a few minutes Captain. You're onboard the medical ship Apollo."

"The Apollo. There weren't any medical ships left when we got back here. Will someone please explain what's happening here!"

"Well sir, it's like this. When Commander O'Connor heard that the arrowhead vessel was heading this way, he split the fleet into two groups. The first fleet, consisting of all the ships that could be armed, were sent to intercept the mother-ship. All other ships were loaded up with colonists and sent to hide behind the star in case the first fleet failed."

"Smart idea, go on."

"To cut a long story short Captain, all but eight ships in the first fleet where destroyed in a matter of minutes. Two of those where heavily damaged and Captain Hemmingway of the Intrepid ordered them to stay behind and search for survivors."

"The mother-ship wasn't manoeuvrable enough to destroy an entire fleet of ships. Why the hell didn't they retreat?"

"Well apparently the mother-ship didn't attack the fleet at all. It released three small fighter ships as it broke through the lines. From the descriptions I've heard they sound like the same kind of ship we took out in Earth's orbit." Hawkins slowly sat up and checked himself for holes.

"O'Connor?" Clarke shook his head.

"The Lynx was destroyed with all hands still onboard Captain. The crews of the Argon and the Intrepid have also been lost to the same kind of breaching-pod attack that we were subjected to."

"What's the status of the infestation on those ships?"

"The Intrepid has been cleansed but the invading machines on the Argon managed to tap into the propulsion systems before an armed team could get onboard. It was destroyed by the fleet under my request sir." Hawkins nodded.

"It's a shame. We don't have that many good ships left." Hawkins sat looking thoughtful for a moment. "How many ships do we have left?"

"The fleet presently consists of twenty-one vessels, all jammed full of pissed off and hungry people."

"Then we don't have time to stand here talking." Clarke helped Hawkins to his feet. "How long have I been laid here? My legs feel like I haven't stood up in months."

"You've been unconscious for over forty-eight hours sir. Most of the repairs to the fleet are well under way."

"Two days. Damn, no wonder I'm so hungry." Hawkins thanked the nurse, dressed himself and walked towards the door. As he reached the archway that led to one of the ship's corridors he stopped and turned back to the crew. "Where is my ship?"

"Those little insect things did a lot of damage to the wiring on decks four and five. She's docked at the port airlock, Kane's over there supervising the repairs." Hawkins turned back to the nurse who was now stood cleaning a small tray of medical equipment.

"How do I get to the mess hall?"

"I'm sorry Captain, we're out of food supplies." Hawkins sighed and looked at Clarke.

"Any idea how long it will be before we're ready to return to Tartarus?"

"Tartarus is no longer an option Captain." Hawkins looked puzzled. "The mother-ship attacked the colony from orbit, destroying several thousand square miles of the planet's surface. The resulting shock wave has totally devastated the atmosphere sir, the planet is no longer inhabitable."

"Hawkins to Kane, what's the status on the repairs?"

"Good to hear from you sir. The wiring on deck four is shot to shit but the hull's back in one piece. I'm just in the middle of repairing the sensor grid."

"How long before we can get under way?"

"She's ready to fly now sir. There's nothing down here that I can't fix on the move."

"Very good Kane, Hawkins out." Hawkins and the crew left the medical bay and headed towards the port airlock. "Where's Commander Redmond and the engineer?"

"Commander Redmond has been given command of the Intrepid. Her and Drake have been over there for over a day."

"The Intrepid is a good ship." Hawkins pressed the inner door activation button as they reached the port airlock. "Not very big but it's supposed to be one of the fastest in the fleet." The airlock door hissed shut behind them as they walked in. The voice of the ship's computer sounded a warning as the crew waited for the button on the outer door to change from red to green.

"Running diagnostic check on interior pressure door seals, please standby."

"Our ship isn't much older than this one is it?" questioned Blaine.

"No, they started building this class of medical ship about three years after the Dark Star was launched."

"So why doesn't our computer talk?"

"It did, I disconnected its vocal processors when I was promoted to captain. Damn thing used to get on my nerves." Blaine pressed the button on the outer door as it turned green and it hissed open. They walked through the airtight passageway of the Dark Star's starboard docking gantry. After a few seconds of waiting in the airlock, the inner pressure door opened and they made their way to the bridge.

"Clarke, give me a systems check," asked Hawkins as the crew sat down at their stations.

"Running diagnostic now Captain, standby."

"Blaine prep us for flight."

"Aye sir. Initiating engine warm up sequence."

"With the exception of deck four's lighting and sensor grid, systems are working within flight tolerances Captain."

"Very well, open me a channel to the Apollo." The view screen flashed up a picture of the Apollo's bridge.

"How are you Aiden?"

"Ah John, I trust you're feeling better?"

"I've been worse. We're ready to get under way over here. I just wanted to thank you for the hospitality."

"No problem my friend. Anything for the saviours of mankind." Hawkins shook his head and grinned.

"We did nothing more than the rest of the attacking vessels."

"Ah, the famous Hawkins modesty. You and your crew saved all our necks and you know it. You got my vote for leader on your timing alone, that was one hell of an entrance."

"Leader? What are you talking about?"

"The fleet captain's had a conference whilst you were healing and unanimously voted for you to replace O'Connor. Has no one told you?" Hawkins turned and looked at Clarke with a frown.

"Oh yeah, I knew I'd forgotten something." Hawkins returned his gaze to the view screen.

"Are you sure about this?"

"Yes, everyone in the fleet has been notified. Congratulations." Hawkins stood silently for a moment still wearing a troubled frown.

"Clarke, detach the docking clamps and retract the gantry."

"Aye sir." The bridge shook slightly as the two ships parted.

"Well Aiden, it would appear I have an exodus to co-ordinate."

"Good luck John, you're going to need it."

"Luck is not a factor Captain. Hawkins out." The view screen switched back to a bow view of space. "Blaine, take us to a position just outside the fleet's main cluster."

"Aye sir." Blaine carefully navigated the Dark Star through the stationary fleet and brought her to a full stop outside the cluster.

"Clarke, I need a channel opening to every ship here."

"Err, hold on a second sir. This is going to take some

doing." Clarke played around for a few seconds on his keyboard before activating the view screen. "All ships have been hailed Captain and are awaiting your message." The view screen brought up a slightly disorientating split-screen view of all the bridges, of every ship left in the fleet. Hawkins stood up and calmly took a moment to scan the faces on the screen. He nodded at the image of Commander Redmond, who smiled back at him.

"Thank you all for responding so quickly. I have called this little meeting to assess the fleet's status. I need to know if anyone is incapable of short-range flight." Hawkins waited for a response.

"If you're planning on taking us back to Tartarus, you should remember that it is no longer habitable." Hawkins fixed his view on the face of a rather scrawny looking young man on the screen.

"Who are you, boy?"

"I am First Officer of the Aurora. My captain was injured in the battle and I have assumed command of this ship until his return," answered the first officer in an extremely snide and pompous tone.

"Tell me, what is the full classification of my ship?" The first officer looked suddenly puzzled.

"Err, your ship is an Earth Fleet mining vessel. Classification Mark Five Dreadnought, call sign Dark Star."

"Very good. I want you to remember that, boy. Because if you ever use that tone with me again, you're gonna need to let the nurses know where to send my boot back to, after they remove it from your ass, do I make myself clear?" The officer nodded nervously.

"Yes, yes Captain. Sorry sir."

"As I was saying," Hawkins continued, "Does anyone have a problem with a relatively short-range flight?" Hawkins waited for a response. "I'll take that as a no. I want all ships to prepare to return to Earth space."

"With all due respect Hawkins, I'd hardly call returning to sector zero-zero-one, a short flight," replied one of the captains.

"Yes, and most of our ships are packed full with people. We don't have anywhere near enough stasis pods for everyone," stressed another captain with a panicked look on his face. Hawkins halted the conversation by holding up his hand.

"Clarke." Clarke nodded and returned to his keyboard. "Gentlemen, and lady." Redmond smiled. "If you calm down for a second, my first officer will put your minds at rest." The heads on the view screen all turned to look at Clarke who looked up briefly before smirking and returning his attention to his console.

"With all due respect people, you need to keep up with the times." Clarke hit the enter key and smiled. In the background of the other ship's bridges on the view screen, Clarke and the crew watched as officers scurried around frantically in response to the now beeping warning sirens on their sensors. Entire bridge crews could be seen looking out of view ports to catch a glimpse of the enormous anomaly that was forming just off the Dark Star's bow. Like a miniature black hole the anomaly concaved into itself. Sucking in the space around it like a whirlpool swallows water. A few of the captains returned their gaze to Hawkins, most of them with gaping mouths and all of them wearing questioning looks. Clarke licked his lips and leant over his console towards the view screen. A huge smile spread across his face.

"Cryo-stasis is a thing of the past."

CHAPTER: 7

Within a matter of hours the last of the fleet's ships had touched down on the welcoming soils of Earth. After weeks of extensive and time-consuming repairs had been made to the battered and rickety vessels, Hawkins returned the Ore Miners to space to continue the task for which they where built. Only this time they were collecting ore for a greater purpose; not to increase the already overflowing purses of greedy corporations; not for minerals and precious metals to make trinkets and expensive jewellery for the fat upper-classes, but to collect any and all materials necessary to create a city for the new colony, the new brotherhood of man. Before one flower had been picked, before more than a few breaths of air were taken, Hawkins called a meeting of the whole colony to dictate the rules of the second age of man.

"Well we made it, we're home." A great cheer rose from the crowd that stood at the base of the Dark Star's main access ramp, in anticipation of their leaders speech from above. "Look around you. Out of the misery of our exile this planet has flourished, and that shows me what must be done. We must live in harmony with this place, we must find a natural equilibrium that benefits the Earth as much as it benefits us. With our crystalline reactor and recycling technologies in place from the very start, there is no reason why this planet should have to suffer the damage that we subjected it to in our past. Never forget that the price for this paradise on which you stand was the slaughter of over ninety-nine percent of our race. Remember this when you breathe the air, when you walk through the hills and drink from the pure water of the streams. Remember the mistakes of the past and remember that what once was, can never be again. Your captains and I didn't choose to land in Peru at random. This is to be the site of the greatest and only stronghold of man. Once we have completed construction of our city, the Earth will be yours to roam but only here will there be evidence of human settlement on this world."

"But what if we wish to settle on our own, away from the colony? One building won't make a difference."

"No, one building won't make a difference, and in times to come neither will ten buildings or a hundred. Have you realised that this day, this moment, is the first and only time that the entire human race has stood together as a family instead of standing apart as factions, as continents. We can't afford to walk the same path as our ancestors. It only leads to destruction." The group broke into applause as Hawkins stopped talking.

The city was designed using the latest of technologies from the AI fighter ship databank. New alloys previously unimagined and state-of-the-art equipment to go with it. All ships that had been deemed unnecessary since the landing on Earth were stripped of their equipment and materials. The propulsion and navigation systems on the Jupiter gas refinery were painstakingly repaired and the entire station was brought back to Earth to be dismantled. Its repair system and hundreds of repair drones were upgraded and used in the city's construction.

Carved deeply into the mountainside, the great saucer-like domes of the city began to take shape. From their lofty positions over the lands below the domes of the city, when finished, would offer a truly remarkable view over miles of open plains and rainforest. The abundance and diversity of the plant and animal life in this region would easily support a colony of this size. As a community they could easily live and grow here without endangering its complex and precious equilibrium. Eventually the city's machine shops were completed and brought online and from them sprung a whole new range of vehicles and equipment such as the world had never seen. Compared to the complexities of maintaining a starship, the construction of the dozens of small open-top vehicles was relatively easy. The first of the sturdy six-wheeled vehicles were built with battle in mind, and were therefore equipped with the first of the prototype Pulse Cannons. These original vehicles were directly responsible for removing all traces of the leftover Reeva units and drop-pods from the former British Isles. After being airlifted in, the small group spent three weeks in the Scottish highlands, tracking down and eradicating the mechanical abominations before returning to the drop-off site for extraction.

"Morning Captain," greeted Kane as he entered the city's partially completed operations chamber.

"Kane. I haven't seen you for days man, where the hell have you been?" returned Hawkins happily as he slapped Kane on the back.

"I've been trying to get the power grid in the third dome working. I'm starting to think that re-using the reactors from the dismantled ships was a bad idea."

"How so?"

"Some of these things look like they've been maintained by chimps Captain. Frankly, I'm amazed that some of them are still working." Hawkins shook his head. "Still, we're making progress. Anyway Captain, how are you doing?" Kane glanced around the cluttered half-built room and out over the rainforest through one of the gaping holes in the wall. Hawkins removed himself from the path of one of the room's four repair drones and shook his head.

"I'm bored out of my fucking mind. If I don't find something to do soon I'm gonna have to shoot myself." Hawkins continued to whine as he strolled across the room and kicked another repair drone that was in the way of his chair. The drone hovered off to the other side of the room and continued the construction work. "All I've done since we got here is look over progress reports." Hawkins sat down at his desk facing Kane. "What brings you here anyway?" Kane held up three small progress reports and shrugged. Hawkins lit a cigarette and sat back in his chair. "You see what I mean. Nothing but progress reports."

"Brent to Kane, come in please."

"Sorry sir, hold on a second. What is it Brent?"

"We've solved the relay problem in the long-range communications array. We're ready to bring it online."

"OK Brent, fire it up whenever you're ready."

"No problem Kane, it'll take a few minutes to warm up. I'll keep you posted."

"Thanks Brent, Kane out." Kane turned back to Hawkins.

"You think you're having a hard time. Since you put me in charge of the construction, all I've done is wipe everyone's asses for them. These guys can't take a piss without asking me my opinion." Hawkins chuckled.

"What about the Dark Star Kane, are the repairs finished yet?"

"I haven't had time to patch into the repair system today Captain. Still, last time I checked the drones had finished integrating the new long-range communications array, so they should have started the weapon upgrades by now."

"Weapons upgrades?" questioned Hawkins, a look of anxiety suddenly crossed Kane's face.

"The new weaponry upgrades. I mentioned it in one of last weeks reports didn't I Captain?" Hawkins shook his head.

"Oh, damn. Well the repair drones were already building the new long-range communications system and Blaine and I thought it would be a shame to just scrap the Laser Cannon. So we sort of found a way to keep it."

"Go on."

"We had it re-installed a little closer to the bow." Kane licked his lips nervously and took a deep breath. "Well, actually Captain, we had the design copied and installed a few." An ambivalent look spread across the captain's face. "All in the interest of being prepared sir," Kane continued as if rambling would somehow soften the news.

"Really?" replied Hawkins questionably. "And how many Cannons does a Dreadnought require before it is sufficiently prepared?"

"Err, well, four sir."

"Four!" shouted Hawkins.

"Yes sir, but in our defence, with the new anomaly jump-drive at our disposal we're gonna be heading deeper into space than ever before. There's no telling what we could run into." Hawkins shook his head and sighed.

"Cut the shit Kane."

"Aye sir."

"How the hell did you manage to get the materials to build three new Cannons without anyone noticing?"

"One of the perks of being the city's chief engineer. All the stock lists have to go through me."

"Where did you get the man power?"

"I sort of, borrowed a few repair drones to do the bulk of the work."

"Damn it Kane, those drones are supposed to be working on this complex."

"Yes I know sir, but I made sure all the teams still met their weekly quotas." Hawkins frowned.

"Well, I suppose there's no harm done."

"Thanks Captain."

"Don't thank me Kane, the only reason you're getting away with it is because I happen to agree with you." Kane looked surprised.

"Sir?"

"Let's just say I like the idea of having a little muscle in case we need it."

"My thoughts exactly sir."

"Where are the new Cannons?"

"Here I'll show you. I should be able to patch into the Dark Star's repair system from here." Kane leant over the desk and started punching keys on the keyboard. Hawkins watched as a blueprint of his ship loaded up on the screen. "We installed one on the belly of the ship directly below the original Cannon." Kane pointed to the spot on the screen. "Then we installed the other two on the port and starboard flanks, again in line with the original Cannon." Hawkins raised an eyebrow and nodded approvingly. "If I ever manage to get the targeting scanners aligned, we should be able to hit four targets at once. Blaine named it the Laser Sword System."

"Colourful. What's this in the spare mid-section crew quarters?" Hawkins made reference to a new blue marker on the blueprints.

"Well technically sir, the spare crew quarters are now known as the Laser Sword Reactor Room. I had to install a separate reactor to be able to run four Cannons at once; they simply draw too much power. Otherwise we'd have been standing in the dark every time we opened fire."

"Brent to Kane, the communications array should be online in a few seconds."

"Thanks Brent. How are the sensor arrays coming along?"

"Well we've managed to integrate them into the computer system but we're having trouble with this AI technology. If I'm honest it doesn't make a whole lot of sense."

"Tell me about it Brent. Keep at it. Co-ordinating the landing times for the Ore Miners will be a lot easier once we can track them at a distance."

"OK Kane, I'll get on it as soon as possible. Brent out." Hawkins covered his ears as a high-pitch squeal suddenly filled the room.

"It's just the communications system coming online Captain. The idiots haven't calibrated it properly." Kane accessed the new communications system through the computer console on the captain's desk. After a few seconds of typing, the ear-splitting sound cleared up into a voice.

"Alabama to anyone who's listening. Is anyone there?" Hawkins pushed the answer button on his keyboard.

"This is Hawkins, go ahead Alabama."

"Finally, I was starting to think something was wrong down there."

"Yeah the new communications system still has a few bugs in it. It's a pain in the ass but it should be working fine from now on."

"Fair enough sir. We're gonna be hitting the atmosphere in about thirty minutes, I'm gonna need a landing plan."

"The landing preparations are being co-ordinated from the Rochdale until we get the operations chamber up and running. You need to contact Captain Newton."

"Thanks sir, oh and it's nice to see those engineers finally figured out how to reproduce that anomaly drive of yours. It will save me weeks of travel time and…"

"Wait a minute," interrupted Kane. "I don't know who you're getting your information from, but the original anomaly drive we took from the fighter we destroyed is still the only one we have."

"Whom am I speaking to?"

"This is Kane, the fleets head engineer."

"Well I'm sorry Kane, but it looks like you're overdue for a progress report or two. There are gravity wells forming all over the place up here. There must be a dozen at least."

"What, are you sure?"

"Yeah, in fact I'm picking up a ship emerging from one off my port bow."

"Alabama can you identify it… Alabama…! Alabama…!"

CHAPTER: 8

The year is 2436 and the Earth is in peril. For the last six hundred year's this small orb has been subjected to a constant and relentless attack by an apathetic and relatively unstoppable force, utilising many hundreds of different methods of attack to poison the Earth. Rendering the ecosystem almost incapable of supporting life.

By the early twenty-fifth century, the planet had all but lost the war. Animals of all descriptions were forced to take shelter on a daily basis from the very thing that once brought life. The dark black clouds that once heralded the life, bringing and replenishing rain, now warned of a burning bombardment of acid from the skies. The great oceans of the planet that once teemed with life existed now as little more than a lifeless cocktail of chemicals that supplied the deadly rains with their power. Plant and animal life grew less abundant by the day and the only hope for salvation lay in the hands of the force responsible for the cataclysm; Man.

In January of 2436 the leaders of the world held a summit to find a solution to the decay. After a long and heated discussion they came to the conclusion that the technologies required to reverse or neutralise all the pollution and poisons simply did not exist. Furthermore, the creation and development of such technologies would take years and the Earth simply did not have that long left before the ecosystem collapsed entirely. The only viable solution came in the form of two unwelcome guests that suddenly burst through the huge doors of the hall and collapsed under the weight of several security officers.

"What the hell is this, how did those men get in here?"

"I'm sorry Mr President," apologised one of the security staff as the two men were dragged towards the door.

"Wait, we can help!" shouted one of the intruders before

being quickly muffled.

"Wait." The security staff halted as the Japanese delegate began to speak. "Are they unarmed?"

"Yes sir."

"Then let them speak." The security staff released the two men who proceeded to brush themselves off as they walked back into the room. "Who are you?"

"Their names are Jake Evans and Thomas Bradley," announced one of the British delegates. "They've been pestering me for weeks regarding funding for a new computer they've designed."

"Is that why you're here?"

"Yes Mr President."

"And how can your computer design solve this problem?"

"It's not a computer system Mr President, it's a design for an artificial intelligence." The sound of chattering filled the room.

"Ladies and gentlemen, please." The noise dimmed. "Go on."

"As you're all aware, the ecological degradation of the planet is developing faster than the technologies that are required to counteract it. What I'm basically saying is that we, the human race, cannot develop our technologies at a sufficient rate to be able to reverse the decay in time."

"But your computer can?"

"Yes sir."

"How is that possible?" questioned the Japanese delegate.

"It's possible because this System is more than just a computer, it is a sentient, free-thinking entity."

"Are you saying it would be alive? That's preposterous."

"It is not preposterous, it is fact." Evans stopped to compose himself. "Our System may not have a beating heart or require oxygen to sustain its muscles, but its brain intelligence will be like nothing the world has ever seen. Capable of remembering everything it has ever learned with perfect clarity and total recall. With the ability to process that information at the speed of a super-computer."

"And you're sure you can build this thing?"

"I have the blueprints right here." Bradley held up a small

disk.

"And you're sure this thing will be capable of developing any ideas we give it?"

"Why even bother?"

"Excuse me?"

"No offence Ladies and Gentlemen, but this System will be perfectly capable of finding it's own solution to the problem. Which coming from a memory that contains all the knowledge in the world, will probably be more effective than anything your scientists can give it to work on." Once again the room filled with the droning sound of a hundred different conversations. After a few seconds the President of the United States of America stood up and leaned over to his microphone.

"What do you need to make it work?"

3:01AM 15/12/2436

Evans knocked over the lamp on his bedside table as he fumbled around in the darkness for the phone.

"Hello."

"Jake, it's me."

"Thomas man, it's three in the morning."

"I've done it Jake."

"What?"

"I've solved the processing problem. It's finished."

"My god. Call the partners, I'll be there in a couple of hours."

"What is it Jake?" questioned a voice from the bed, as Evans hurriedly got dressed.

"Bradley's cracked the processing problem on the system. I have to go down to the lab to meet the partners." Evans' wife sighed and sat up.

"I suppose this means the bed's mine for a few days." Evans sat down on the bed beside her.

"If I'm not back in a week you have my permission to remarry." Evans kissed his wife goodbye and quickly exited the apartment. After taking one of the complex's many lifts down to the transport storage area he climbed into his vehicle and headed out of the building.

The complex's main door slowly opened and Evans drove

out into the darkness of the city. He hovered down the vast network of roads that weaved through the looming forest of dull metal and concrete that stretched out before him. Enormous cylindrical skyscrapers and towering apartment complexes that rose high into the sky, covering the whole area as far as the eye could see in an attempt to house the ever-growing population.

5:59AM 15/12/2436

"Ah, here he is now," introduced Bradley as Jake entered the room.

"Mr Evans, nice of you to join us," remarked one of the many people who had gathered in the room.

"Sorry to keep you all waiting, the hyper-link was packed solid, I couldn't get above one-fifty all the way here. If you'll follow me." Bradley and Evans led the group into a large lift at the far end of the room. Upon entering they each placed their left hand on a small pad on the wall. A sweeping beam of light moved back and forth from their palms to their fingertips several times and as it stopped the lift doors closed and it began to move.

"Now I see where my money's been going," remarked a member of the group as he watched the numbers on the floor indicator ticking over. "How deep are we going Evans?"

"The System chamber is exactly one mile down."

"One mile?" replied another member of the party. "Judging from that counter we should have stopped shouldn't we?"

"The chamber is exactly one mile underground Miss Walker, but this lift shaft is over two miles long. You see we built the chamber as far under the mountain as possible for extra security."

"Oh I see."

"Don't you think you're being a little paranoid Evans?"

"You said to spare no expense on this System's security. This complex can withstand a nuclear strike, and I assure you that no sensor system in the world can penetrate this much rock. Your System couldn't be any safer if God himself was protecting it." The lift stopped and the doors opened to reveal a long, well-lit corridor. The group followed Evans and Bradley along it until they reached an extremely large door.

"Cry havoc and let slip the dogs of war."

"Voice-print identification verified," indicated a light feminine voice from nowhere as the great doors opened. "Welcome Bradley."

"Is that it?"

"No Miss Walker, that's just a standard series seven security system. What you're interested in is through that door." The group was startled as they walked towards the door by two large chain cannons that suddenly dropped out from the ceiling in front of them. Positioned at either side of the unopened door, the cannons sprung to life and trained in on the group.

"Warning, retinal scans required to access this section. You have thirty seconds to comply." Evans and Bradley quickly walked over to two small panels on the wall at either side of the door. They both looked into a small round opening that pulsed with a green light. After a few seconds the pulsing stopped and as the immense solenoid locks retracted, the doors began to open.

"Ladies and Gentlemen, let me introduce you to the first and only Artificial Intelligence System ever created." The group looked in awe around the small room as they entered. In the centre of the room stood a large black cube of at least ten feet in height. Built into the walls of the chamber were dozens of large computer monitors and keyboards, presently powered down and inactive. Below the raised metal grid floor, hundreds of wires and cables stretched out from the cube and disappeared into the walls.

"So that's it."

"Don't let the look fool you. The cube is only to shield the System from electromagnetic pulses. Inside that shell is the most complex computer processing system that's ever graced the planet. It is capable of accessing any and all satellite and information systems with up-link capabilities. This complex has been fitted with fifteen state-of-the-art machine shops and with the amount of raw materials stored down here, the System should be able to create just about anything it can dream up to aid it in its quest." Whilst Evans gave the group a rundown of the System's capabilities, Bradley attached the final component to the System.

"That's all very impressive Evans, but is this thing actually capable of reversing the damage to the ecosystem?"

"Jake, it's ready." Evans nodded at Bradley.

"Well General, if you'll be good enough to wait a few moments. You can ask it yourself." Evans turned to Bradley. "OK Thomas, fire it up." With the flick of a master circuit-breaker positioned in a deep crevice in the wall, the dozens of monitors and lights exploded into action.

"Thomas, you did it man, it's working," congratulated Evans as Bradley started to laugh.

"We did it Jake." The pair excitedly shook hands, taking their eyes off the flickering screens for barely a moment.

"What's it doing?"

"It's learning, Miss Walker."

"What do you mean it's learning?"

"Well General, at this point it only has the mental capacity of a newborn child. You see, it would have taken months to programme it with all the information it requires to function as a sentient being. But with its Web and other information links, it should be able to learn everything there is to know in a matter of minutes."

"What exactly do you mean, everything there is to know?"

"Imagine this thing as a life form with the processing power of a super-computer. It only has to be told something once and it will remember it indefinitely with perfect clarity. Our minds are childlike in comparison to this System." Suddenly the racing monitor screens shut down and the sound from the busy processors stopped. Everyone in the room stood silent and looked at Evans and Bradley.

"Jake look." Bradley drew Evans' attention to the monitors covering the walls. On every single screen, one word had appeared in small green writing.

"STATUS."

"What does it mean?" questioned one of the group members in a whisper. Evans gestured for the group to be quiet with a raised hand. He walked over to one of the keyboards on the wall and began to type.

"RE-PHRASE THE QUESTION." Immediately a new line of text scrolled across the screen.

"REQUIRE INPUT. WHAT IS PURPOSE?"

"It's not making any sense."

"It's making perfect sense. This thing has essentially just been born. It wants to know why it is here, what its purpose is." Evans turned to Bradley. "Are we ready to give it its orders?"

"Everything seems to be working just fine," answered Bradley who was looking over the complex's systems on one of the consoles. "It's as ready as it will ever be."

"OK General, time to answer your question." Evans began to type. "PRIMARY OBJECTIVES: CLEANSE THE EARTH BY ERADICATING ALL POLLUTIONS AND INFECTIONS. PROTECT THE EARTH FROM ALL POSSIBLE THREATS." The AI System immediately responded.

"PRIMARY OBJECTIVES INPUTTED @ 6:27AM 15/12/2436. MISSION PARAMETERS ARE ACCEPTABLE." Once again the monitors in the room began to scroll through information faster than the group could read. Every so often a noticeable image would flash up on the screens, such as a picture of the Earth or the anatomy of a recognisable animal or plant.

"Well, that answers your question General."

"Very well done, both of you. The president will be pleased."

"As will my government," added Miss Walker with a smile on her face. "This is the start of a new era and it's all thanks to you two gentlemen."

"Well we can't take all the credit," replied Bradley. "It took hundreds of people to make this place a reality."

"You are too modest I think," added another member of the group in a broad Russian accent. "My superiors will be pleased by this news."

"Does anyone have any questions?"

"What powers the System?"

"We managed to acquire a crystalline reactor to run the facility. The entire complex is completely self-sufficient and has even been equipped with its own repair drones in case it runs into any problems."

"What about security? I didn't see any guards at the front entrance."

"The security system I installed is second to none. The

entrance alone is equipped with two anti-tank guns, a set of chain cannons and three surface-to-air missile launching systems. Human guards are not required to defend this installation."

"Well it seems like our government's funding has been put to good use."

"Any other questions?" Evans paused to allow for a response. "Very well, then if there's nothing else I wonder if you would all like a tour of the complex. Bradley needs to concentrate on the online checks." The Russian delegate chuckled.

"Da, we will leave him in peace."

"This way please."

9:30AM 22/12/2436

Several days later outside the White House in Washington D.C, Evans and Bradley joined the president and delegates of the other nations involved in the project to announce their exciting news. T.V companies from all over the world were invited, allowing the conference to be sent out on a live feed to homes across the globe. A gathering such as this had not taken place since the discovery of the Magnasite crystals that revolutionised the power industry in the form of the ecologically-sound crystalline reactors.

"That's a good question, I'll let the AI System's designers answer that one. May I introduce Jake Evans and Thomas Bradley." A slight, half-hearted applause came from the crowd as Evans and Bradley stepped up to the podium.

"Thank you Mr President. Morning, my name is Jake Evans and this is my associate Thomas Bradley. I've never been in front of an audience before but if you bear with us we'll try to answer all your questions. Let's start with you sir, would you mind repeating the question."

"I was wondering how it works. Obviously the term Artificial Intelligence states that this computer can think for itself, but are you actually saying that it can comprehend like we can?"

"Not exactly. You see it isn't really a computer technically, it is silicon-based life. The System is sentient in the respect that it has its own consciousness and even its own views and opinions. However, it doesn't process information the same way we do. You see, the information in our brains is stored and processed in a way that allows us to experience emotion and become confused. The AI System's brain, or neural-net as we like to call it, stores all information in neat separate files that can be referenced at any time with perfect recall and clarity. This means that the System's train of thought works on pure logic and is not affected by the hindrance of emotion or confusion. It can also process information thousands of times faster than us without becoming overwhelmed."

"Is it dangerous?"

"Excuse me?"

"If it thinks for itself isn't it possible that it could decide to take over the world or something?" Bradley laughed and stepped up to the microphone.

"At the risk of sounding judgemental, the System isn't interested in power or profit as we are. It simply does what it's been asked to do."

"Then how do you explain the new sickness?"

"I assume you're referring to the mystery illness that's sweeping the globe. Let me clear this up once and for all, right now. The AI System does not have the type of equipment necessary to create viruses or pathogens of any kind. Any information you have heard to the contrary is little more than rumour and speculation spread by fools."

"So you expect us to believe it's a coincidence that the world is being plagued by a deadly virus, only seven days after the AI System was brought online?"

"That's exactly what I expect you to believe because that's the truth." Evans and Bradley were removed from the stage as the crowd began to get unruly. They were surrounded by the president's men and ushered into the White House and upto the famed oval office where the president and his aids were already sat waiting.

"It is confirmed gentlemen, the virus that is sweeping the planet has been traced to contaminated crops and reservoirs in thousands of different locations across the globe. The report states that the virus works on a genetic level. Apparently it is spread by touch and ingestion and I have it on the best authority that no one in the world is capable of creating a virus of this complexity."

"So we were right, it is the System."

"What the hell is it doing?"

"That's exactly what you two are going to find out."

"Sorry sir?"

"The European Alliance are sending an armed response team to the AI facility to find out what's going on. We are sending a squad of our own to accompany them and you two are going with them. We've had clearance from your government to take you along." Evans and Bradley nodded. "Sergeant Miller here will have tactical command but you two will be responsible for getting the team into the complex and working out what's gone wrong."

"OK boys, you're with me," demanded Sergeant Miller as he walked towards the door. "You can inform me of anything I need to know on the way to the drop-ship."

"We're leaving now?" questioned Bradley.

"That's right, the team is already prepped and waiting."

Evans clung tightly to his safety harness as the military drop-ship lifted off and began to climb. From his window he watched the concrete covered ground of the military base grow smaller and smaller as they ascended towards the clouds.

"Entering low orbit now sir. Igniting primary boosters." Bradley's seat rocked as the engines of the drop-ship ignited, propelling them forwards. "Flight path is stable guys, E.T.A. for re-entry window is six minutes." Bradley watched the soldiers for a few minutes as they talked amongst themselves. Wearing white, grey and black camouflage and covered in many different pieces of equipment and weaponry the soldiers made him a little nervous. The soldier across from him undid his harness and leaned over. He was a large African-American man with muscles that seemed to strain the stitches on his uniform, and a long thin scar that ran down the left side of his face.

"Names Zeus, what's yours little man?" The soldiers laughed.

"Thomas. Thomas Bradley."

"So what the hell are you two doing on this mission?"

"Maybe they're the backup," mocked another soldier and once again the squad broke into laughter.

"Actually asshole we're the brains of the operation. They brought us along in case your bootlaces come undone." The soldier suddenly looked unimpressed as the rest of the squad pointed at him and laughed. Evans just gave a small victorious grin and turned his attention back to the view through the window.

"So why are you here?" questioned yet another member of the squad.

"We're the only ones who can get into the complex without kicking down the door."

"So you're the genius's that built this thing. All this is down to you two fruits."

"All this was built at the request of government agencies from around the world. Including your government before you get started."

"Look who's suddenly on the defensive. What's the matter boy, is the 'saviour of the world' title starting to slip away?"

"What the hell is your problem, redneck?"

"Redneck? You're dead boy." Sergeant Miller stood up and grabbed the soldier as he started to head towards Evans.

"Check that shit, Deacon."

The soldier didn't move.

"I gave you an order soldier!" shouted Miller about two inches from the soldier's face. "Now sit down before I knock you down." The soldier grunted at Evans before nodding at Sergeant Miller and returning to his seat. "Now cut the shit all of you. This is a military operation not a fucking picnic."

"Aye sir," shouted the squad.

"And you," shouted Miller as he pointed at Evans. "Stop fucking with my men or I'll kick your ass myself, I shit you not." Evans nodded and sat back in his seat.

"Everyone better be strapped in back there, we're going in." Bradley's stomach churned as the ship suddenly began to dive. It was descending at such an incredible rate that he had to push to keep his feet on the floor. He watched the soldiers as their looks hardened and they checked over the equipment that was already strapped to their bodies. "Picking up a small contingent of troops about half a mile from the installation Sergeant. Do you want me to set down near their co-ordinates?"

"Affirmative, stay frosty, this place is equipped with aerial defences." The squad was on its feet within seconds of the drop-ship touching down.

"Frost, Stone, prep the APC."

"Aye sir."

"Deacon, Zeus, check the equipment."

"Aye sir."

"You two come with me." Evans and Bradley followed the Sergeant to the hatch at the front of the chamber. Miller typed a code into a small keypad on the wall and under the groan of its pistons the hatch opened. The snow around the base of the hatch's ladder had been melted by the heat from the drop-ship's engines and Bradley almost lost a boot in the resulting muddy ground. A man from the European Alliance team was walking towards the ship. Sergeant Miller saluted the fellow soldier as he stopped.

"Good afternoon Gentlemen."

"Afternoon Sergeant, I'm Sergeant Smith of the British army. Nice to know we can still count on the Yanks to make an over-the-top entrance." Miller grinned.

"I'm Sergeant Miller, and these two sorry looking specimens are the reason we're all out here freezing our asses off."

"Ah the System designers I take it." Smith hazarded a guess as he shook the pair's hands. "So we're relying on you two to get us in here."

"Yes, I suppose so."

"Well you have the engineers Miller. How do you suggest we approach this situation?"

"I think these two are the best one's to answer that question."

"We'll need to get inside and down into the System chamber."

"Fair enough, we'll take a nerd each."

"That won't work," replied Bradley. "Either of us can get into the complex but it takes both our retinal scans to activate the System chamber door."

"Why isn't there some kind of remote shut down for this System?"

"There's not a remote signal in the world that could pass through that much earth and rock. The only shut off switch is located inside the System chamber."

"Damn it. OK then both of you will have to go in." Miller turned back to Sergeant Smith. "I suggest we hold one team back in case there's any surprises." Smith nodded.

"Sounds reasonable, but who gets to go in first?" Deacon ran in from somewhere behind the drop-ship as Miller was pondering the question.

"The equipment's still in one piece Sarge." Deacon handed Miller one of the two Plasma Rifles he was carrying.

"Thanks Deacon, carry on."

"Aye sir." Deacon quickly turned and ran back behind the ship. Miller pushed a button on a small black piece of equipment that was attached to his ear.

"Miller to Frost, what's your status?"

"APC is prepped and ready to roll sir."

"Fire it up."

"Aye sir." The roar of another engine became apparent through the din from the waiting drop-ship. From the rear of the ship emerged a heavily armoured six-wheeled vehicle that advanced out into the open and stopped. The wheels on the vehicle were mounted on six long struts that spread out from its raised rectangular body. The ground clearance of the machine was high enough for Evans to view its entire underside without even having to stoop.

"Impressive hardwear Miller," remarked Sergeant Smith. "With that kind of fire power your team would best serve the mission by covering us as we advance."

"Agreed. I'll set up position a few hundred yards from the main entrance, check the place out before your boys move in." Smith nodded.

"See you on the inside Sergeant." After saluting Miller, Sergeant Smith took Bradley and Evans and returned to his troops. A large section of the underside of the APC lowered to the floor as Miller walked over.

"OK Marines, this ain't no social gathering, let's go." The

squad ran over and joined Sergeant Miller on the lift and it retracted back into the APC.

"Miller to Davidson, get that bird in the air. Back off to a safe distance and wait till I call you."

"Consider me gone Sergeant." The APC shook as the dropship's engines fired up.

"OK Frost, take up position a few hundred metres from the installations entrance."

"Hold onto something guys, we're going in." The APC engines roared as it started to advance towards the complex.

"Deacon, how's it look?"

"Quiet Sarge'. No sign of any activity from the installation."

"What about the Allied team?"

"Their two vehicles are right behind us sir." A couple of the men fell over as the APC bounced over a large snowdrift at high speed.

"Damn it Frost."

"Sorry." The sound of pistons filled the compartment as Deacon activated two large chain cannons that emerged from the roof of the APC.

"Coming up on co-ordinates Sarge' E.T.A thirty seconds."

"OK Deacon, keep your eyes open." The APC jerked to a halt in the deep snow surrounding the complex. Deacon trained the chain cannons on the large steel door as the Alliance vehicles raced past.

"Still no reaction from the installation's security systems sir. Maybe the Nerds were right about it being a simple glitch."

"Maybe." The Alliance vehicles slid to a halt by the outer doors of the complex. After the British and French soldiers rushed out and secured the area, Evans and Bradley exited the vehicle and walked over to the door. As they did so, the entrance's anti-tank guns rose from their compartments in the ground and a large set of chain cannons quickly followed.

"No wait!" shouted Evans as the soldiers raised their rifles. "It's just the security system. It's supposed to do that. They won't fire unless you give them a reason to fire." Evans nodded at Bradley who opened a small concealed panel on the wall and began to type a code into the keypad.

"Gentlemen, welcome to the AI installation." Bradley hit the enter key and stepped back.

"Oh yeah, best built complex ever," mocked one of the soldiers after a few seconds of nothing happening. Bradley gave a confused frown and re-typed the code.

"Jake, it won't accept my code." Upon Bradley stating this fact, Evans noticed one of the anti-tank guns very slowly turning towards the Alliance vehicles.

"Oh god." A great swell of fear ran through Evans as he realised what was happening. "Get outta here, it's a trap!" he screamed to the squad. In instant response to his warning, the chain cannons perched above them began to fire. Bradley was splattered by blood as the bullets from the cannons tore mercilessly through the screaming soldiers.

"Stone."

"On it sir." The chain cannons on the APC screeched into action. Evans shielded his face from the speeding chunks of concrete that were now flying chaotically through the air as the cover fire laid waste to the entrance frame above him. Three men were crushed under the weight of the complex's mangled twin cannons as they were sent crashing to the ground.

"The installation's anti-tank guns have opened fire on the Alliance vehicles."

"Take em out."

"I can't sir, not without hitting the troops."

"Fuck. Frost, take us in." Frost hit the throttle and the APC burst into action. "One of the Alliance vehicles is retreating sir, the other's under heavy fire."

"Get us to those scientists now."

"Brace for impact." Miller took hold of a roof support as Frost smashed the APC through the battered Alliance vehicle. Zeus and Stone ran onto the lift followed by another two members of the squad. Miller pulled a rocket launcher from its rack on the wall.

"Hanson!" he shouted as he threw it to one of the soldiers. The lift quickly descended and before it had even reached the floor the troops opened fire on the antitank guns.

"Down!" shouted Hanson as he raised the rocket launcher. The gun was totally demolished as the rocket hit it and exploded.

"Get over here!" shouted Zeus to Evans and Bradley who were still cowering in the doorway. "Now damn it now!" The other marines concentrated their fire on the remaining gun as Zeus dragged Evans and Bradley on to the lift.

"We have to go back down sir, there's still men alive out there." The APC began to shake lightly as the soldiers pushed Evans and Bradley off the lift.

"Deacon, report."

"I don't know Sarge, some sort of low level seismic activity I guess."

"No," stated Bradley as he tried to wipe the blood from his face. "It's a machine shop door."

"A door?" questioned Miller in disbelief.

"Sergeant, with respect, I suggest you get us out of here." Miller stood and looked at the expression on Bradley's face for a few seconds.

"Frost, fall back."

"Aye sir."

"What about the Alliance troops sir?"

"We'll come back for them. I want this area secured." As the APC cleared the wreckage of the damaged Allied vehicle, Frost spotted the opening door of the underground machine shop. "Err, Sarge." Miller looked out of the window in disbelief as he watched the snow parting.

"Jesus that thing's bigger than a football pitch."

"Twice as big if you want to get technical," informed Evans. As they watched, a large tracked vehicle sped out of the gaping chasm that opened before them.

"Now there's something you don't see every day." Standing as tall as the APC the shiny steel vehicle slightly resembled a battle tank. Even under the weight of its veritable arsenal of turrets and cannons, it moved with ease at incredible speed across the rugged terrain. The machine was lost behind the debris of a large explosion as the surviving Alliance vehicle opened fire. Emerging unscathed from the blast-cloud, it raised a single cannon and returned fire.

"Shot fired sir, the Allied vehicle managed to get out of the way."

"Deacon, teach that thing why it shouldn't fire at our

Allies."

"With pleasure sir." Once again the sound of moving pistons filled the compartment as three large multiple missile launchers emerged through the outer armour of the APC. Deacon hit the fire button and two of the three launchers fired.

"Hellfire's launched, impact in three, two, one."

"Status?"

"Target remains."

"What the hell? Hit it again."

"Hellfire's away sir, standby. Target is still moving Sarge, and it's turning towards us."

"Use the Firestorm missiles."

"Aye sir, Firestorm's away." The APC rocked as the missiles impacted with the attacking tank. "Target is down sir."

"I should fucking hope so."

"Picking up four more vehicles emerging from the opening sir. They appear to be of the same configuration as the first."

"Give 'em hell Deacon."

"Aye sir, priming Firestorm missiles." The sound of an explosion rattled through the compartment as one of the tanks opened fire.

"Report."

"I don't know what those things are firing Sarge, but the Allied vehicle is no longer on my scopes."

"Sarge." Frost drew Miller's attention to yet more tank-like vehicles as they burst into the open through the immense doorway.

"Get us outta here."

"Hold on." Frost pushed the steering assembly forward and the APC began to move.

"Deacon, do you think our armour will hold long enough to rescue the Allied troop's."

"Armour or no armour, one direct hit from those weapons and we're toast Sarge."

"Frost."

"I know Sarge." Frost turned the APC away from the complex and the wounded Allied troops and began the retreat.

"Incoming." The soldiers stumbled around the compartment as a number of explosions narrowly missed their vehicle. Frost strafed erratically as they sped away, desperately trying to avoid being hit.

"Pedal to the metal Frost."

"I'm going as fast as I can sir."

"Incoming," warned Deacon. "Veer left now." The proximity of the latest explosion caused one side of the APC to momentarily leave the ground. The soldiers struggled into their seats and strapped themselves in.

"Miller to Davidson, we need evac' now."

"On my way Sarge." Another assault covered the windscreen in snow and dirt, temporarily obscuring Frost's view.

"God damn it, return fire."

"I can't get a missile lock while we're bouncing around like this."

"Then use the cluster missiles, do the whole area."

"Cluster missile locked and loaded, launching now." The central missile launcher rose high into the air before launching the large cluster missile. After gaining altitude for a few seconds the missile's outer shell burst off to reveal several smaller, tightly packed missiles. Launching in slightly different directions these small projectiles effectively blanket-bombed the whole area behind the APC where the attacking tanks were positioned.

"Confirmed hit on two targets. Five more are still in pursuit."

"We're running out of road Sarge," stated Frost as the valley before the APC began to rise into the base of a mountain.

"It's not that steep Frost, we can make it."

"Not fast enough to dodge the weapons fire Sir."

"Enemy vehicles are closing Sarge." Through the noise of the APC engines, Miller picked up the sound of distant explosions.

"Boo yeah, hear comes the cavalry." Deacon referred to the drop-ship that was approaching rapidly from behind, laying waste to the enemy tanks as it passed overhead.

"Davidson to APC, prepare for extraction."

"Copy that Davidson, nice timing man." The drop-ship blasted over the APC and slowed to a stationary hover. As it descended towards the ground the large entry ramp at its rear began to open. The APC slid from side to side as Frost braked heavily and with a final screech of the rubber tires on the metal ramp he brought the vehicle to a halt.

"Frost to Davidson, we're in, get us outta here." The vertical thrusters of the drop-ship burst into action and it began to ascend up the mountainside. Miller and the soldiers quickly placed their weapons back in the APC weapons locker and hurried towards the ship's seating area. Miller ran into the ship's cockpit as Evans, Bradley and the squad strapped themselves in.

"Open me a channel to Command."

"Channel open sir."

"Arch Angels to Command, come in please. Command this is Sergeant Miller, please acknowledge."

"This is West, go ahead Sergeant."

"Be advised General, we are under heavy attack from an extremely well-equipped and hostile force. The United Nations team has been neutralised and the enemy has control of the area."

"Elaborate, Sergeant."

"The AI System has some sort of new battle tank sir. Bigger and more heavily armed than anything we have."

"Report back to base for debriefing on the double Sergeant."

"Yes sir, Miller out. You heard the man Davidson."

"Aye sir, best speed for Washington."

CHAPTER: 9

5:00 PM 22/12/2436

Evans and Bradley followed Miller into the meeting room. Several men stood around the large oval table that all but filled the room. All easily over forty years old and wearing finely pressed uniforms, the men returned Miller's salute before calmly sitting down.

"Let's get to it Sergeant," opened the man furthest away from Miller at the far end of the table.

"Well General, as you know, my team was ordered into the Alps to assess the AI situation. After these two men and the European Alliance team reached the complex they came under fire from its sentry guns. We managed to rescue the scientists and take out the entrance's armaments but were engaged by hostile vehicles before we could rescue the Alliance troops."

"Yes these hostile vehicles I've heard about. Didn't you say they were some form of tank?"

"Yes sir. The vehicles were heavily armed and had armour like nothing I've ever seen. We had to hit the first target with a high-yield Firestorm warhead in order to take it out."

"If I'm not mistaken Sergeant, Special Forces drop-squads are equipped with the new Mark Four Armoured Personnel Carriers aren't they?" questioned another member of the group.

"That's correct Colonel."

"Are they not equipped with Hellfire missiles?"

"Yes sir they are, however, they proved ineffective."

"How do you mean, ineffective? Be more specific Sergeant."

"We hit one of the tanks with at least a dozen Hellfire's sir and they didn't even slow it down. I'm sure that enough Hellfire's would stop one of these things but not fast enough to be effective in battle."

"Thank you Sergeant, please continue."

"Yes sir. The tank emerged from a huge door in the ground that apparently leads to one of many subterranean machine shops."

"Yes, thank you Sergeant, we are aware of the facilities design parameters," interrupted the colonel.

"Of course Colonel. Anyway, we took out the first tank just before several more emerged from the machine shop entrance. After witnessing the destruction of the Allied vehicle, I decided it would be a good idea to fall back."

"You mean run Sergeant."

"I mean remove my team from a non-survivable situation, sir," snapped Miller who was obviously offended by the colonel's remark. "The Allied transport was totally destroyed with a single direct hit from one of those vehicles. My squad would have been dead in seconds if I hadn't ordered the retreat."

"You should have tried to secure the area, soldier."

"I blanketed the whole area with a cluster missile and those tanks still kept coming. The only way to secure that area is with a full contingent of hover tanks and preferably air support. Which if I may be so bold sir, is exactly what I suggest we do."

"The European Alliance has already dispatched three tank squadrons to mount an assault on the complex. We have a Command Carrier positioned over the site in orbit to offer assistance if it is required." The general slid a small folder across the table to Miller. "Your mission is to return these two to the site and make sure they survive long enough to fix this mess. You will rendezvous with the Command Carrier and wait there until the Allied forces are ready to engage the AI's defences. Do you have any questions Sergeant?"

"Permission to speak freely and make a request sir."

"Anytime Sergeant."

"I'm gonna need my APC re-arming with Firestorm missiles. I can't guarantee the safety of these men if my arsenal is still eighty percent Hellfire's." The general nodded.

"Agreed, I'll have the Command Carrier's armoury at your disposal by the time you get there."

"Wait a minute," interrupted Evans. "I'm not going anywhere near that place. It was pure luck that we got out the first time."

"I was under the impression that you two were the only people that could access the AI System chamber."

"Well, yes but…"

"Then you're going."

"But…"

"Stop fucking me around man!" shouted the colonel as he stood up and slammed his fist against the table. "I have fighter squadrons napalming crops and small towns all over the country to contain a deadly virus that your invention created. If we don't come up with an antidote soon I'm going to have to order my troops to start wiping out cities." Evans and Bradley suddenly looked horrified at this news. "Yes that's right. New York, Seattle, even Washington are starting to show signs of infected people, in mass." The colonel leant over the table towards the scientists and continued in a calm, disturbing tone. "If you two don't find a way to fix this soon, American troops are going to have to start burning their own people."

6:30PM 22/12/2436

"Black Hawk to Philadelphia, come in please. This is the drop-ship Black Hawk to Command Carrier Philadelphia, please respond."

"This is Philadelphia, what can we do for you Black Hawk?"

"We have orders to report here and re-arm before joining the UN ground forces in the Alps."

"Standby Black Hawk." Davidson sat and waited.

"My god, that's a big ship," remarked Bradley as the Carrier came into view of his porthole.

"Yeah, the Command Carriers are the biggest things up here. Bigger than the Dreadnought class Ore Miners even."

"Really?"

"Yeah, only three of them were ever built, and two of them are ours. This computer picked a fight with the wrong assholes." Back in the cockpit Davidson received his confirmation.

"No problem Black Hawk, you're cleared for bay two."

"Thanks, Black Hawk out." With a short burst of its thrusters the drop-ship began to move slowly forward. A bead of sweat ran down Davidson's brow as he concentrated intensely on avoiding the sides of the docking bay entrance. The ship rose slowly through the entranceway and into the stillness of the deserted bay area. As the bottom of the ship cleared the floor level, the huge pressure doors closed beneath it and Davidson lowered the landing struts.

"Standby for re-pressurisation." Through the view port of the drop-ship Davidson could make out a young man standing behind a small window in the landing bay's wall. The man nodded at Davidson before pulling a lever on the panel below him. As he did so a great flood of air began to rush into the room and the drop-ship fell a few inches and hit the ground as the gravity-field in the room was restored.

"Bay re-pressurised Black Hawk, exit at your leisure and report to the bay's control room."

"Acknowledged Control." Davidson locked down the drop-ship and removed his flight harness and helmet. After double-checking that the flight systems were on shutdown he exited the ship through the seating chamber hatch and joined his squad.

"I've been told to report to the landing bay control room Sarge. I'll sort out the extra missiles we were promised while I'm there."

"Thanks man but I've got it. The Allied squadrons are moving in over ground, they won't be in position to start the offensive for at least three hours. Why don't you guys see if this place has a mess hall or something?" The rest of the squad thanked the Sergeant and quickly exited the area before he changed his mind. Zeus dragged Evans and Bradley along under the chant of:

"Come on you two, let's get some red meat into those skinny little body's of yours. God knows you could use the protein."

"You sure sir?"

"Yeah Davidson, I have to go up and see the captain anyway."

"OK sir, see you in the mess." Davidson turned and ran after the squad. Miller walked into the landing bay's control room and returned the salute of the controller.

"Sergeant Miller of the twenty-fifth, I'm going to need

access to your armoury." Miller handed the officer a copy of his orders.

"Hmm, clearance from General West himself." The officer closed the folder and handed it back to Miller. "Our armoury is at your disposal Sergeant."

Having found the mess hall, the squad got down to what seemed to be the very serious business of eating. Bradley was quite shocked by the way the soldiers piled food onto their trays. Huge mounds of cold mashed potato and as many fat, bloody pieces of steak as the food re-hydrators could handle.

"Here you go ladies." Deacon smirked as he dropped a couple of trays in front of the scientists. "Enjoy it, probably gonna be the last meal you fags ever eat." Zeus walked over and sat down across from Evans, the metal bench creaked under the weight of his enormous frame.

"Don't pay any attention to Deac'," he said loudly. "He's just pissed because I fell asleep on his mother." Frost covered Hanson and Stone in potato as he burst into laughter.

"Damn it Frost, watch where you're spitting that shit."

"My mother's a saint, spear chukka."

"Ooh." The squad responded to Deacon's insult. Zeus just nodded and grinned.

"That's funny man, cause she's a demon under the sheets." The squad laughed. Deacon gave a defeated smirk and threw an orange at Zeus.

"What's with the sudden knight in shining armour routine anyway Zeus. They're big boys, don't you think they can look after themselves?"

"Perhaps he's taken a fancy to them," returned Deacon, seizing the opportunity to throw another insult.

"Well it's understandable Deacon. They are both prettier than your mother." The squad roared.

"So, what are we gonna be running into inside that installation?" Williams mumbled with a mouth full of food.

"Well, let's work on the assumption that the security system layout hasn't changed," answered Evans. "For a start we know our codes are no longer accepted, so we're gonna have to blow the main doors. Then there's the lift that takes us down into the installation."

"Providing it still accepts our palm prints."

"Yeah, good point Thomas. We might have to waste a bit of time hot-wiring it so we'd better take the right equipment. Then there's the pressure door to the complex itself. Now it doesn't have any weapons systems to worry about but it's gonna take some getting through if the code doesn't work."

"You let us worry about that," reassured Stone. "Never seen a door yet that a Plasma Grenade couldn't open."

"Fair enough. OK where was I, ah yes. Once we get into the main chamber we'll have two chain cannons to take out. Now they're situated in the roof at either side of the AI System chamber door."

"Is their anything to use as cover?"

"No, the room is entirely empty. Come over here." The squad all picked up their trays and relocated to Evans' table. Evans took his fork and began to sculpt a clumsy overhead view of the room out of his mashed potato.

"OK, this is the main chamber. This over here is the AI System chamber and this door leads to the lower levels."

"We're gonna be sitting ducks against chain cannons in a space as open as that."

"What's in the lower levels?"

"The lower levels consist of the machine shops and storage bays."

"Great, so our choices are the chain cannons, or the rooms with the tanks. It's gonna be a long fucking night, that's all I know."

"Are you boys playing nice?" joked Miller who had entered unnoticed and was standing behind Evans.

"We're just going over the installation's security system Sarge. Trying to get a head start." Hanson pointed at the makeshift mash potato blueprints. "This is the main chamber and these…"

"Yes I know, roof-mounted chain cannons. I've been standing here for over two minutes."

"Ah, right. So, what do you think?"

"I think we're gonna need a way of taking out both cannons at once."

"We could take something down with us to use as a shield

while we hit them. I don't know, maybe one of the lift doors or something."

"No, that isn't going to work," explained Bradley. "The cannons are armed with the same armour-piercing rounds as your Personnel Carrier."

"Jesus, you really went to town on this System didn't you."

"Well something as revolutionary as the AI was always going to be under threat from extremists and thieves. Why the hell do you think we built it in the Alps? There aren't many groups with the equipment to mount an operation against a target on this sort of terrain."

"What about taking out the installation's power source?" questioned Stone. "I mean, you two must know some way of shutting the place down." Evans sighed.

"When I designed the security system, I didn't account for the fact that it would be firing at us. You guys aren't listening to me, there is no easy way into the AI System chamber. The crystalline reactor is positioned directly under the System itself. The only way to get to it is through an access hatch in the floor of the System chamber and the only way to get into the System chamber is through the door with the chain cannons."

"Then we're just going to have to do it the hard way," remarked Miller as he started walking towards the mess hall door.

"And what exactly is the hard way?" questioned Evans. Miller stopped just long enough to answer the question.

"Devastators and a lot of luck."

"What's a devastator?" asked Bradley as Miller walked off through the door.

"It's a hand-held rocket launcher about the size of a Plasma Rifle. It holds a fully automatic thirty round clip that contains missiles about the size of a nine-millimetre shell casing."

"Damn."

"Oh yeah, it's an ass kicker no doubt."

"Then why do you all look so worried?"

"Cos only a fool or a headcase would use one in a confined space." Suddenly the room began to rumble and shake followed by a flood of flashing red light as the ship's warning system kicked in.

"What the hell?" Evans watched his tray as it rattled its way off the table and crashed to the floor.

"This is the Captain," came a loud echoing voice over the ship's speakers. "All hands to battle stations." Evans and Bradley followed the squad out into the corridor where crew members were rushing around to get to their posts.

"What the hell's going on?" shouted Evans through the screeching sirens.

"We're under attack."

Now on the bridge, Miller could do nothing but watch as the crew frantically ran around trying to get the situation under control.

"It's the Asteroid Defence Satellites, Captain. They're not responding to our command codes."

"What do you mean they're not responding? Double-check the codes."

"The codes are right sir, it's the Satellites, they're not responding to the shutdown order."

"Divert all emergency power to the shields."

"Aye sir."

"Tactical, return fire. Helm, hard to port."

"Sir, I'm detecting dozens of objects entering the atmosphere. Many of the satellites have launched missiles towards the surface."

"Neutralise those platforms now damn it."

"Missile launchers are online, commencing assault." The sound of multiple missile launches could be heard through the chaos as the Philadelphia's starboard batteries fired. The lights and monitors on the bridge flickered as the inbound bombardment continued.

"The crystalline reactor has been damaged Captain. Primary power is offline."

"Bridge to engine rooms, we need that reactor back online. The shields won't last long on backup power."

"Gillian to bridge, the reactor's been damaged by a falling bulkhead Captain, I'll have to replace the crystals before I can get it back online."

"I need every spare kilowatt of power diverting to the shields Gillian. Now!"

"On it sir." Miller fell into one of the bridge's diagnostic consoles as a large explosion shook the ship.

"Hull breach section seven, decks five through eight. Energy seals are holding Captain but they won't last long with the shields drinking all the juice."

"Understood." Once again the sound of firing thrusters could be heard as another bank of missiles were launched at the satellites. "Tactical report."

"Forty percent of the platforms have been neutralised Captain."

"That's not good enough, soldier."

"Aye sir." Another bank of missiles were launched from the ship as the tactical officer tried to target the dozens of satellites.

"Shields are starting to buckle Captain." Miller took his communications device out of his pocket and put it back over his ear.

"Miller to Davidson."

"Davidson here, what the hell's going on out there sir?"

"Is the rest of the squad there?"

"Yes sir, they came back to the hangar when the red alert sounded." Miller walked into the bridge's lift.

"Good, prep the ship for take off, I'm on my way."

"Aye sir."

The squad was struggling to carry a number of large missiles up the drop-ship's ramp as Miller entered the landing bay.

"Hurry up, this ship's getting its ass kicked. We need to get airborne and take out some of those defence satellites." Frost and Stone looked at each other as Miller ran straight past them and up the drop-ship's ramp. Stepping up the pace they hurried to load the missile they were carrying into the ship, before heading for the seating compartment.

"What's the plan Sarge?" asked Davidson as Miller burst into the cockpit.

"Can you out-manoeuvre missiles from the asteroid defence platforms in this thing?"

"Atmospherically maybe, in space I doubt it."

"Try Davidson, we need to start taking out those platforms before this ship…"

"This is the Captain," interrupted a loud echoing voice through the P.A system. "All hands abandon ship. Repeat, all hands abandon ship." Davidson and Miller looked at each other.

"Sounds like we're too late man, just get us outta here."

"Err, we might have a problem sir." Davidson pointed to the empty control room of the landing bay.

"God damn it, don't go anywhere till I get back." Miller exited the cockpit.

"What's happening Sarge?" questioned Deacon as Miller opened the seating area's hatch.

"The asshole in the control booth has left already. I'm going to start the decompression sequence."

"I'll get it Sarge," offered Williams as he undid his safety harness. "I used to run one of these things." Miller nodded and stepped aside.

"Hurry up."

"Aye sir." Williams ran down the exit ramp and clumsily crossed the now shaking floor of the landing bay. He closed the pressure door of the control room behind him and began to push buttons on one of the control panels.

"Williams to Davidson, starting depressurisation sequence now." A great hissing sound filled the room as it began to depressurise.

"Williams, what are you doing? Set it on a delayed sequence or you'll never get back here in time."

"The ship's computer's off line Davidson, I'm having to do this manually."

"Then reset the damn thing and run."

"Sorry man it doesn't work like that. The sequence won't run unless the control room's pressure door is sealed and the door won't open until the sequence is complete."

"But…"

"Just get ready to depart."

"What the hell's he doing?" asked Miller as he re-entered the cockpit."

"He says we can't get outta here without leaving him behind." Miller pushed the button on his earpiece.

"Williams stop fucking around and get back here soldier."

"Sorry sir, but it's not possible to get out of this room while the depressurisation sequence is running."

"Damn it Williams, I'm not leaving you here." The huge pressure doors of the landing bay began to open, revealing the light from the surrounding explosions.

"You don't have a choice Sarge. I'll find a life-pod or something when the room re-pressurises. Now go." Miller punched the wall of the cockpit.

"Get us outta here Davidson."

"Aye sir, engaging manoeuvring thrusters."

"It's been an honour serving with you sir."

"Don't give me that shit Williams. I'd better be receiving your life-pod's location beacon in less than ten minutes or you're in deep shit." Williams chuckled.

"Aye sir."

"Sarge, if you're staying up here you might want to take a seat." Miller sat down and strapped himself in. "See you on the ground Williams."

"Catch you later Davidson. Give the AI one from me man."

"Consider it done bro. OK marines, hold onto your asses, we're going in." Williams watched as the drop-ship shifted position over the now fully open door of the landing bay. Raising the tail of the ship until it was perched at a ninety-degree angle with the cockpit now facing the open door, Miller tightened the straps on his safety harness as the tail of the ship lightly scraped against the roof of the bay.

"Err, Davidson."

"Relax Sarge, I'm just making sure we get a good start." Miller sat staring out into the dark expanse of space that filled the window. His head slammed back into the headrest as Davidson hit the engine ignition button and sent them screeching out into space.

"My god," remarked Evans as the Command Carrier's flank came into view through his porthole. The entire starboard side of the huge ship was in pieces. Large sections of the interior decks could be seen through the craterous holes in the outer hull. Many large plumes of fire reached out into space fuelled by damaged pipelines and ruptured oxygen storage tanks. Small flashes of blue light caused the whole surface of the vessel to twinkle as dozens of life-pods were launched.

"Incoming."

"Yeah I see it." Davidson strafed the drop-ship from side to side desperately trying to avoid the incoming missiles.

"What's that?" questioned Bradley, pointing at a flickering blue tint around the Command Carrier.

"Its shields are buckling."

"Jesus, Sarge the Carrier's shields have failed."

"Ah shit, Davidson."

"I'm going as fast as I can sir."

"Are we far enough away Frost?"

"I don't think so."

"What?" questioned Bradley unaware of the new danger.

"If one of those warheads hits that ship with the shields down…" Stone's explanation was cut short by a large blinding flash of light that suddenly filled the compartment.

"Incoming."

The shields of a Command Carrier are effective enough to deflect up to 75% of the force from an Asteroid Defence missile. However, with the shields down the enormous blast-yield of the warheads tore through the vessel with ease.

"Brace for impact." The drop-ship shook violently as speeding pieces of debris from the exploding Carrier bounced off its hull plating. The enormous amounts of power required to form and sustain ablative energy shielding could only be achieved by use of a crystalline reactor. Unfortunately the Raptor class drop-ships were not large enough to house a power source of that size and instead ran on a number of rechargeable power cells. The only thing between the squad and the advancing hail of shrapnel was the armoured hull plating.

Miller shielded his face as the console in front of him exploded under a shower of sparks. Davidson struggled to keep the vessel at thirty degrees as they descended through the atmosphere.

"Hanson!" shouted Frost as a large steel beam tore through the hull, skewering the soldier to his seat. Hanson grabbed hold of the beam in shock as blood began to drool from his mouth. A great wind swept into the compartment from the breach in the hull as the drop-ship sped towards the ground.

"I've lost propulsion!" shouted Davidson through the din.

"Starting emergency landing procedures." Miller watched through the window as the ship cut through the cloud layers.

"Hold on." Davidson pulled a lever and a large set of wings emerged from the sides of the ship. Miller almost lost consciousness from the force as Davidson quickly pulled out of the dive.

"The debris that's pierced the hull is causing too much drag. I'm having trouble holding her." Davidson radically altered direction. "I'm gonna have to put her down soon Sarge, I need you to find me a landing site." Miller looked over the global positioning map on the charred and smoking console in front of him.

"What about one of the coastlines, it should help soften the landing."

"We're going too fast, I'll never slow down in time to hit the coast."

"Use the breaking thrusters."

"If I use the breaking thrusters while we're in an emergency glide we'll fall like a rock. I need to slow down gradually or we're not going to make it. Pick a site further away."

"What about the British coastline."

"Well at least their weather makes for plenty of soft ground."

"Bear right four degrees."

"Confirmed, E.T.A thirty seconds."

"This is Miller, we're going in, brace for impact."

By the time the Asteroid Defence Platforms had launched the last of their missiles the Earth was in chaos. Washington, London, Moscow, Paris and many more of the world's capital cities were in ruin. Reduced by the brief but devastating bombardment to little more than tombs of burning rubble. The swiftness and ferocity of the assault could not have hit the world harder. No one had anticipated that the System would be able to crack the security codes that protected the satellites from outside interference. In the ultimate ironic nightmare the unprepared leaders and governments of the world were obliterated in a single attack. A tactically brilliant assault staged from their own defence system that lasted little more than five minutes.

Four miles inland from the port of Dover, in the cornfields

surrounding the town of Lydden, a great plume of black smoke rose into the still evening air. A deep scar and trail of devastation that stretched as far as the eye could see betrayed the final resting-place of the battered drop-ship. Miller stood over the shallow, freshly dug grave of corporal Hanson as Zeus and Stone covered his poncho-wrapped body with dirt.

"Want the good news or the bad news Sarge?" asked Frost as he approached.

"How's it look?"

"Well the APC is still in one piece but the drop-ship's totally screwed." Miller nodded.

"Get all the gear you can into the APC and load those Firestorms into the launchers."

"Aye sir."

"Sarge, you might want to take a look at this!" shouted Deacon through the open window hatch of the APC. Miller ran over to the lift and after waiting for it to retract back into the vehicle, he walked into the drive compartment.

"What is it?"

"We're receiving standard broadband updates from Hunter."

"Ah, I was wondering whether both of the Command Carriers had been destroyed. What do they have to say?"

"It's a repeating message Sarge. It says that all America's strategic operations are being run through Fort Thomas in Nevada." Deacon paused and turned to look at Miller. "Since the destruction of Washington and the Pentagon." Miller's face dropped.

"What?"

"Apparently that missile strike from the defence platforms was more co-ordinated than we thought. The Pentagon, the White House and several major military bases across the continent have been destroyed. It's not conclusive but it appears that the President and the Vice-President were killed in the attack." Miller sat down in the driver's seat beside Deacon. For a few seconds he said nothing and simply sat staring out of the window with a troubled look on his face.

"Any news on the rest of the world?"

"The airwaves are flooded with it. Every station, military

and civilian is screaming about the fall of one place or another."

"That would explain why it's so quiet out here."

"Sir?" questioned Deacon.

"We came in over Dover like a bat out of hell and our landing was anything but stealthy. We should have British troops all over us by now, or at least a voice on the Com system reminding us of the airspace restrictions. I'd say it's a good bet that Britain got hit too." Miller stood up and slapped Deacon on the back. "Call in an evacuation request, I'll inform the men."

"Aye sir."

Miller called over his men as he and the lift returned to ground level. Stopping what they were doing, the squad took up position in front of Miller's position and waited.

"Stand easy guys. Evans, Bradley!" Miller shouted to the distant scientists. "You should hear this too." Evans and Bradley walked over and joined the squad. Miller sighed and started to speak.

"As you already know, the attack from the orbital missile platforms was directed at the surface as well as at the Command Carrier. I've just received intelligence on the effectiveness of the surface damage from the Hunter Command Carrier, which I'm relieved to say is still in one piece." Miller stopped as he struggled to think of a way to break the news to his men. "Well there's no easy way of saying this so I'll just say it. The Pentagon, the White House and most of our military strongholds have been destroyed." The squads composure broke into a chaotic din of questions and profanity.

"What the hell are we gonna do?"

"The White House, where's the President?"

"Be quiet. This is no time to go to pieces." Miller gave the squad a few seconds to calm down. "The President, the Vice-President and all the Chiefs of Staff are presumed dead."

"Jesus Christ."

"What are our orders Sarge?"

"The message we received was just a recording, as of yet I haven't received any updated orders." Deacon lowered himself down from inside the APC.

"I managed to reach the Hunter, Sarge. Apparently there are no ships available for an evacuation at this time. We've been ordered to secure our own means of transport if possible and head for Fort Thomas."

"Fuck me." Miller kicked one of the lift struts. "OK guys, we're on our own."

"What's the plan Sarge?"

"Our best bet is to head for London. If it's still standing we should be able to secure some form of transport large enough to carry the APC."

"Sergeant Miller."

"Yes Evans."

"I wonder if I could have a word with you in private." Miller nodded.

"OK Marines, move like we got a purpose." The squad quickly returned to their tasks and Miller turned his attention to Evans. "What is it?"

"It's my wife. I want your approval to fetch her and bring her with us. You know as well as I do what the major cities will be like over here once the population starts panicking. It's gonna be chaos." Miller sighed and shook his head.

"This is a Marine squad not a Bingo outing."

"Damn it I know that Miller. I also know that the safest place on this continent right now is right behind you." Miller stood and stared at Evans.

"Where from?"

"Hawkhurst, Kent."

"Damn it Evans, that's in the opposite direction to where we're going." Evans said nothing and just stared at Miller with a look of uneasy anticipation. "Stone, Davidson, front and centre." The soldiers quickly complied.

"Yes sir."

"Take the Speeders. Go with Evans to fetch his damn wife." Stone and Davidson took the lift up into the APC.

"Thanks Miller."

"Don't thank me Evans. I'm just trying to keep you alive so you can fix this shit storm you've created." Miller reached into his pocket and took out an earpiece. "This is Hanson's communicator, push the button if you want to talk, but speak up so the microphone gets a clear signal. It has a built-in locator that I can track from the APC, so don't even think about disappearing." Evans nodded and put the communications device on his ear.

Evans' attention was suddenly drawn to the loud humming sound of motors as the hatch on the rear of the APC slowly opened. Davidson and Stone roared out into the air on two large bike-like machines that circled round and hovered down to the ground with a loud blast from their thrusters. Evans gave one of the machines a quick look over as they waited. Except for a number of small pistons that controlled the directional flaps, the whole of the machine was a dark green colour. Attached to either side of the main frame just below the handlebars were two large gun barrels. Evans didn't know what type of guns they were, but he decided to hazard a guess.

"Twin machine guns?" Stone shook his head.

"Devastator Cannons," he informed with a rather disturbing grin on his face. Evans nodded and climbed on the back of the machine. "Ever been on a Speeder before?"

"No, I've seen them but they always seemed a little too dangerous for my liking. Although, those models didn't carry warheads." Stone handed Evans a helmet and smiled. After slipping on his helmet he nodded at Davidson and began to rev the engine. Evans' feet left the floor as the Speeder ascended into the air.

"It's not the warhead you need to worry about." With a twist of the throttles, the Speeders screeched into action and tore off into the distance. Miller watched as they disappeared over the horizon.

"OK Marines, get a damn move on, this isn't a school outing."

CHAPTER: 10

"Assault Squadron to Command, come in please. Pearson to Command, please respond." Colonel Pearson shook his head. "Where the hell are those guys? Command, if you can hear me be advised, we have arrived at the battle zone. The AI System complex will be within firing range in approximately two minutes." Again Pearson got no response. "This is Colonel Pearson, all flanks stand ready."

"Area is quiet sir, no sign of any hostiles."

"Keep your eyes open Private."

"Yes sir."

"Artillery batteries report armed and ready Colonel."

"Second wing move in when ready."

"Copy that sir, we're going in."

"All scopes still report no movement or traceable power sources of any kind. Second wing is closing on the installations entrance."

"Second wing be advised, all Perimeter Defence Systems have been reported as neutralised, but keep your eyes open anyway."

"My thoughts exactly Colonel."

"Sergeant Naylor to Colonel Pearson, first wing is ready to advance at your discretion."

"Negative Sergeant, hold position till the area has been secured."

"Second wing has reached the installations entrance sir. Still no response from the AI."

"Second wing here, requesting permission to see who's home."

"Confirmed wing two, knock when ready." The sound of a large explosion filled the air as the second wing's lead hover tank fired on the main doors of the complex. The doors were blown apart with ease, exposing the empty interior of the ground level chamber.

"Door is open Colonel, chamber is clear, there is no one home."

"First wing spread out and secure the surrounding area. Remember to watch out for the machine shop doors."

"Affirmative Colonel."

"Sergeant Kelly, is the Speeder squadron ready for deployment?"

"Ready and willing sir."

"Intelligence states that there are only three surface-to-air missile launchers to take out. Keep a lookout for any additional platforms while you're out there."

"Aye sir."

"All remaining vehicles stand ready, this is a little too easy." The sound of Speeder engines briefly filled the main chamber of the Mobile Command Vehicle as the squad left the safety of their APC and sped past. As Sergeant Kelly and his squad rocketed over the site he glanced around for any sign of hostile vehicles. Except for a few frozen bodies and the twisted remains of the Allied vehicles, there was nothing to be seen but snow-covered mountains and ridges.

Suddenly the sounds of multiple explosions filled the area.

"Shots fired, shots fired, the Artillery batteries are under attack."

"What, where the hell is it coming from?"

"I don't know sir, everywhere."

"Damn it Private, where?"

"From the surrounding ridge-lines, the scopes say there's nothing there."

"All units to battle stations. Sergeant Kelly, do you have a visual on the enemy targets?"

"Negative Colonel I don't see..." The sound of static replaced the Sergeant's voice.

"Speeder squadron is under missile fire."

"Damn it, can anyone see what's firing at us?" The Mobile Command Vehicle shook as an adjacent hover tank exploded.

"All units open fire on the surrounding ridge-line." The dozens of tanks raised their turrets and opened fire. As the first wave of shells hit, the snow-covered ridge-line began to flicker like the faltering picture on a television set with faulty reception. As the second wave of shells hit the illusion shattered.

"The ridge-lines are false sir, it's some sort of mirage." The projection of the long surrounding ridgelines gave way to reveal menacing lines of waiting vehicles. Enemy battle tanks that spread out in several positions, waiting in ambush and totally surrounding the squadrons. Colonel Pearson felt a sudden cold shudder of fear as he realised the reality of their situation.

"My god." The surrounding aggressors fired, indiscriminately targeting the Allied vehicles with deadly accuracy and no sign of mercy. It took Pearson a few seconds to pull himself together as he witnessed the slaughter of his battle force through the Command vehicle's view screen.

"All units break formation, fall back to grid forty-six mark three-two-five." In the hellish noise and confusion of the constant onslaught, the disorientated squadrons did their best to obey. Tank after tank the squads engaged their afterburners and retreated away from the ambush area. Relentlessly the attack continued as the enemy battle tanks pursued.

"Pearson to Command, Pearson to Command, we are under heavy attack. At least thirty percent of the battle force has been destroyed. Attempting to fall back to a neutral position."

Unit after unit the retreating battle force grew smaller as the enemy targeted them from behind.

"We are clear on three sides sir. All hostiles are on our six."

"Pearson to squadrons, hold and attack." The raging afterburners of the hover tanks silenced as they began to slow and turn. "Destroy them, all units fire at will." The fast approaching enemy vehicles broke formation and scattered as a hail of Firestorm missiles filled the air. A great cloud of snow and dirt cloaked the aggressors as the hover tanks turrets fired shell after shell into their ranks.

"Yes!" shouted Pearson as the Firestorms arced back downwards and laid waste to the entire area causing the cloud of debris to swell in size. "All units hold fire." Pearson grinned and whispered. "Take that you bastards."

Meanwhile on the outskirts of Hawkhurst, the growing sound of approaching engines had begun to draw a crowd.

"Where?"

"Over there, the third street on the left." Several people quickly moved out of the way as the two Speeders swung round the corner and sped along the street.

"Jesus, look at this place." Evans made reference to the long row of buildings surrounded by glass from their smashed windows.

"Here, stop." The Speeders swung round and came to a halt outside the entrance to the large apartment complex. Evans quickly jumped off and ran inside.

"Never fails, man," Stone remarked to Davidson as he glanced around the street.

"Yeah, introduce a little panic into the status quo and everyone thinks they're Robin Hood."

"It don't make any sense to me man."

"Ooh the worlds ending," mocked Davidson. "Let's go steal some television sets." Stone laughed.

"Pussy's."

"You said it."

Evans burst through the door to his apartment.

"Jayne! Jayne!" he shouted as he ran from room to room.

"Jayne!"

"Jake!" Evans ran into the bedroom where his wife was sitting on the bed. Evans ran over and hugged her.

"Thank god."

"What's happening Jake, where have you been?"

"I'm sorry I didn't call after the presentation at the White House. I had to go back to the lab to find out what was wrong with the System. They didn't exactly give me time to use the videophone."

"I've been worried, the attacks started and you didn't call and I wondered what…"

"Shush, stop crying. We don't have time now, there are some people waiting for us outside."

"Who? Where are we going?"

"They're soldiers, American soldiers."

"But…"

"Look," he interrupted. "I'll explain everything once we get under way, but we have to go now OK?" Jayne nodded. "Have you been eating like I told you last time I called?"

"Yes, only tinned foods and bottled water that's over a week old." Evans gave a relieved sigh.

"Good girl. Put everything you think you'll need into a rucksack, and hurry."

"What about a suitcase?"

"Trust me there's no room, now go. Oh and wear some flat shoes."

Evans ran back out of the apartment complex's main entrance with his wife directly behind him.

"Wow, nice ass," Stone complimented through the headsets.

"Yeah, I wouldn't mind a couple of hours with that one."

"Hey assholes." Stone and Davidson stopped as Evans' voice came through the earpieces. "You're not the only one's with communicators." Davidson and Stone grinned at each other.

"Jayne, this is Stone and Davidson. Stone and Davidson, this is Jayne."

"Pleased to meet you ma'am."

"Err, thanks."

"Afraid we're gonna have to cut the introduction short, I'm picking up a large storm-front heading this way."

"Don't suppose it's heading in from a clear zone?"

"Yeah, you wish. It looks like it formed somewhere into the south-west." Davidson sighed.

"Definitely going to be acidic. Think we can make it back to the APC before it hits or do we need to find some shelter?"

"It ain't moving that fast, out-running it shouldn't be a problem."

"Evans, we need to get moving." Evans reassured his wife as he helped her onto the back of Davidson's Speeder. He quickly jumped onto the other vehicle behind Stone and wrapped his arms around the marine's waist. As he did so, Stone set the machine into motion and sped off through the streets towards the edge of town.

"Dear god." Miller couldn't believe his eyes as he stared out of the APC windscreen. He looked in dread over the broken heaps of flaming debris that occupied the space where the great

City of London once stood.

"Deac' get me a reading."

"I'm only picking up a few dozen life form readings Sarge, and most of them are too small to be human. Except for the unstable structures the place should be relatively safe."

"Can you tell if any of the airports are still in one piece?"

"Hold on a second sir, I'll try to patch into one of the surveillance satellites."

"Surveillance satellites?" repeated Bradley in a questioning tone.

"Yes Bradley, surveillance satellites."

"Big Brother really is watching you," Deacon boasted wearing a smug grin.

"OK I think that's got it." A small screen on the drive room's dashboard crackled into action as Deacon typed on the keyboard in front of him. From what Bradley could make out it appeared to be a view of the planet from orbit.

"Zoom it in."

"Aye sir, going to twenty times magnification." The picture quickly changed to a tighter view of what was now more obviously the British Isles. "Going to thirty times magnification." Bradley could now make out the city through the monitor screen. Or at least what was left of it.

"Damn, this place was hit big time. The whole city's been completely levelled."

"Is there anything that resembles a mode of transport?"

"Nothing sir, the whole place is on its ass. I can't make out an airport let alone any aircraft." The squad's attention was suddenly drawn to another small monitor screen as it started to beep and scroll line after line of unreadable text.

"Getting a message Sarge."

"No shit," replied Miller sarcastically. "What does it say?"

"Bear with me a second, it's encrypted." Deacon pushed a few buttons on the keypad beside the monitor and the still scrolling text suddenly became legible. "It's another message from the Hunter, apparently a major offensive is being launched on the AI System in response to the attack. The United Nations, Korea, Russia, it looks like everyone wants a piece of that thing."

"When?"

"It say's the attack is planned for zero-eight hundred tomorrow morning." Miller smiled.

"What happened to the European Alliance squadrons that we were supposed to meet?" questioned Bradley.

"It doesn't say." Deacon looked across at Frost who slowly shook his head to signal his lack of optimism for the Allied squadron's survival. Deacon continued to read the message.

"We have special instructions to get the scientists back to the System complex by whatever means necessary." Miller nodded and thought for a moment.

"Open a communications line on broadband."

"Line open sir," whispered Deacon.

"This is Sergeant Miller of the United States Marine Core. Any members of the British military that can hear this message please respond. Repeat, any members of the British military who are hearing this message please respond."

"This is General Savage of Scarab squadron eight, I read you Sergeant go ahead."

"I assume you just received the same message I did."

"If you mean the times for the reunion then yes."

"I need your help General, me and my boys are currently stuck in London. I have two V.I.P guests that need to get to the party. Trouble is we can't get a taxi."

"So, you need a lift Sergeant?"

"Basically sir, yes. Do you know anyone that might be close enough to lend a hand, preferably someone capable of carrying a rather large present."

"Well it's a little out of the way but I don't see why I can't swing by. I shouldn't have a problem getting clearance to leave a little earlier. I'll meet you at co-ordinates five-thirty-six point one."

"General, I owe you one."

"Don't worry, I get the feeling you'll have a chance to pay me back. Savage out."

"Deac', get on the line to Stone, tell him where to meet us."

"Yes sir."

"Frost, you heard the man, co-ordinates five-thirty-six point one."

"No problem Sarge."

"Report," demanded Pearson as the cloud of debris began to settle around the enemy vehicles.

"Nothing yet sir the cloud is still too thick." Pearson stared out through the view screen of the Command vehicle into the dingy mass of settling particles.

"Did anyone see that?"

"Sir?"

"Look there, some sort of orange glow."

"Yeah I see it."

"What is it?" The crew of the Command vehicle watched as the strange orange glow became more and more apparent in the settling cloud.

"My god." As the cloud dispersed the whole fleet of battle tanks came back into view, standing motionless and virtually unscathed in one solid line before Pearson's squadrons.

"That's not possible." The Command vehicle shook as the enemy vehicles commenced firing, sending parts of an adjacent hover tank crashing into its hull.

"All squadrons fire at will, repeat, fire at will." The orange aura of the enemy tanks grew brighter and more apparent as Pearson's squadrons opened fire.

"The glow is some sort of energy shielding sir. Our attack isn't even scratching those things."

"Open me a channel to Command."

"Channel open sir."

"Command, this is Colonel Pearson, come in. Command sound off damn it." Pearson kicked the communications console in frustration. "Why is no one answering?"

"Sir the enemy vehicles are starting to advance, eighty percent of the battle fleet is down or destroyed."

"Signal the retreat."

"All exit routes from this valley are on the other side of the enemy forces sir. We're cut off." Pearson dropped back into his seat; his eyes fixed on an advancing battle tank through the view screen. He watched calmly as it sped straight towards his Command vehicle, its weaponry trained and locked.

"Damn!"

7:59AM 23/12/2436

A storm had settled over the agreed pick-up site, it had been raging for some hours now. A single figure could be seen standing watch, covered from head to toe in green plastic overalls. Standing beneath the hull of the APC offered some protection from the toxins in the rainfall, but in a downpour such as this, the Bio-suit was still necessary.

"Miller to Stone, how's it going out there?"

"All quiet Sarge."

"You've been out there long enough, come back inside, I'll send Zeus out to relieve you."

"On my way." Stone suddenly became aware of a new noise piercing the sounds of the storm. "Stone to Deacon, you got anything on the scanners?"

"Yeah, one big ass storm."

"No, there's something else, I hear thrusters."

"There's nothing on the scanners that's small enough to be a ship, Stone. All I got is a shit load of low clouds." Stone directed his view to the sky as six large ships descended into view through the thick black clouds.

"Deac', that ain't clouds you're scanning." Deacon leaned over and looked up through the windshield.

"Sarge, our ride's here." Miller walked into the drive room as the drop-ships touched down.

"Jesus, I don't think they're gonna have any trouble carrying the APC." Miller watched as a large ramp in the rear of one of the ships slowly descended to the floor.

"Sergeant Miller, come in."

"This is Miller, nice of you boys to be on time."

"We're guilty of a lot of things Sergeant, being late isn't one of them." The locking mechanism of the APC entry lift drew Davidson's attention as Stone came back inside. "Bring your Personnel Carrier inside whenever you're ready."

"No problem, Miller out." Frost powered-up the motors and slowly rolled the APC up the ramp and into the back of the drop-ship. He was surprised at the chaotic set-out of the ship's hold as he carefully manoeuvred between many protrusive and bulky struts that spanned its walls. Except for a few scattered munitions crates and the half-dozen troops that stood awaiting their arrival, the entire hold was empty.

"APC powered-down Sarge, stabilisers are locked and holding."

"Deacon, get me a check on all systems." Miller walked out of the drive chamber and headed past the squad before stepping onto the lift.

"Need any company sir?"

"No I got it Zeus. Then again, Evans, you might prove useful." Evans joined Miller on the lift-pad. He smiled reassuringly at his wife as he descended out of view.

Evans steadied himself on the lift's guardrail as the huge drop-ship took off, its rear hatch closing but still more than half-way open. The sound of the roaring take-off engines was deafening. If the room hadn't been full of hardened soldiers he would have covered his ears in a second.

"Sergeant Miller I presume!" shouted General Savage, his voice barely distinguishable through the din.

"Thanks for the help General." Miller shook Savage's hand. "We'd have been lost without you."

"Don't thank me till you know what I'm flying you into."

"Do you have any word on the progress of the squadrons your boys sent in?" Savage shook his head.

"The entire Alliance was hit pretty bad by the satellite defences. All our primary Command installations were destroyed. By the time we got our shit together the whole of Europe was in chaos. All attempts to reach Colonel Pearson or his battle force have failed. In case that wasn't bad enough, the damn virus has taken more than half my men. Don't get me wrong, their replacements are all worthy soldiers, but they're not exactly trained to use these Scarabs." Miller frowned.

"Scarabs?" Miller followed the general's pointing finger to the roof above him, and suddenly the chaotic layout of the room made sense. The large protrusive support struts that spanned the walls of the chamber were actually legs. Legs that held up the huge bulky chassis of the war machines that loomed above them. It was a few seconds before Miller could make out the full shape of the enormous machines. There were three of them standing tightly packed along the length of the shadowed chamber. True to their name the machines vaguely resembled large beetles that towered above the twenty-two foot high APC.

"Jesus Christ." Miller looked at General Savage. "And I thought our intelligence network was up-to-date on Alliance weapons technology." The general grinned.

"Six months ago these things were just a concept, most of the Alliance countries aren't aware they exist yet."

"Very impressive."

"Wait till you see them in action." The general suddenly diverted his attention to a call that was coming in through his headset. A couple of seconds later Miller also received a call.

"Deacon to Miller come in."

"What is it Deac'?"

"We've just received an update from the Hunter, France is under attack on several fronts sir." Miller watched General Savage's face drop as he listened to his message. "Should I forward the message to General Savage's men sir or do you want to tell him yourself?"

"I think he knows Deac'." General Savage released the button on his headset and ended his transmission. After a few seconds of contemplation he looked at Miller.

"I'm sorry Sergeant we're gonna have to drop you off a little short. We've been re-directed to France to reinforce the city of Grenoble, apparently they're under heavy fire."

"I heard. We'll help out as much as we can General but understand, I have orders to get these scientists back to the AI System complex and…"

"I know Sergeant," interrupted the general. "There's no need to explain, we all have our orders. I'm not sure how much your APC could do against these things anyway. Our intelligence report's that they have energy shielding." Miller nodded.

"We've faced them before. Shields would explain how they managed to withstand a direct hit from one of our cluster missiles."

"All hands to their seats, we're going down in three minutes." The intercom message from the cockpit ended the conversation. Miller and Evans headed back to the APC as the general and his men disappeared through a small door in the wall of the cargo hold.

Miller rushed off the lift as it locked into position inside the APC. Evans took his seat beside his wife and strapped himself in.

"What is it?" she asked as she noticed the look of worry on his face.

"I shouldn't have brought you here. You were safer at home."

"I was scared out of my wits at home. Hundreds of people were rioting in the streets below the apartment and the reports on the news kept getting worse and worse. I want to be here, with you Jake." Evans shook his head.

"I've put you in more danger than you ever would have been in at home."

"It doesn't matter, at least I'm not alone." She grinned.

"What's so funny?"

"I knew you'd come and get me as soon as you could, I just can't believe you turned up with the army." They both chuckled.

"Don't worry man," added Zeus, who had been quietly listening in on the couple's conversation. "Anyone who tries to harm this little beauty while I'm around is gonna get a visit from the hurt fairy."

"Thanks Zeus." Evans frowned. "I think."

Miller had strapped himself into the command seat, which was set back between Deacon and Frost's control chairs in the drive room.

"General Savage is on the line sir."

"Patch him through."

"Miller, the local intelligence network shows that the enemy vehicles are trying to secure the west side of the city. That entire area is full of automated construction yards and other industrial buildings."

"Are those construction yards capable of creating military technology?"

"They're top-of-the-range Miller, they'll build pretty much anything they're programmed to build, and the raw material stores for the buildings are reported to be just about full."

"We have to secure or destroy those buildings General."

"Negative. I've been ordered to preserve the construction

yards to aid in the war effort."

"Very well, but I can have our Command Carrier's arsenal trained on this area within five minutes if you need it."

"Nice to know Sergeant, get ready, we're touching down."

The Alliance drop-ship landed with a jolt. The large exit ramp opened and under a cloud of burning rubber from the wheels the APC quickly backed out. After a tyre-screeching one hundred and eighty degree turn, Frost hit the power and the team rapidly and noisily accelerated away.

"Miller to Savage, I'm heading towards the west side of the city. With a little luck I can find out what the state of play is before I'm noticed."

"Copy that Miller, we're right behind you. Good hunting Sergeant."

"And you General, Miller out." Suddenly the Personnel Carrier's auto-drive system kicked in and the bulky machine turned towards the buildings on the side of the road.

"Frost, what the fuck..." Miller's question was cut short as the APC smashed through the front of the building, rocking him violently in his seat. "Frost, what the hell are you doing?"

"It's not me sir, the auto-drive system's kicked in."

"Turn it off for gods sake." Another violent shaking of the compartment silenced Miller.

"I can't sir." The APC burst back into the open streets through the opposite side of the building. The demolition continued however, as it continued straight through the wall of the adjacent structure across the street.

"The computer's been hacked sir. Command codes have been re-directed to an outside source."

"Can you get control back or not damn it?"

"No sir!" shouted Deacon, frantically pushing buttons.

"Move." Deacon turned to look at Miller. Noticing the Plasma Pistol in his hand he quickly ducked out of the way of his console. Miller opened fire and under a shower of sparks the console flickered and shut down.

"That did it Sarge, I have control back."

"Then for god's sake stop." Frost brought the APC to a halt as it smashed through the exterior wall of the building and back into the open air.

"Receiving a message from General Savage, Sarge."

"Patch it through."

"Sergeant Miller, come in."

"This is Miller."

"If your vehicle is equipped with an auto-pilot, disconnect it now, the AI System has figured out how to…"

"Yeah I know," interrupted Miller "I've just had to blow out a whole Command console to stop this thing."

"Any major system damage?"

"Standby. Well Deac', how's it look?" Deacon shook his head.

"It's bad, we still have sensors but the weapon system controls are fried."

"Do we have anything left to engage the enemy?"

"Nothing but insults and bad language."

"Fuck." Miller slammed his fist into the armrest on his chair. "Miller to Savage come in."

"What's the prognosis Miller?"

"The weapons system control unit is fried. It doesn't look like we're gonna be much help until we can get it fixed."

"Sorry to hear that, we're gonna have to continue to the western industrial zone."

"Understood General, good luck."

"Sarge, I'm picking up three large objects moving in from the north-west."

"Identification?"

"Couldn't say, the sensors can't match them to anything on record."

"Can you tell if they've spotted us?"

"They're heading straight for us."

"Frost, get us out of here."

"Yes sir." Frost powered-up the motors and headed away from the sensor blips that were slowly closing on their position. He changed roads as many times as he could to prevent the pursuers from getting into visual range.

"They're splitting up, trying to flank us." Deacon relayed the positions of the blips on his sensor screen as they slowly but surely closed in.

The Special Forces Armoured Personnel Carrier was one of

the only remaining wheeled vehicles used by the US army. Since the invention of the anti-gravity platform, wheeled vehicles had been deemed as obsolete. However, anti-gravity platforms required tremendous amounts of power and were unsuitable for lengthy operations. As some Special Forces missions involved weeks, even months in the field, the sturdy and reliable APC became standard equipment.

"Vehicle at three o'clock," warned Deacon as they crossed a large intersection. The APC shook as a large explosion narrowly missed its rear end.

"Definitely hostile." Frost struggled to hold the APC steady under the blast from another explosion, this time on their left side.

"Jesus that was close. Hold on." In a desperate attempt to avoid further shots, Frost ploughed the APC into the closest building. The sheer bulk of the vehicle made smashing through the bricks and mortar relatively easy.

"Frost, the building on the other side of this one is made from…" Deacon's warning was cut short as a large decelerating jolt racked the APC. The huge machine suddenly dropped and slammed into the floor as the forward-most wheel supports broke loose. It continued to skid along under its own momentum for a few seconds before coming to rest, still in the centre of the buildings. "Alloy." Deacon sarcastically finished his sentence as he climbed out of his seat.

"OK, everyone up, we have to move now." Evans was checking over his wife as the squad leapt from their seats.

"Stone, Zeus, I want Devastators and Rocket launchers."

"Yes sir."

"Davidson, Frost, as many Plasma Grenades and Landmines as you can carry."

"No problem."

"Deacon, get the portable communications up-link. Bradley, give him a hand." Miller and the squad quickly grabbed as much equipment as they could carry and hurried into the rear section of the APC. Davidson and Frost began the Speeder start-up sequences as Miller tried to give his passengers a fighting chance.

"You three put these on."

"What is it?" questioned Evans as he looked at the small badge-like piece of equipment.

"They're Bio-Dampeners. They mask all the traceable signals that your body gives off. They'll help hide you from vehicle sensors." The rear hatch of the APC opened as the Speeders powered-up.

"Bradley, Evans, get on the Speeders."

"What about my wife?"

"She's only small sir, I don't think the extra weight will be a problem," Frost reassured.

"Fair enough, just go."

"What about the rest of you?"

"We'll meet you one mile due East of here. Now go." Evans and his wife climbed aboard Frost's Speeder and with Davidson and Bradley in tow they sped off through the battered building. Miller and the rest of the weapon-laden squad climbed down from the battered APC and started looking for another way out.

"Over here." Stone directed the squad's attention to a small hole in one of the walls. One by one they started to squeeze through the gap. As they did, the sound of squealing tank tracks grew closer and closer, then suddenly stopped.

Miller slowly turned and looked through the gaping hole left by their entry. The turret of a large AI battle tank loomed over the entrance. It slowly moved until it was pointing straight towards him; then fired.

CHAPTER: 11

The battle in the city's western industrial zone had been raging for almost twenty-six hours now. Over a day and still the sound of distant weapons fire showed no sign of easing. Every so often the sound of terrified screaming could be heard as the patrolling AI battle tanks found another cluster of hiding civilians. They swept through the all but deserted city in a spiralling search pattern that grew ever wider, guaranteeing that they would cover every inch of the streets in their search for victims. No matter where people hid, no matter which streets or buildings were chosen as sanctuaries, the tanks would find them; and the squad knew it.

"OK Davidson, here it comes."

"Are you sure about this Frost?"

"Yes, they can't be totally shielded on their undersides or their tracks wouldn't touch the floor. Trust me this will work."

"It'll be hitting the landmines in about ten seconds, are you in position?"

"Yeah, I'm ready. Now keep your damn voice down."

"Come on baby, just a little closer." Frost and Davidson ducked as an exploding landmine sent dirt and pieces of twisted metal hurtling in all directions.

"Boo yeah, score one for the home team," Davidson shouted in delight.

"Told you it would work."

"Damn that felt good. Are you reading any more?"

"I got two more heading this way. We'd better fall back." The pair stealthily retreated back into the battered building behind them and headed upto the roof.

"Well done," congratulated Evans, who had been watching with his wife and Bradley from the rooftops.

"Won't that explosion bring more tanks this way?"

questioned Jayne nervously.

"Don't worry Ma'am, we have this whole area rigged with explosives. Nothing's getting through here unless it comes through in pieces." Frost stood looking at the personal sensor panel on his left forearm as Davidson reassured Evans' wife.

"Davidson, the other two tanks are gonna be here in about two minutes. The sneaky bastards are splitting up and coming in from two different sides."

"Where?"

"One's coming in down the main carriageway, the other should be coming in past the shopping precinct. Both routes are rigged, we shouldn't have a problem."

"Confirmation of the tank on the carriageway. It's heading in fast."

"OK Evans, be careful not to take those binoculars out of the shade. The sun reflecting off the lenses would give away our position."

"No problem." The group's attention was drawn to a large explosion, somewhere off the other side of the rooftop. Bradley ran over and took a look through his binoculars, being careful to keep the lenses out of direct sunlight with his jacket.

"Well?" questioned Frost impatiently.

"Nothing but a smouldering hole in the floor. I think we got it." Frost took a look at his sensor screen.

"Yeah, it's gone." Another large explosion drew the group's attention back to the tank on the carriageway.

"Did we get it Evans?"

"I'm not sure."

"What do you mean you're not sure?"

"Here, take a look." Davidson climbed under the fallen concrete slab that Evans was using as a vantage point and looked through the binoculars. The tank was sitting motionless in the middle of the carriageway with several pieces of its equipment and armour plating surrounding it. The only sign that the vehicle was still functioning at all was an orange aura that surrounded it, flickering like a faulty light-bulb.

"It could still pose a threat."

"Should I take a Speeder and check it out?"

"No, there's no point giving away our position for one tank.

We'll give the Sarge one more hour, then we'll get moving."

"What if he doesn't show?" Davidson moved closer to Frost so that the others wouldn't hear him.

"We've been waiting here for over a day. If they were able to do so they would have been here by now."

"What are you saying?"

"You know exactly what I'm saying Frost." Frost suddenly looked troubled.

"We should break radio silence, try to contact them."

"We can't and you know it."

"So what if we're detected. We can outrun these things."

"We can't outrun their energy weapons. I don't like it any more than you do but you know it makes sense." The group's attention was drawn to the Speeders as their consoles started to make a beeping sound.

"What is it Frost?"

"An update from Hunter."

"What does it say?"

"Hold on, the translation matrix is still decoding it." The look on Frost's face became more and more troubled as he read through the message on the Speeder's monitor screen. Suddenly his legs gave out from under him and he fell to his knees. He sat motionless with his head down and whispered one single word. "No." Davidson walked over and started to read the message. The same discomforted look spread across his face as he ingested the passages on the screen.

"What is it?" questioned Bradley in an uneasy tone.

"The States are gone."

"What?"

"Three hours ago the entire US nuclear stockpile launched by itself. Russia, China and the whole of North America have been obliterated." Davidson sat down on the Speeder beside Frost and stared out into nothingness. "There's nothing left."

Bradley and Jayne walked over to the edge of the roof where Evans was sitting. Jayne sat down and Bradley placed his hand on his shoulder.

"How you doing man?"

"My god Bradley, what have we done?"

"It's not your fault," reassured Jayne.

"Yes it is."

"It doesn't make any sense. Nuking continents will kill everything, not just humans. The radiation from those missiles will stop life returning to those continents for years. It's totally against the System's programming to do that."

"Actually it makes perfect sense." Everyone turned and looked at Davidson, awaiting any kind of explanation for this madness. "The only two American military sites that survived the orbital attack from the defence platforms, were Fort Thomas and a missile base in the Rocky Mountains. The missile base was supposed to be a closely guarded secret, so we assumed that it was missed because the AI System didn't know it was there." Davidson stood up and walked around as he continued his explanation. "That complex was constructed to build and house a new type of nuke. The basic warhead and missile housing was the same but the missile also carried something called E24. A bio-engineered chemical that's capable of neutralising radiation."

"How fast?"

"With three grams of this stuff, the radiation from a Class Five warhead can be neutralised in three to four years."

"Jesus."

"I know."

"What's to stop it nuking the rest of us?"

"It can't nuke the whole planet," interrupted Evans. "Only a small percentage of the surface can be hit at any one time without kick-starting a nuclear winter. Besides, its programming won't allow it to wipe out any species entirely. It has to allow for the re-population of the plant and animal life after it's finished."

"If that's true, how can it be trying to wipe us out?"

"I'm not sure."

"The only way it could possibly kill us is if it didn't consider us as animal life," Bradley offered.

"Quite possibly."

"What the hell are you talking about?" shouted Frost angrily. "Any idiot can see that we're a life form."

"Yes, but it's not programmed to protect all forms of life." Frost gave a confused frown.

"I don't understand."

"The System was programmed to find ways of destroying certain forms of life as part of its primary objective. Unnecessary, destructive forms of life such as the Aids virus and malaria for instance."

"So you're saying that the AI System considers us a virus?" questioned Davidson, seeming a little offended by the accusation.

"It would explain why it's attacking us."

"That's bullshit."

"Is it?" Evans paused to consider the best way of expressing his response. "Define a virus."

"What?"

"Define a virus." Davidson stood quietly for a few seconds looking thoughtful.

"A life form that uses other life forms to survive."

"Yes, a life form that infests something and feeds on it, using it to survive no matter the cost. An infestation that breeds and spreads exponentially, until the sheer scale of its infestation starts to damage or even kill the thing it inhabits. Do you agree with that definition?" Davidson nodded.

"Yes, that sounds about right." Evans sat and stared at the soldier, wearing an intensely serious look.

"Now, consider the Earth as the thing that we are inhabiting…………..Then define mankind."

The group's conversation was stopped as the distant explosions from the western industrial zone ceased. Evans, Bradley and Jayne stared nervously at the soldiers. The battle for control of the construction yards was over, but who had won? Jayne jumped as Frost's forearm sensor-pad started to beep.

"We got incoming."

"Where?"

"Coming in from the North-West. Three small objects, coming in fast." Frost looked up at Davidson. "They could be missiles." Davidson ran across the roof and jumped on his Speeder, frantically trying to get it started. "No time man, they're almost here!" Frost shouted at Davidson as he and the others ran past. Davidson continued to fiddle with the Speeder.

"They'll be here in seven seconds damn it, get inside."

Davidson gave out a frustrated roar as he abandoned their only mode of transport and sprinted towards the stairwell door. Frost counted down the seconds till impact.

"Four, three, two..." Davidson dove through the door at the last second. He rolled uncontrollably down the metal stairs as the objects rocketed overhead.

"They're some kind of aircraft," explained Frost as he watched the speeding objects fly off into the distance.

"Aircraft? You fucking asshole." Frost turned at this remark and looked down the stairs. Davidson was laid on his back in a heap on the first landing of the stairwell; at least ten steps down.

"Err, sorry." Frost's quivering lip betrayed his insincerity as he desperately tried not to laugh. "Wait a minute." Frost's expression turned to one of concern. His lack of concentration had caused him to miss another movement confirmation on his forearm sensor pad.

"What?"

"Multiple targets, several of them heading this way."

"From the industrial zone?"

"No, their course heading suggests that they came from the direction of the Alps."

"What's their E.T.A?"

"Estimated time of arrival for the leading objects is two minutes."

"Can you identify them?"

"Not yet." Frost grabbed Bradley's jacket as he tried to walk out onto the roof for a look. "Stay in here."

"What about the equipment?" Frost gestured to Davidson and the soldiers ran out of the stairwell and across the roof.

"No, get the water and the food supplies," corrected Frost as Davidson headed straight for the last of the landmines.

"What? Are you crazy, we're screwed without these things."

"We're screwed if we run out of water." Frost pointed to a number of dead bodies laid out in the streets ten stories below. "We can avoid the tanks, we can't avoid the virus if we run out of bottled water."

"We can take the Speeders."

"Think about it man, their energy signatures will light us up

179

like a beacon now that the battle's over. Every enemy vehicle in the city will know where we are the second we twist the throttle." Davidson grunted and picked up a backpack full of supplies.

"I'll get the supplies," offered Evans who had left the relative safety of the stairwell and walked over to lend a hand.

"God damn it I told you to stay inside." Davidson passed Evans the bag full of landmines and patted him on the back as he walked past towards the stairwell door.

"Come on, they'll be here any minute."

Frost and Evans hurried back into the doorway and turned to watch the skies. Several small aircraft sped silently overhead at incredible speed, as they did so Evans warned his wife to cover her ears. She jumped in fright as a deafening noise exploded from nothing all around them, shaking the building beneath their feet.

"They're firing at us!" she screamed.

"Calm down," snapped Evans as he stopped her from running down the stairs. "Calm down, they're not firing at us. That blast is called a sonic boom, it happens when an aircraft is travelling faster than sound."

"They looked like our boys to me," stated Davidson, an obvious air of relief in his tone.

"Not quite," responded Frost as he pushed buttons on his arm pad.

"What do you mean?"

"They were American fighters alright but I didn't detect any life form readings from them."

"Aren't most military aircraft equipped with sensor jamming equipment?"

"I know what you're thinking Bradley, but this sensor pad is equipped with the codes to neutralise American jamming signals." Frost continued to push buttons on the pad. "Hmm, that would explain it."

"What?"

"All of those jets are missing their ejection-pods." Frost looked at Davidson. "They're being remotely piloted."

"The sneaky bastard must have broken the codes for the remote piloting systems."

"Yeah, probably at the same time as the APC. I wonder how many vehicles it managed to take."

"The crews of any affected ground vehicles could simply smash their auto-navigation computers like we did on the APC." Davidson sighed as he considered the problem further. "Now aircraft, that's a different story. Ejection-pods separate from a ship in something like two-thirds of a second, there's no way any pilot could react fast enough to stop it."

"So what you're saying is that the AI System could potentially control every aircraft in the area?"

"Worse," interrupted Evans. "We gave the damn thing access to just about every communications up-link that exists. With the exception of certain military frequencies." Frost looked at Evans, defiantly shaking his head in anticipation of his next sentence. "The AI could potentially control every ship in the world that's capable of being remotely piloted." The group covered their ears again as another wave of aircraft shot overhead. Dust fell from the shaking support beams of the ceiling as the sonic boom hit.

"Five more. Two fighters and three British drop-ships, all without pilots."

"This is a fucking nightmare." Davidson rubbed his head and sat down on one of the steps.

"How many aircraft can be remotely piloted?" questioned Jayne nervously.

"About eighty percent."

"Jesus Christ." Bradley sat down beside Davidson and stared blankly down the stairs.

"Definitely every military ship that exists. Plus probably thirty, forty percent of commercial aircraft and starships."

"Be quiet." The conversation stopped as Frost turned towards the door. "Davidson, can you hear that?"

"Yeah, it sounds like an anti-gravity engine."

"I'm not reading it on the sensors. It must be coming in low behind the buildings."

"It sounds like a hover tank, maybe the Allies won the battle." Davidson stood up and followed Frost out onto the roof.

"Sounds close. Somewhere in the street below us." Evans, Bradley and Jayne joined the soldiers out on the rooftop.

"What is it?"

"Shut up!" snapped Frost. "Listen."

"It's getting closer."

"It's not that close, it's too quiet." The group watched as a small metallic object slowly ascended into view over the side of the building. Measuring about two metres in diameter the machine resembled a large rugby ball, hovering on its end in the sky. Except for one counter-sunk pit in its centre, the object was totally smooth and reflected the scenery around it in its shiny surface.

"Don't move," whispered Davidson. The machine quickly turned towards the sound of his voice. As the group silently and motionlessly watched, the sound of another humming anti-gravity engine could be heard approaching. The machine quickly turned its attention to Jayne as she took a step back in panic. The deep pit in its centre began to glow and the machine backed away, further from the rooftop. Under a shower of sparks and dispersing blue plasma, the machine fell from the sky and out of view behind the edge of the rooftop. After checking themselves for holes the confused group turned to Frost and Davidson, who stood casually behind their smoking rifle barrels.

"What…" The marines spun quickly around as another machine rose up the building-side behind them. They quickly took aim and fired. Two speeding, blue plasma bolts smashed into the adjacent building across the street as the object quickly dodged to one side.

"Shit."

"Run." The soldiers ran backwards still firing at the object as they followed the civilians through the roof access door. With a great release of energy the machine fired, sending the entire upper section of the stairwell and all surrounding walls flying explosively in all directions.

"Go! Go! Go!" shouted Frost as the group ran down the stairwell towards the street, ten floors below. Another explosion sent a hail of debris crashing down around the group from the battered floors above.

"Take the next door into the building." The group exited the stairwell as a section of the roof collapsed and bounced down the shaft, taking large sections of the bolted metal stairway with it.

The shape of their fast moving pursuer almost immediately filled the window beside the group.

"Don't stop, keep moving." Frost slammed into the back wall of the room as the windows blew under the force of another assault. The machine quickly disappeared out of sight as Davidson opened fire to cover his team-mate.

"Come on damn it!" he shouted as he dragged Frost to his feet. The soldiers continued to run through the corridors and offices of the building in the direction of the still moving civilians. All the while the pursuing machine continued to lay down fire in their direction.

"Quick, into the lift."

"The lift, but…"

"I know, I know." The group rushed into the large cylindrical lift and the doors slowly closed behind them. The lift shook violently as it descended through the relentless onslaught towards the ground. Suddenly it began to fall as a shot from the machine's energy weapon severed the cables. The sound of the screeching emergency brakes was second only to Jayne's screams as the lift crashed into the floor of the ground level.

"Is everyone OK?"

"Fuck you Frost."

"I'll take that as a yes, what about you three?"

"We'll be OK."

"Davidson, help me with these doors." The pair pulled at the now buckled doors as hard as they could but they would not budge.

"Stand back." The lift door surrendered to the force of Davidson's Plasma Rifle. After only three shots a smouldering circular hole had formed through the two-inch thick metal alloy, allowing the team to carefully squeeze out between its glowing hot edges.

"How the hell is this thing tracking us, I thought these armbands masked our bio-signs?"

"They just block our life form readings from sensors. The damn thing can still see us."

"Frost!" Davidson shouted as the machine descended into view in front of the building's main entrance. Frost turned just in time to see the glowing energy build-up from its priming weapon.

"Get down!" he screamed.

The ceiling of the large reception area collapsed as the machine fired a shot through the door. Darkness and disorientation gripped Frost as the entire area filled with thick dust from the shattered structure.

"Frost, Frost where are you?" shouted Davidson as he struggled to work out which way he was facing. In the distance through the rumbling of the still falling rubble, he could hear the weapon of the machine as it began to charge. He quickly made his way towards the sound, stumbling on the scattered rubble as he tried to get a clear view of his target. As he finally reached the clear air of the main entrance a screaming Frost ran past him, carrying what appeared to be an emergency fire axe. He ran unwaveringly at the machine and as it turned to intercept this unexpected onslaught from the murk, he swung the axe as hard as he could and jammed it into its side.

"Fucking die!" he screamed, spitting with rage as he shouted. The machine made a loud crackling sound before dropping from the air and rolling to a silent halt. Davidson, looking rather shocked, lowered his rifle and slowly turned to look at Frost. Frost just raised an eyebrow and shrugged his shoulders.

"I lost my rifle in the blast. I was improvising." Davidson nodded approvingly

"Fair enough."

The pair walked calmly back into the building. The dust was starting to settle now and the pair could just about make out the floor of the room.

"Where are you guys? Hey, Evans, Bradley, Jayne."

"Help!" A shaking hand rose from beneath a pile of rubble across the room. Davidson ran over to lend a hand.

"Damn Bradley, are you OK man?"

"How is he?"

"Not sure. He's passed out."

"That's probably a good thing. He doesn't want to see this." Davidson turned and looked at Frost.

"Both of them?" Frost nodded. "Fuck. Now we're really screwed." The pair suddenly noticed the distant humming of another anti-gravity engine.

"Ah shit. Come on, we'd better get outta here." The pair both grabbed one of Bradley's arms and quickly dragged him out of the building.

"How close is it?" Frost looked at his armband.

"Close. We need to find cover fast." The soldiers dragged Bradley out of the building and headed as fast as they could down the street.

"Over there, in the apartment complex." Frost tried the keypad on the large metal door of the building.

"Amazing, there's a fucking mass evacuation to escape the killer robots, and the bastards still manage to find time to lock their doors." Frost took out his knife and pried the keypad off the wall.

"Frost."

"Just a minute, there's not a door in the world I can't hotwire."

"Tell that to them." Frost looked up at the two rugby ball shaped machines that were speeding towards them along the street.

"Shit."

"Come on."

"Shit, shit, shit."

"Hurry up."

"I know, I know."

"Damn it." Davidson picked up his Plasma Rifle and walked out into the middle of the street. He took aim at the closest machine and began to fire.

"Hold 'em off for a few more seconds."

"A few more seconds and they'll be close enough to spit on us." Strafing from left to right across each other's paths the drones dodged his plasma bolts with relative ease. Closer and closer they drew, speeding straight towards him, their now glowing energy weapon pits signalling their readiness to fire.

Davidson couldn't help wondering how painful the next few moments were going to be. His attempts to hit the fast moving machines were futile at this range and he knew it. Maybe he would have a better chance of hitting them if he waited awhile. Maybe they would have a harder time dodging his shots at close range. Maybe he should have picked up more power cells from the rooftop instead of rations.

"Oh shit, Frost I'm out of ammo, throw me another power cell."

"I don't have the power cells, they're in the bag with the landmines."

"Oh fucking beautiful."

"What?"

"Evans was carrying the landmines."

"Fucking priceless." The pair jumped and fixed their attention on the middle of the road as the lead machine exploded.

"What the…" As the second machine altered direction to avoid the force of the blast, it too exploded. They stood silently wearing frowns of confusion as they watched pieces of the machines raining down to the ground. Walking down the street behind the blast, clutching their smoking Devastator Cannons, were the large shadowed forms of Zeus and Stone. Frost shook his head and began to laugh.

"Now that's what I call timing!" Davidson shouted as the pair approached. "We thought you were dead."

"Nah, just got detained slightly."

"Slightly, you guys should have been here hours ago. Where the hell have you been, and where's Deacon and the Sarge?"

"We've been pinned down in the sewers, trying to avoid the tanks. I guess we got a little lost. We found a small transport ship at a public transport station about two miles south of here. It looks like it was left behind in the evacuation because of engine damage. The Sarge and Deac' are working on it now." Zeus looked around. "Where are the other two?" Davidson shook his head.

"They didn't make it." Zeus sighed.

"How?"

"One of those fucking hovering things chased us through a building down the street. The roof collapsed on Evans and his wife, Bradley isn't gonna last much longer if we don't get him out of here." Zeus stood silent for a moment.

"The Sarge isn't gonna like this. Come on, we'd better get

going."

Back at the transport ship, Miller and Deacon had finished the repairs and were attempting to disarm a large docking clamp.

"I can't crack the security code on this thing. We're gonna have to do it the hard way."

"Fair enough Deac', keep out of the way." Miller removed two Plasma Grenades from one of the many bags they had brought with them. After removing the safety covers on the tops of the grenades, he pushed the small red buttons and placed them under the docking clamp. The clamp blew into several pieces as the grenades went off, sending large pieces of metal bouncing noisily across the concrete floor of the transport station. Miller stepped back as the ship's forward landing strut, which was attached to the security clamp, groaned and collapsed. He winced as the nose of the small craft slammed into the floor.

"Nice work."

"Kiss my ass Deac'." Deacon grinned as Miller climbed in through the now slanting door of the ship.

"Any damage?"

"No I don't think so, all systems seem to be operating within tolerances." Miller stuck his head back around the door. "Except for the landing gear." Deacon took a second look at the ship's new position.

"Take-off should be interesting," he raised an eyebrow and grinned smugly.

Deacon quickly fixed his attention on his forearm sensor pad as it began to beep. Several small yellow circles on the pad's screen were slowly moving towards their position. He turned himself to face in the direction of the incoming objects, attempting to work out where they were in relation to the surrounding structures.

"Sarge, you'd better get out here." Miller quickly jumped down from inside the ship.

"What is it?"

"I got movement, somewhere behind that scraper."

"Could it be our guys?"

"Quite possibly sir. Whatever they are, they're moving slowly and keeping close to cover."

"OK take cover." The pair picked up their Plasma Rifles and quickly moved off. Deacon took cover behind the fallen front end of the ship and Miller crouched himself behind a stack of metal crates. Deacon lay on his belly and watched the adjacent building-line from under the ship's hull, his rifle aimed and ready. He nodded at Miller as the objects reached the edge of the building that concealed them.

Miller stood up and rested his rifle on the top of the metal crates. Looking through the rifle's scope, he trained the crosshairs on the edge of the building and waited for a target to present itself.

"Deac' hold your fire!" Miller shouted as Davidson and Stone came into view. Deacon relaxed his grip on his rifle and stood up.

"Have they found the others?" Miller's answer came in the form of a frowning look as he started to jog over to the returning team.

"What the hell happened to him?" Miller questioned, pointing to the still unconscious body of Bradley, which was slumped over Zeus' shoulder.

"We were attacked by some kind of small hovering Cannons sir. Bradley was hurt by a collapsing roof." Frost paused for a second. "Evans and his wife didn't…"

"Don't say it Frost," Miller interrupted. "Don't tell me he's dead or I'm gonna fucking shoot you."

"I'm sorry sir." Frost hung his head in shame.

"Sorry!" Miller bellowed. "Fuck me!" He stood silently for a moment and rubbed his eyes, taking long deep breaths as he contemplated their options. "Zeus, put him in the ship."

"Yes sir."

"Davidson."

"Sarge?"

"Do you think that thing will take off in that position?"

"Shouldn't be a problem sir."

"Good, prep it for launch."

"Yes sir."

"Frost."

"Sir?"

"I want a tally on all remaining supplies and equipment."

"Yes sir."

"The rest of you set up a perimeter, keep your eyes open." Miller walked back over to the transport ship and climbed onboard. He opened the large box containing the communications up-link, flicked a couple of switches and with a calming sigh, began to speak. Outside, Deacon and Stone talked as they patrolled the area.

"This mission is fubar man."

"I hear that. How the hell are we supposed to get into the AI System installation now?"

"No idea man, probably expect us to blast our way in."

"Screw that man, I didn't sign up for no suicide mission."

"We'll be OK."

"OK my ass, did you sleep through the briefing on that place? The lift shaft's two miles long and that's the fucking easy part. After that there's chain cannons and god knows what to get past."

"Not going soft on me are you Stone?"

"Everybody listen up!" The conversation was halted by Miller's bellowed order from the transport ship's doorway. The squad closed in for the briefing.

"What is it Sarge?"

"We can't get into the AI System complex without both of the scientists. So unless anyone has a plan to resurrect Mr Evans, this mission is scrubbed."

"It's about fucking time."

"Shut up Deac', I'm not fucking laughing."

"Aye sir."

"Why don't we try knocking Sarge?" offered Stone as he cocked his Devastator Cannon suggestively.

"Stone, right know we don't have enough ammo to successfully assault a schoolgirl. I've been given clearance to take Bradley directly to the medical centre on the Hunter; we'll replace our equipment and supplies while we're there. Any questions?" Miller paused to allow for a response. "OK, get everything into the ship, we lift off in ten minutes."

CHAPTER:12

The nose of the transport ship crashed clumsily into the metal floor, as the docking bay's artificial gravity-field was re-established. After the spinning yellow warning lights, which spanned the walls of the large rectangular bay, ceased to flash, the ship's door slowly hissed open, and Miller stepped out.

"OK guys, I don't remember authorising a break, get out here and secure me some supplies. Deac', clear it with the Load Master, he's expecting us."

"Yes sir."

"Sarge." Davidson and Frost followed Miller across the bay.

"What is it Frost?"

"We want to come with you sir. It's our fault that the mission was compromised, it's not fair that you should take the flack." Miller nodded.

"Thanks, but it's not your fault. When you're under fire shit happens." Miller turned and continued across the bay, pointing out the ship to two medics as they ran towards him.

"But Sarge."

"Damn it, get over there and help the others. I want everybody fully tooled-up by the time I get back." Miller continued across the bay to its main exit, where two guards stopped him.

"Hold on please sir, no one can exit the docking bay until they've been scanned for the virus."

"I don't have time for this Corporal. I have orders to report to the bridge." One of the guards placed himself in the doorway as Miller tried to exit.

"You will comply sir." Miller stared at the guard for a moment, then stood down and took a step back. "Thank you sir." The guard ran a small cylindrical device up and down Miller's body, creating a rather detailed medical diagram of him on a nearby wall monitor.

"Won't take long now sir." They all watched the monitor as it ran its search cycle. After a few seconds a light female voice replied with an answer.

"Biological contamination negative. Subject clearance granted." The guard stepped aside.

"Thank you sir."

"No problem."

The Command Carriers were the largest vehicles ever built by man. Measuring in at just over two miles in length these mammoth vessels dwarfed even the Dreadnought mining ships. The weight of the vessels easily exceeded several hundred million tons and as a result they were totally space-bound, incapable of atmospheric flight. Equipped with a crystalline reactor and many hydroponics bays for onboard food growth, the Command Carriers were capable of actively sustaining themselves and their crews for years at a time. The ships were also equipped with a record-breaking amount of cryogenic stasis chambers to enable them to carry large amounts of troops into deep space.

"Captain Shepherd sir, a Sergeant Miller is here to see you."

"Send him in." Miller walked into the captain's ready-room and saluted.

"Sergeant Miller of the Arch Angels reporting Captain." The captain was stood staring out into space through a large porthole. He answered without turning around.

"Sit down Miller." Miller sat quietly awaiting some sort of response. "You realise how many men are going to die trying to force their way into that complex."

"Sir, I request permission to handle that personally. The scientists have already briefed my team on the complex's security systems and…"

"I've already sent a team in," the captain interrupted. "In fact, they should be arriving in a few minutes."

"What about my team Captain?"

"I'm sending you back to Grenoble. The western industrial zone has fallen to the AI forces and we can't afford to let them keep control of those construction yards. I can't rally the forces for a large-scale attack right now, and neither can the Alliance. I need you to use your talents to sneak in and level the place."

"Just give me access to a ship and point me towards the armoury." Miller paused for a second. "Thank you for the second chance sir." The captain sighed.

"I've been kept upto speed on your movements over the last few days Miller. Personally, considering what you've been up against, I think you've done one hell of a job. The fact that you managed to keep any of your team alive against those odds is exceptional. Many other squadrons have fallen under far more favourable circumstances."

"Thank you Captain."

"Your re-entry window is in three hours, make sure you're ready. Dismissed Sergeant." Miller stood up and headed towards the door. As it hissed open he stopped and turned back towards the captain, who was once again staring out through the porthole.

"Sir."

"Yes Miller?"

"There really was nothing we could do."

"I know Sergeant." Miller steadied himself on the doorframe as the ship suddenly shook.

"Shepherd to bridge, report."

"We've lost helm control sir, the ship…" The voice through the communications system turned into static as the transmission was cut off.

"Shepherd to bridge, say again. Come in bridge." The captain looked at Miller.

"What is it?"

"I don't know." Captain Shepherd grabbed his desk as the shaking intensified. "It feels like we're descending."

"Can this ship be remotely piloted?"

"There's no way the AI could crack the command codes for this ship, the system's too advanced to hack into."

"Even for a super-computer?" The look on the captain's face was one of uncertainty.

"Get your team ready, you might be leaving sooner than planned." Miller nodded and headed out of the door.

Crewmen were running frantically from console to console when Captain Shepherd entered the bridge.

"Report."

"Helm control is still not responding Captain. The navigational computer has started a descent towards the planet."

"By pass it."

"Already tried sir, the engineering stations won't respond either."

"Shepherd to engineering. Engineering come in."

"The communications system is offline too sir."

"God damn it. You there, get down to the navigational computer room and shut that thing down."

"It can't be shut down sir, the safety overrides won't…"

"Find a way."

"How sir?"

"I don't care how. Shoot the fucking thing."

"Aye sir."

"Helm, do we have anything?"

"I still have control of the emergency thrusters sir but they aren't helping."

Miller tore back through the door of the docking bay and ran over to the ship.

"Davidson, Deac', get the transport prepped, this thing could be going down." Deacon sighed.

"What, again, what is it with these things?" Suddenly the warning sirens in the bay sounded and the yellow lights began to flash. "Warning, warning," came the echoing female voice of the computer as the communication system came back online. "All hands to battle stations."

"Helm, full thrust on all engines, maximum power."

"Aye Captain, all engines full ahead."

"Engineering come in."

"Engineering here."

"Finally, I need all emergency power diverting to the engines."

"Way ahead of you sir, the engines are already at one hundred and ten percent of safety limits."

"Increase it to a hundred and twenty percent."

"But sir."

"Now damn it."

Miller and the squad ran back out of the transport ship and headed for the bay exit door.

"What the hell do you mean we can't leave?"

"We're too deep into the atmosphere." Davidson pointed at one of the windows, which glowed bright red from the heat and friction of the re-entry.

"So?"

"Anything trying to leave this ship under re-entry conditions, without a calculated entry vector, would be toast in about two-thirds of a second."

"But—"

"Trust me sir."

"Sarge, what's the plan?"

"Find an escape-pod."

"Same result sir."

"God damn it. OK, I'm open to suggestions." The squad stopped as the captain's voice came over the communications system.

"All hands abandon ship, repeat, all hands abandon ship."

"Oh great."

"Davidson, where's the best place to go on a crashing Command Carrier."

"How the fuck would I know Deac'."

"You're a pilot."

"Yeah I'm a pilot, not a fucking tour guide." While the squad argued, Frost typed away on the keyboard of a wall monitor beside them.

"What about this?" The squad looked at the internal map that now filled the screen.

"What is it?"

"A hell of a lot of Cryo-stasis chambers."

"Jesus, there must be a hundred of them in there."

"One hundred and fifty to be exact," informed Frost as he looked over at Miller. "All equipped with independent inertial dampening systems."

"Frost you're a fucking genius. Which way?"

Back on the bridge the crew's composure was starting to break.

"Where do you think you're going crewman? Get back to your station, you'll abandon this ship when I tell you to."

"Hull stress has exceeded tolerance Captain. Bulkheads on decks twelve through twenty-two are starting to buckle."

"Hull breach detected in cargo bay two, sealing section now."

"Engineering to bridge, the engines aren't gonna last much longer at this output level."

"Keep those engines burning or we're all dead."

"Descending through upper atmosphere, we're in free fall sir."

"We're gonna die!"

"Get him outta here. Helm, level off our descent as much as possible, target sector seven for crash landing."

"Please confirm sir, sector seven reads as the Atlantic Ocean."

"I know where sector seven is damn it."

"Aye sir."

"Sir, at this speed…"

"I know, we need to level off more. Give me a three second burst, all ahead full."

"Faster sir?"

"We need to get the nose up."

"All ahead full, aye sir. Reheat engaged, burn is at three, two, one, engine shut down."

"It's working Captain, our pitch has changed."

"Sir, we could create more drag if we open all the underside bays."

"Good thinking son. You heard him, open all the doors on our belly."

"Aye sir."

"Ten seconds till impact Captain."

"What's our angle of descent?"

"Forty-three degrees Captain."

"Not good enough, our angle needs to be shallower. Engineering, all power to engines, now."

"Hail Mary, full of grace…"

"All hands, brace for impact."

Miller climbed out of the cryo-chamber and lowered

himself down onto the now sloping floor of the room. Zeus and Stone were already up and were attempting to open the room's large and only door.

"Everybody OK?"

"Yeah, nice call Frost, didn't feel a thing."

"Inertial dampening fields, the best thing since the invention of airbags."

"The door's jammed Sarge. Looks like something's hit it from the outside, twisting it into the bulkhead."

"Can you move it Zeus?"

"Not a chance. Maybe if I had my rifle I could blast us out, but this thing ain't going anywhere." Zeus shook his head.

"Great."

"Sarge?" Miller turned.

"The air vents aren't working." Miller sighed.

"Even better."

"Guys listen." The squad fell silent. "Do you hear that?" A barely audible tapping sound could be heard through the floor of the room.

"Someone's down there."

"Shut up a minute."

"What's it say Deac'?"

"Nothing, it's just tapping."

"Well someone's obviously down there."

"Where the hell are we?"

"I think we're back on the ground."

"Deac', see if that wall monitor still works."

"Yes sir."

"We can't be on the ground. There's no way this ship would still be in one piece if we'd hit."

"How do you know it is in one piece? There could be a field on the other side of that door."

"Nah, the Captain must have managed to escape the planet's gravity."

"Then how do you explain the fun-house floor?"

"Maybe the Artificial Gravity Generator is damaged."

"Bullshit, this is real gravity, can't you tell the difference?"

"He's right." The squad turned to Deacon, who was sitting on the floor in front of the wall monitor shaking his head.

"What is it Deac'?"

"Take a look." Miller walked over and looked at the screen. "Jesus."

"What is it Sarge?" Miller stepped back to allow the squad a look at the screen.

"We're under water."

"Over three hundred feet down if this information is correct. Captain Shepherd must have brought us down into the sea."

"What about the ship, it should be in one piece right? The water would have made for a soft landing wouldn't it? Wouldn't it Davidson?" Davidson shook his head.

"Deac', can you find out what state the ship's in?"

"Already tried man. I can't get a damn thing."

"Can you tell us where we went down, send a distress call or something?"

"No, this monitor's jammed on the external sensors. It won't show you anything you can't see now."

"We're screwed man."

"He's right, game over."

"Shut up!" snapped Miller. "We're not dead yet. We know there's at least one person still alive out there, and on a ship this size there are bound to be more. We'll signal through the hull like our friend down there until someone hears us."

"All due respect Sarge, but I don't think that's gonna work."

"What do you mean?"

"Well this is a big room sir and that'll work in our favour. Trouble is, with the ventilation system not working we're gonna be running out of air real soon."

"Any idea how long?"

"I'd say two days, tops."

"Jesus Sarge, it could take a week to get us outta here. We don't even know if anyone's close enough to hear us."

"There's at least one person close enough, if we can hear him tapping then he can hear us."

"He's trapped too, why else would he be banging on the hull." Miller quietly paced back and forth while the squad bickered, trying to think of a logical solution to their problem.

"Deac', Frost."

"Yes sir?"

"Do these things have a backup power supply in case the reactor shuts down?" Miller made reference to the cryo-stasis chambers that littered the room.

"They should do sir. Safety regulations state that these things should be linked to at least one set of emergency power cells in case of reactor failure."

"Any idea how long these things will operate for on backup power cells?"

"If I remember correctly, except for the initial freezing and revival processes, these things run on very little power. They should be able to run for a long time if the power cells are large enough."

"Longer than a couple of days?"

"Easy."

"OK, prep six chambers, we'll wait this out in deep-freeze and hope the rescue teams pickup the power signatures from the chambers." The squad suddenly looked very nervous.

"What if the rest of the crew are dead Sarge? What if there are no rescue teams?"

"If anyone has a better idea I'm listening." The squad remained silent. "Then it's agreed. Prep the chambers."

Under the direction of Frost and Deacon, the squad spent the next two hours disconnecting the unused cryo-chambers to reduce the power drain. Using a large metal rod, which he tore off one of the cryo-chambers, Stone continuously tapped out a message in Morse Code against the bulkheads of the room. "Cryo-room three, trapped." After setting the cryo-chambers to run until they were manually turned off, the squad prepared themselves to be frozen. Cut off from time itself, waiting to be found.

CHAPTER: 13

The humming motors of the cryo-chambers lid woke Miller as it slowly opened. The sensation of awakening from cryo-stasis was new to him and it took him a few seconds to overcome the unexpected feeling of nausea. As his awareness slowly returned to him, he realised that the room was still in darkness. All except for the strafing beams of light from what must have been two torches.

"Who's there?"

"Swan, they're waking up." He shielded his eyes as one of the torch beams shone directly into his face.

"I said who's there?"

"My name's Sykes. How are you feeling?"

"Like shit." Miller pulled himself out of the stasis pod and stretched his legs.

"You've been in deep-freeze for a long time, it'll take your body a while to re-adjust."

"Get that fucking light out of my face." Miller looked out into the darkness of the room towards the shouting. It sounded like Deacon, who was now obviously awake and less than impressed by the brightness of Swan's torch. "Who the fuck are you?"

"Deac', stand down."

"That you Sarge?"

"Yeah, do me a favour and wake the others." Miller turned his attention back to the man in front of him. He was wearing a scraggy, torn pair of overalls and carrying nothing but his torch. The only other piece of equipment on him was a communicator device that was fixed to a band on his left arm. "Well you're obviously not military. What are you doing here?"

"We're part of a salvage team. We were just checking this room for anything that we could use, you guys are lucky we found you."

"Salvage team?" Miller's look turned to one of confusion.

"Yes, err, Sergeant was it?"

"Yes." Miller took another look around the darkened room and shook his head. "This ship was the last US stronghold, carrying over five thousand Americans," he sighed. "Now my country is truly dead." He looked at Sykes. "I'm gonna need to speak to someone in your military, I still have orders to carry out, I'm in need of equipment and transport." Sykes had a very strange look on his face.

"I don't know how to tell you this Sergeant, but the war as you know it is over."

"Then we won." Sykes shook his head.

"We were slaughtered."

"What? But you…"

"With the exception of your team, every human that couldn't escape the planet was killed. Over ninety-nine percent of the population was lost. As far as we can tell, this ship has been down here for almost a hundred years." Miller stood silently, his eyes betraying his confusion and anguish as he struggled with the news.

"This doesn't make any sense. If the AI System has control of the planet how did you get down here?" The rest of the squad was awake now and attempting to move around. Sykes looked over their faces and uniforms and returned his gaze to Miller.

"Are you all soldiers?"

"We're Special Forces. Arch Angel squadron." Sykes smiled.

"Old Iron-hand is gonna love this!" shouted Swan from across the room.

"Iron-hand?" questioned Miller.

"Iron-hand is what we call our leader. We'd better get you and your squad back to the Sanctuary Sergeant. I'll fill you in on what you've missed once we're aboard our ship." Miller nodded.

The squad followed the two men through the twisted and buckled corridors of the Command Carrier. Miller had a hard time believing his eyes as he looked around. Long corridors of the ship that he had previously walked through now ended abruptly due to their collapsed and crushed bulkheads. Dripping seawater from hairline fractures in the hull had rusted and eroded the walls and floors of the corridors. Small dribbles no greater than those from a leaky tap had over time formed impassable water barriers that filled entire decks of the ship.

After making their way to the outer corridors of the ship they entered a rusty airlock. Through one of the airlock's two small viewing windows, which were positioned at either side of the outer door, Miller could make out what seemed to be a relatively large ship.

"Is that a starship?"

"Yes, the Polaris. She's a science vessel."

"What the hell is a starship doing down here?"

"Granted she's clumsy underwater but it beats swimming." The airlock's rust-covered outer door squealed open and the group walked onto the Polaris. The clear air of the ship was welcoming after breathing the old, stale air of the Command Carrier.

"So, where is this Sanctuary? Let me guess, the lunar shipyards?"

"No they were destroyed as well." Miller raised an eyebrow as he tried to think of another place.

"Pluto's Duridium mines?"

"No, the Sanctuary is much closer than that."

"Then where?"

"You'll see."

Over three hours later the newly informed and updated squad were called out of the mess hall and up to the bridge. Miller looked out through the view port, straining to make out the shapes through the dark murky water. He could see a glow coming from the seabed in front of him. He couldn't tell what it was but it was definitely a light-source.

"Helm, slow to approach speed."

"Aye sir." The sandy seabed in view of the ship's lights gave way to a large sea-shelf. The squad gazed in awe as the scattered lights and domes of the Sanctuary came into view below them.

"Damn Sykes, you weren't kidding. This place is huge."

"Size is relative Mr Stone. Compared to the amount of people it holds, this place is a shoebox."

"You say they built this in under six months?"

"Some of it. The repair drones are still building domes now, I think there are three under construction at the moment."

"Impressive."

"I suppose so. Trouble is the construction of the new sections is taking up just about all the repair drones we have." Sykes sniggered. "Nothing much works around here."

"Sanctuary to Polaris, I'm not going to keep telling you Sykes, transmit your damn code before you cross the ridgeline."

"Sarah, honey, you have to learn to relax. All that negative energy can't be good for you."

"One of these days Sykes, I'm gonna follow procedure and activate the Laser Cannons. Let's see how relaxed you are after I cut your ship in half." Sykes grinned.

"Transmitting code now, honey."

"Use docking port six. The gantry on port four is flooded again, and stop calling me honey." The speakers fell silent as the controller ended the transmission.

"Oh yeah, she wants me." Miller and the squad continued to gaze out at the surrounding structures as the ship made its final approach towards the airlock.

"Look at that." Davidson looked out into the water, towards the area indicated by Stone's pointing finger. He could just make out five small craft as they sped by below them.

"They look like Sub-Orbital attack fighters. Mark Six if I'm not mistaken."

"Very good," praised Swan. "Are you a pilot?"

"Class Six clearance," interrupted Miller informatively. "If it has an engine Davidson can fly it."

"Yeah, he's crashed more ships than most people will ever fly," Deacon added sarcastically. The squad started to laugh.

"Well I wouldn't have to risk my ships extracting you assholes if you could shoot straight Deac', you cross-eyed fuck." The squad chuckled again.

"I had to co-ordinate the Personnel Carrier's missile launchers to fire at multiple targets, moving targets might I add. All you have to do is avoid hitting the ground. I believe the technical term is flying." Davidson grinned and nodded.

The deep and meaningful conversation continued until the

ship had successfully docked with the Sanctuary. After locking down the ship, Sykes and Swan led the squad into the relevant airlock. After the brief pressure equalisation cycle had finished the airlock hissed open and the group walked out.

"This is dome three, it houses most of our machine shops!" Swan shouted to be heard over the dozens of busy repair drones that all but filled the large chamber.

"What are they doing?"

"They're upgrading the roof supports. The engineers have just finished converting the level above this into a dry dock for the starships. We need to start treating the hulls before the rust from this damn salt water eats the whole fleet." Two fast approaching guards with Plasma Rifles halted the group's conversation.

"Do you have clearance to be in this dome sir?"

"Yes, we're going to see Iron-hand. I forwarded a message hours ago, he's expecting us."

"Who are you sir?" questioned one of the guards as he pulled a small computerised pad from its belt pouch. Sykes sighed.

"Captain Sykes of the Polaris. This is my first officer Swan and these are honoured guests." The guard checked the information on his pad.

"Sorry about that Captain, you're free to go."

"Thank you." The team walked on.

"Why do you call him Iron-hand?" Sykes grinned.

"You'll see." Swan and Sykes led the group through several corridors of the dome and into a turbo-lift. After Sykes gave the command the lift began to move, taking them all the way to the very top of the dome.

"Captain Hawkins sir, these are the soldiers I told you about. Sergeant Miller and his squad."

"Don't salute me Sykes, you know I hate that shit." Hawkins stood at the far side of the circular room stubbing out a cigarette into an ashtray on his desk. Miller couldn't help but notice the shiny metallic limb that hung in the place of his left hand and forearm.

"Sorry sir."

"Sergeant Miller." Hawkins asked as he scanned the new

faces.

"That would be me Captain." Miller kicked his heels together and saluted.

"Don't you start, he's bad enough." Miller grinned.

"Very well sir."

"I trust you and your squad have been properly briefed on our current situation."

"Yes sir. Might I say that from what I've heard, your ingenuity during the battle with the AI attack fleet, was worthy of a US Marine." Hawkins laughed.

"Well thanks Sergeant, but as I'm sure you'll agree, a commander is only as good as the men he commands." Miller nodded.

"Too true sir." The doors of the lift hissed open again and a young man stood nervously in the doorway. Clutching a stack of computerised pads.

"What is it Jacobs?"

"Progress reports from sector three Captain." Hawkins sighed.

"Put them on the desk." The young man deposited the stack of pads on top of the virtual mountain of pads that already graced the desk. In his rush to leave he accidentally knocked the desk as he turned and sent the entire pile clattering to the floor.

"I'm sorry sir." The boy's voice trembled as he began to scoop up the pads, his face displaying a look as though he was about to be flogged. Hawkins sighed and closed his eyes.

"Just leave it."

"Yes sir." The boy stood up and quickly made his exit into the turbo-lift.

"Jacobs." The boy turned.

"Yes, yes sir?"

"Relax."

"Yes sir, thank you sir." Zeus grinned as the lift doors closed.

"Good lad but he's too damn timid, you'd think growing up in this environment would have hardened the boy but..." Hawkins shrugged.

"Exactly how long have you all been down here Captain?" questioned Miller as he gazed out through one of the room's many large windows.

"We've been down here for almost eighteen months."

"How long have you been back on the planet?" asked Frost. "Sykes and Swan mentioned something about living on the surface for a while. Peru wasn't it?" Hawkins nodded.

"Yes that's where we decided to settle after we destroyed the mother-ship," he sighed and shook his head. "We thought it was over. We returned to Earth and began to build ourselves a new home, the great city in the highlands of Peru, overlooking the great rainforest. I don't know why the AI waited so long to mount its attack, maybe it was waiting for us to drop our guard, who knows, but attack it did. One morning dozens of spacial gateways opened above the planet. Through them came an armada of arrowhead fighters that headed straight for the planet, destroying any ship in their path. By a stroke of luck the city's defences had been completed earlier that day." Hawkins smiled. "Murphy's prototype Plasma Cannons," he sniggered. "We obliterated every last one of those bastards before they even cleared the atmosphere."

"Strange that something as logical as a computer would underestimate your defences."

"Ah but that's the thing. The Plasma Cannons were developed once we got back to Earth, until the AI attacked the city it had no idea that the Cannons existed."

"I see."

"At that point it was obvious that the city's location was no longer adequate. The site was chosen for its abundant resources and its aesthetic properties, not its tactical location. We all knew that the element of surprise was the only thing that saved us that day, we wouldn't have lasted five minutes against an all-out attack." Hawkins lit up a cigarette and took a long drag. "The only place we could go that gave us a chance of survival was under water."

"To hide yourselves from sensor scans?"

"Exactly. We already had huge stockpiles of raw materials at our disposal that were going to be used on the city. We relocated the materials and a veritable army of repair drones to the coast, changed the landing co-ordinates for the Ore Miners and started again. Most of the colonists spent weeks living out of submerged ships until enough of the new Sanctuary had been built to sustain them. Me, my crew and a few others stayed at the Peru site to keep up the appearance that someone was home."

"What happened to the Peru site?"

"We managed to fend off a couple more attacks. The System continued to send fighters down through the atmosphere every three weeks or so. Every time they attacked it got harder and harder to stop them. One evening it sent another contingent of fighter ships, this time they were accompanied by a mother-ship. The complex was destroyed in minutes, we were lucky to escape in one piece." Hawkins raised his prosthetic arm and clenched its metallic fist. "Well, almost one piece."

"The AI must know that you're down here, under the water somewhere. If that mother-ship's still in orbit, it will be searching for this place."

"Oh it's still up there alright. The fucking thing started sending drop-pods into the oceans about three months ago."

"Drop-pods?"

"Yeah, full of strange sea-bound machines. Its technology is getting better and better all the time. At first they were clumsy and slow, but it learns real quick. Every time it sends another wave the machines get better, faster, harder to stop."

"So you hunt the machines down and destroy them before they get a chance to start searching for the Sanctuary?"

"Yes, there are always at least two full sub-fighter squadrons on patrol around the clock."

"Where did you get those fighters? We saw some on the way in here. They appeared to be standard military issue."

"Well actually, we got the fighters from the Command Carrier you were found on. There was a flight bay full of hundreds of them. Although, with the force of the crash-landing only twenty were salvageable. Still, the crew of that thing made one hell of a landing considering it was never designed for atmospheric flight."

"How did you manage to get them to operate under water?"

"That I have no idea about. The engineers get the credit for the technical shit, I just run this circus."

"So what do you intend to do Captain? I mean it's only a matter of time until the AI finds this place."

"Yes I know. The trouble is we don't have a target to attack."

"Sorry Captain?"

"We don't have the technology to trace the origin of the jump-gates, the Anomalies that allow the AI to travel so fast."

"So they could be coming from anywhere?"

"Exactly, the only thing we can do is have a ship ready and waiting in space next time the AI jump-gates open."

"So you're gonna let the enemy vessel exit then send a ship back through the anomaly before it closes. Does it work both ways, can you send a ship back through an incoming gateway?"

"Yes."

"With all due respect Captain, how can you be sure?"

"Because we've been doing tests with our jump-drive system."

"You have jump-drive technology?"

"Not exactly, we have an Anomaly Drive Generator that we took from the first arrowhead fighter we destroyed. We managed to connect it to our ship but we haven't been successful in duplicating the technology. The engineers have tried to reverse engineer it, but we just can't seem to get any of the copies to work."

"So let's say that we can get a ship through one of the AI System's jump-gates, what then?"

"Then the ship would have to relay its co-ordinates and any useful info back to the Sanctuary before it was destroyed. It would be costly but at least we'd have a strike point. It's about time we got back on the offensive in this war." Hawkins walked over to one of the command chamber's windows and stared out into the darkness of the deep ocean. "We could use my ship, then at least there would be a chance of getting back without being killed but…" Hawkins stopped to find a reasonable way of putting the next sentence. Before he had chance Miller began to speak.

"But your Anomaly Drive Generator is too important to risk." Hawkins turned and looked at Miller, who continued to speak. "I understand how hard it is to justify sending men to their deaths Captain. God knows I've done it more times than I care to remember, but if you intend to attack the AI itself, you're gonna need that piece of technology." Hawkins nodded.

"I know Sergeant, but it still seems wrong."

"What if I offered you another solution?"

"I'm open to suggestions."

"What if it wasn't your only Anomaly Drive Generator?"

Inside one of the other domes of the Sanctuary, Kane was busy training a group of would-be engineers.

"Yes Johnson, it is faster to adapt a type three sensor node for underwater use. But the type four's have a far superior effective range."

"Sorry sir."

"Don't be, a good engineer should always be trying to make things more efficient, well done."

"Hawkins to Kane."

"Hang on guys. Kane here, what can I do for you Captain?"

"I need you to find Clarke and Blaine and meet me in the command chamber."

"Problems Captain?"

"Time to test the Laser Sword. Hawkins out."

"What is it Kane?" questioned one of the trainees as he noticed the concerned look on Kane's face.

"Not sure, I'll see you guys later." Kane walked off through the long dark passageway of the corridor away from the puzzled trainees. His boots splashed in the thin layer of water that always covered the floor down here on the lower levels under the domes. No matter how many times the repair drones swept the area for cracks and loose seals the water still managed to seep in.

Still, he thought, with the speed this place was built it was a miracle that it held the water out at all.

Clarke was flicking through pages of information on an enormous monitor screen as Kane entered the computer core room.

"You Clarke, how's it going man?"

"Slow, real slow. Where the hell have you been? I haven't seen you in weeks."

"Ah you know, here and there. I've been spending so much time in the tunnels under the domes that the trainees have started calling me tunnel rat." Clarke chuckled.

"Well if the shoe fits."

"How's the data-logging going?"

"I'm starting to think we've got all we're gonna get out of this databank. The rest of this stuff is either incomplete or too complicated for the computer to translate. Anyway, I doubt you came here to discuss my progress, do you need my help or something?"

"Or something. Hawkins wants to see us in his office."

"Any idea why?"

"Not really but he did say it was time to test the Laser Sword System."

"Oh shit."

"Funny, that's just what I was thinking." Clarke typed the security code into the keypad on the door as they left, locking down the whole chamber.

"I just know I'm gonna hate this." As the pair walked through the corridors Kane tried to reach Blaine on his communicator.

"Kane to Blaine come in please. Blaine, sound off. Where the hell is he?"

"He'll be in the flight bay with the pilots." Clarke looked at his watch. "If I'm not mistaken it's time for the weekly match."

The doors of the Sub-Fighter hangar opened to reveal a fight. Just about every chair and table in the hangar's seating area had been knocked over and cards were spread across the floor. A large group had gathered in the far corner of the bay and Kane and Clarke quickly walked over.

"I'm telling you, I had a straight flush," choked Blaine, who was being held up against the wall by a rather large and muscular man, his feet not quite touching the floor.

"Kiss my ass Blaine, you're a fucking cheat."

"Hey!" The crowd turned as Clarke shouted, he and Kane pushing their way towards Blaine. Taking advantage of the distraction, Blaine punched the large man as hard as he could in the face. His feet suddenly returned to the floor as the man dropped him. Ripping a wrench out of Kane's utility belt pouch, he swung it as hard as he could before the man had a chance to retaliate.

"I've told you before Rosa," Blaine boasted as he looked down at the now unconscious giant. "You bring the ass, I'll bring the whupin'." Blaine, Kane and Clarke waded back through the group and headed towards the door. "Nice timing guys."

"No problem."

Kane, Clarke and Blaine exited the turbo-lift and glanced around the room at the camo-clad soldiers. Clarke had no idea what was happening yet, but he knew he wasn't going to like it.

"You called Captain."

"Thanks for coming guys. This is Sergeant Miller and his squad. Sergeant, this is Kane, Clarke and Blaine; my crew." The squad and the Dark Star crew exchanged handshakes.

"You're the guys from the Command Carrier aren't you?" Miller looked surprised.

"Yes, does everyone know we're here already?"

"Small colony, news travels fast. Besides, it's not every day we find survivors from the massacre." Miller nodded.

"Should we get down to business?"

"By all means Captain." Hawkins looked at his crew.

"We're going to attack the mother-ship in orbit."

"Oh goody," remarked Blaine sarcastically.

"We're gonna attempt to take its jump-drive generator. We're gonna be handling the attack personally so I need our jump-drive generator disconnecting and leaving here, just in case." Kane nodded. "Sergeant Miller has volunteered to infiltrate the ship if we can disable it. If any of you don't want to do this tell me now, I won't hold it against you." Hawkins got no response. "OK, this is the plan. We're working on the assumption that the shield generators in this mother-ship are in the same place as those in the one we destroyed. If they are, the first thing we need to do is take one out with the Dark Star's Cannons."

"What if they're not?"

"You get to prove your skills at dodging incoming fire. We'll take two fighter squadrons with us to deal with any arrowhead fighters that might be up there." Hawkins pressed a few keys on his desk's keyboard and the blueprints of the Dark Star flashed up on the monitor. "Kane, we're gonna need a cargo bay converting into a launch deck."

"No problem."

"Mind if I make a suggestion?"

"Fire away Deac'."

"The Dark Star's torpedo tubes would be much more effective if they were repositioned." Deacon pointed at the monitor screen. "If they were placed in the bow, five on the port side and five on the starboard side, your shots would be much more accurate. Plus two or three in the stern about here, to slow down anything that might end up chasing us." Hawkins nodded.

"Is it possible Kane?"

"It's possible sir but it won't be easy."

"I'll give you whatever resources you need." Kane took another look at the blueprints on the screen.

"Yeah, I think I can pull it off."

"How long will it take?"

"From scratch about six weeks. If I reposition the torpedo launchers we already have, about three. Although, losing the underside launchers would make mining a lot more difficult."

"We have enough mining ships, what we're in need of is a gun ship." The group turned their attention back to the monitor screen as Hawkins brought up a copy of the arrowhead mother-ship blueprints. "Our scanners are unable to penetrate the hulls of the AI ships. We only have a small section of the internal deck plan that we obtained through an open cargo bay door, but it could be enough." Hawkins pointed at several spots on the diagram. "We think these are some sort of up-links to the ship's computer. If you can patch into one of them you should be able to find the location of the ship's jump-drive generator." Miller nodded.

"Do you think you can pull it of Deac'?"

"With Frost's help it should be possible."

"We'll keep the Dark Star docked with the mother-ship for as long as we can, but you're gonna have to hurry."

"Your team will have to do this in spacesuits Sergeant," enlightened Clarke. "The AI ships have no breathable atmosphere."

"That's gonna slow us down Sarge."

"I know Stone, but how long can you hold your breath?" Miller turned to Hawkins. "You know, if there are any of those AI fighter ships up there, you're gonna be sitting ducks when you're docked. I suggest we find another way to get my team in and out."

"We still have that breaching-pod that the last mother-ship hit us with. It shouldn't take too long to repair it."

"Good idea Blaine but no human could survive that kind of impact."

"Could we equip it with Cryo-pods, use their built-in inertial dampening systems like we did on the command Carrier?"

"You know, that just might work."

"Nice thinking Frost."

"Can you make it work Kane?"

"Maybe Captain, I'll have to take a look at it. We'd have to cut a hole into the mother-ship before we launched it. That pod wouldn't even scratch that thing's hull plating."

"Shouldn't be too much of a problem, all going well."

"How would the team get back out?" The room fell silent. Everyone looked around waiting for someone to offer an answer.

"Let me worry about that," offered Miller. "Just be ready to pick us up, we'll think of something."

"Anything else?"

"Yes Captain." Hawkins turned his attention to Davidson.

"What is it?"

"No disrespect intended, but how good are your fighter pilots?"

"As good as can be expected considering that they've only been flying military craft for a short time. Most of them were trained to fly starships."

"If you'd like I can give them a brief training course. We're gonna be waiting around for about a month anyway, whilst your ship is upgraded." Hawkins nodded.

"What do you think Sergeant?"

"It's a good idea. In fact, Davidson's piloting skills would be invaluable on the mission. I'll miss the backup inside the mother-ship but if I'm honest, I'd feel a lot better with him engaging the enemy vessels." Hawkins looked at Davidson.

"Are you really that good?"

"Class Six rating sir."

"Then I'll give you command of all twenty fighters. Can

you handle co-ordinating both wings?"

"No problem."

"Clarke, make sure the pilots understand. I don't want any of their shit on this mission."

"Aye sir. One hint of dissension and I'll drown them myself."

"OK then, if there's nothing further." Hawkins paused. "Let's get to it."

The next few weeks were extremely gruelling for the whole colony. Kane and his hand-picked team of engineers worked around the clock to complete the changes to the Dark Star and the other tasks set for them. Cargo bay three was painstakingly converted into a hangar and equipped with twenty separate launchers for the Sub-orbital fighters.

"Murphy, get those rails straight before you attach them. If they're not perfect when the fighters launch we could lose half the bay."

"No problem Kane, it's under control."

"Tony, bring me a laser torch. This bulkhead's gonna have to learn the hard way."

In between border patrols, Davidson trained the pilots ruthlessly. Leaving no manoeuvres untried, no scenarios unexplored. Slowly but surely the group of fighters became a squadron. Two combat ready Wings forming one solid group, with confidence and a thirst for the fight.

"That was the best run yet," congratulated Davidson as two of the squadrons climbed out of their ships. "If you can perform those manoeuvres under water you'll be untouchable in space." Davidson nodded approvingly.

"Davidson, how goes the training?" shouted Miller as he and Hawkins strolled into the hangar.

"Squad, fall in." The pilots quickly obeyed Davidson's bellowing and grouped up. "Who are we?"

"We have no name!" shouted the squad in unison. "You will know us by the trail of dead!" Davidson grinned smugly.

"Well they can talk bullshit well enough but can they fly?"

"They could fly a cargo ship backwards through an asteroid belt." Hawkins grinned.

"We'll see."

The day of the launch finally arrived and the atmosphere in the Sanctuary was chaotic. Equipment loaded and teams strapped in, the Dark Star, for the first time in months, lifted off. The wake from the great ship rocked patrol vessels and sensor towers as it slowly left the Sanctuary. Huddled together to find a view through the windows of the domes, the colonists watched and cheered. All that stood between the Dark Star and the mother-ship now was a few hours worth of undersea travel.

"OK Blaine, I think we're far enough away from the Sanctuary."

"Copy that sir, prepping ion engines for ignition."

"Sir, before we get started. Do you think we should send Reeva with the soldiers?" Hawkins raised an eyebrow.

"You know I'd completely forgotten about that thing." Hawkins activated his communicator. "Hawkins to Miller, how do you feel about a little extra manpower over there?"

"No disrespect sir, I know your crew is capable, but I think a civilian would just get in the way."

"Well I was thinking of a crew member, but something a little more impressive than the ones you've already met."

"Sorry Captain?"

"Open the breaching-pod door, I'll send her down. You can decide when you see her."

"Her?" questioned Miller in a rather startled tone.

"Trust me Sergeant." Hawkins stopped before disconnecting the transmission. "Oh and Miller."

"Yes Captain?"

"Don't shoot her, that's an order."

"Err, yes sir." Hawkins grinned as he ended the transmission and looked over at Clarke.

"Go for it." Clarke nodded and began typing on his keyboard.

"Reeva is back online sir." Clarke pushed the communications button on his armband. "Reeva, report to cargo bay one."

Miller and the squad were waiting in the cargo bay for the captain's last minute addition to their team. No one knew what to expect as the cargo bay door opened, but the sleek metallic cat was the last thing they had imagined.

"What the fuck?" Miller grabbed the front of Deacon's Plasma Rifle as he trained it on Reeva.

"Hold your fire."

"What is it Sarge?"

"I don't know Stone but I hope to god it's friendly." Reeva slowly crossed the cargo bay, the blades on her metal paws clanging on the grid metal floor as she walked. "Miller to Hawkins, what the hell is this thing?"

"It's an AI Hunter Drone, we acquired it a couple of years ago in Scotland. Don't worry we reprogrammed her, she's on our side."

"Where the hell was this thing? I'm pretty sure I would have noticed it running around the ship by now."

"We keep her powered-down when we don't need her. It conserves her power and, well, she has a habit of chewing things when she's bored."

"When she's bored? You mean this thing can think?"

"Oh yes. We've discovered that most AI drones have a rudimentary intelligence, roughly equal to that of a dog. But it only kicks in when they don't have an order to follow."

"So this thing can do whatever it wants to do?" Hawkins grinned.

"Don't sound so worried Sergeant, we'll keep her on a leash from up here. Hawkins out." Hawkins turned to Clarke. "Her programming prevents her from harming them, right?"

"Her programming prevents her from harming the four of us." Hawkins looked a little worried.

"Keep an eye on her."

"No problem." Hawkins sat back down and strapped himself in.

"Blaine, whenever you're ready."

"Aye sir, ignition sequence engaged." The bridge began to rumble as the engines built up power.

"Hawkins to all hands, anyone not strapped in is gonna be a stain on the back wall in exactly ten seconds."

"Confirm that Blaine."

"Ignition in eight seconds."

"There's gonna be a burst of acceleration as we break free of the water."

"Thanks Clarke."

"Here goes nothing." The force pushed everyone back against their seats as Blaine hit the power. The Dark Star swayed from side to side as it forced its way through the water.

"Breaking the surface now." A sudden jolt of acceleration forced back Blaine's cheeks, as they broke free from the resistance of the water.

"Clarke, I need a course heading."

"Hold on a second, switching to non-aquatic sensors. OK, course heading two-thirty-six mark four-five."

"Two-thirty-six mark four-five confirmed. Coming about."

"What do you see up there Clarke?"

"I'm still getting some interference from the water on the sensors sir, but it looks like an arrowhead mother-ship and three arrowhead fighters." Hawkins looked at the small tactical display screen on his chair-arm as Clarke patched the information through.

"Correct course heading to bring us up behind the mother-ship."

"Aye sir. Blaine, new course heading zero-two-five mark four-eight."

"No problem."

"We should be breaking orbit in about twenty seconds Captain."

"Let me know the second it's safe to open the pressure doors on cargo bay three."

"Aye sir."

"This is Hawkins, all fighters prepare for launch."

"We've been detected sir. All three arrowhead fighters are on the move."

"Activate the Laser Sword System."

"Aye sir, system activated."

"Shields armed and holding sir."

"Thanks Kane."

"All cannons are raised and locked. Breaking orbit now sir, it's safe to open the bay doors."

"Do it. OK, here we go. Hawkins to cargo bay three, all fighters launch." Led by Davidson, all twenty fighters screamed out of the Dark Star as she sped past the arrowhead mother-ship.

"Davidson to first wing, engage the first two ships to your left. Second wing follow me." The arrowhead fighters split up as Davidson's squadrons fired their Plasma Cannons.

"Davidson to Hawkins, we have the fighters under control. The mother-ship's all yours."

"Well done Davidson, keep 'em off us for as long as you can." Hawkins took a deep breath. "OK, same attack plan as last time, get me a lock on that shield generator."

"Cannons charged and ready, frequency modulator is online."

"Coming about, we'll be in position in ten seconds." Once again Clarke brought up the internal deck plan of the arrowhead mother-ship. He superimposed it over the picture of the actual ship on his targeting screen and locked all four cannons on the superimposed picture of the generator.

"All stop sir."

"Target locked."

"Fire." Through the main view port the crew watched the mother-ship's shield glow as it absorbed the energy from the lasers.

"It didn't work."

"Hold on, I'll increase the frequency modulation rate."

"The mother-ship is turning towards us."

"Come on Kane, come on."

"OK."

"Fire." The orange glow of the shield faltered and dispersed as the lasers passed through it and cut into the hull.

"Got it, the generator is toast sir."

"Blaine back us off. Hawkins to Miller, get ready."

"Full-yield torpedoes prepped and ready Captain."

"Fire."

"Torpedoes away."

"The ship will be facing us in about twelve seconds sir. I'm detecting an energy build-up." The light of the blast caused Hawkins to squint as the torpedoes hit.

"Shock wave incoming." The ship rocked as the shock wave hit.

"Report."

"Direct hit to the mother-ship's port mid-section. I'm

detecting a hull breach with a rough diameter of about ten metres."

"Perfect. Hawkins to Miller, you're up in five. Clarke launch the breaching-pod."

"Aye sir, cargo bay door opening."

"Sir we need to move."

"Strafe right Blaine, turn with it."

"Aye sir."

"Bay doors open, launching pod now." The tracking monitor on Clarke's console began to beep as the breaching-pod rocketed out of cargo bay one.

"OK Blaine, punch it." Blaine threw the power lever as the mother-ship discharged its energy weapon. The energy beam blasted past the stern of the Dark Star, missing her by sheer inches as she moved.

"Sweet Jesus!" shouted Blaine in sheer panic. "Was that as close as it felt?"

"Any closer and we'd be missing our ass end."

"What's the status of Miller's team?"

"The pod hit its target perfectly sir, they're fine. I can't reach them on the Com, it must be that damn hull plating. I'm still getting a strong signal from Reeva though."

"Put her on point in front of the squad, tell her to protect them."

"The mother-ship is still trying to get a lock on us Captain."

"What about the fighters?"

"Davidson's squadrons are still engaging. The arrowhead fighters are faster than ours, but they're being easily out-manoeuvred."

"Put it on the main view screen." As the view screen lit up Hawkins grinned. The small, six metre long sub-fighters were swarming like bees around the half-mile long arrowhead fighters. Many explosions lit up the blackness of the surrounding space as shot after shot was fired towards the four overwhelmed vessels. Blaine continuously made course changes as rapidly as the Dark Star's design would allow. Spinning around the mother-ship, utilising its lack of manoeuvrability.

Miller and the squad had survived the initial impact from the breaching-pod's landing and were attempting to get their bearings.

"Speak to me Deac'."

"Hold on sir." The squad had located one of the devices that were assumed to be computer up-link consoles. Frost and Deacon were attempting to tap into the system.

"Don't tell me to hold on, tell me where the fucking generator is." Deacon hooked up a small pad to the device and began to type on its keypad.

"This thing is hooked straight into the main computer, it's trying to block me."

"Zeus, Stone, secure those two corridors."

"Yes sir."

"Damn this thing's fast."

"Can you tap into that thing or not?"

"It's not that simple, I can't just ask it where the generator is, I'm trying not to give away what we're looking for."

"Sarge, we're not alone in here."

"What is it Stone?"

"Not sure sir." Stone stood looking at his forearm sensor pad. "There's a lot of movement about a mile down this corridor and it's heading this way."

"You hear that Deac'?"

"Almost got it."

"How fast is it moving Zeus?"

"Not that fast, but fast enough to catch us while we're in these pressure-suits."

"Got it, ah shit."

"What is it?"

"The reactor is in a large chamber about three quarters of a mile from here." Miller sighed.

"You know, I'm starting to think I'm being punished for something I did in a previous life."

"With the luck we're having you must have been Hitler."

"Zeus, do you think we can keep ahead of whatever's heading this way?"

"Not a chance sir."

"Try to contact the Dark Star again. See if they can take out the artificial gravity on this thing, we'll use the thrusters on the pressure-suits."

"Dark Star come in please. Come in Dark Star." Frost waited for a response. "Dark Star, respond." Frost shook his head. "The transmission's not getting through, it must be this thing's hull plating." The floor of the corridor suddenly began to rumble and overhead lights flickered.

"What the hell was that?"

"It must be the Dark Star."

"They couldn't have heard us, the message never got through the hull." Miller jumped as Reeva rubbed her nose on his leg.

"What the hell is this thing doing?" Miller looked thoughtfully at her as she stood in front of him. "I wonder." He knelt down and looked into Reeva's eyes. "If you guys can here me, make this cat sit down." Sure enough Reeva sat down on the floor of the corridor. Miller smiled. "Perfect."

"OK guys, we can contact the ship by talking to the cat."

"This shit gets stranger by the minute man." The ship rumbled again and this time the lights failed completely.

"They did it, the power's offline."

"No shit Frost," replied Miller sarcastically as he floated around in the dark.

Back outside the now crippled mother-ship posed little threat to Hawkins and his crew.

"OK Blaine, bring us about. Bearing one-seven-three mark zero-one."

"Aye sir, one-seven-three mark zero-one."

"Clarke, let's lend our fighters a hand."

"My pleasure sir, targeting closest arrowhead fighter. The targeting scanners won't lock onto its hull, I'm gonna have to do this manually."

"Hawkins to Davidson, make your boys aware that we're gonna fire."

"Davidson here, no problem."

"Ready when you are Captain."

"At your leisure Clarke." Clarke trailed the targeting crosshairs in front of the speeding AI fighter. He made one final check to ensure that no friendly ships were in his line of fire and engaged the cannon on top of the Dark Star.

"Dorsal Cannon activated." The cannon fired out a beam

directly in the flight path of the fighter as it approached. Hawkins watched through the main view port as the vessel flew straight through the beam, betrayed by its own momentum, and then dropped out of view.

"Track it Clarke, don't lose it!"

"Which half?"

Meanwhile, inside the mother-ship, the squad was making record-breaking progress.

"Boo-yeah, this is the only way to travel." The squad was travelling through the zero-gravity environment of the corridors at speed. Using their pressure-suit thrusters to propel them forward.

"How long Deac'?"

"At this speed, we'll be there in under a minute." Deacon followed the internal map he had downloaded from the computer up-link.

"How's the trail look Zeus?"

"Whatever I'm detecting is still behind us. Although we seem to be gaining ground on it."

"How the hell is that thing staying on the floor?" questioned Stone in reference to Reeva who was running along in front of them.

"I don't know man, but if that one can do it you can bet your ass the rest can too."

"Oh, great."

"Sarge, I'm picking up a lot of movement in the section ahead of us."

"How far?"

"The closest signal is about eight hundred metres ahead."

"Be ready guys." Miller cocked his Plasma Rifle.

"How much of the internal layout did you get Deac'?"

"Looks like all of it. I've got deck layouts, technical schematics and what looks like co-ordinates for something."

"Any idea what?"

"No, but it'll probably make more sense to Hawkins."

"Coming up on the generator's co-ordinates Sarge."

"What about the movement?"

"The closest signal is coming from the same location."

"Of course it is. What about the movement behind us?"

"Still with us Sarge." The reverse thrusters on the spacesuits hissed noisily as the squad slowed down. As they came to a halt, they engaged their magnetic gravity boots and returned to the solid metal floor of the corridor.

"Are you sure these are the right co-ordinates Deac'?" Deacon checked the deck plan.

"Yep, right behind that wall."

"So, no door?"

"Not that I can identify sir." Miller shook his head.

"OK, let's do it the hard way, for a change. The centre of that panel on my mark." The squad took aim with their rifles. "Fire." The soldiers all opened fire at the same spot on the wall. The intense heat from the superheated plasma easily melted the metal alloy. When he was satisfied that they had created a large enough hole Miller ordered the team to stop. "Hold your fire!" he shouted over the racket from the discharging weapons. The shiny smooth wall now gave way to the glowing edges of its freshly installed and smouldering door. "OK, two by two, left and right, move, move, move." The squad carefully made their way into the adjacent chamber, their rifles raised in readiness.

"Left side clear."

"Right side secured sir." Miller looked around the room.

"I thought you said something was moving around in here Zeus?" Frost's face suddenly disappeared as he spat blood over the inside of his helmet visor. Zeus looked upto the roof above Frost, where a large spherical object was clung to the ceiling. One of its many limbs stretched out, skewering Frost in the back.

"No!" he raised his rifle and fired at the machine, blowing it loose of the roof. The rest of the squad opened fire as Miller made his way over to Frost.

"Frost, speak to me man." Frost clutched Miller's arm tightly, his eyes flicked around the room in a state of shock and panic. "Hold on man, I'll get you outta here." Frost managed to compose himself slightly as he drew his face closer to Miller's. His words were barely audible as he choked on his own blood.

"Anything you want me to tell Williams and Hanson?"

"Stop talking shit soldier, you're gonna be fine." Miller could feel Frost's grip on his arm loosening. "Don't you fucking die on me Frost, that's an order." Frost released his grip as his body went limp. Miller screwed his eyes up and hung his head.

"Sarge, the movement in this section is getting awfully close." Miller took a deep breath and stood up. Frost's body slowly drifted away from him as he released it.

"Stone, Zeus, go and stand over by the door with the cat. Keep your eyes open."

"Yes sir."

"Deacon, give me a hand with this generator."

The bridge of the Dark Star was calm and quite. Hawkins stood at the main view port in front of Blaine's station, looking out into space with a contented grin on his face.

"Davidson is requesting permission to bring his squadrons in sir."

"Any casualties?"

"All fighters present and accounted for." Hawkins nodded.

"Bring them in."

"Aye sir."

"Kane, what's the status of the Laser Sword System?"

"All cannons read as fully operational. I noticed that the beam on the ventral cannon was fluctuating slightly under sustained fire, but it's nothing I can't adjust."

"Perfect, a successful test."

"Captain, shouldn't we try to salvage the technology from one of those fighters?" Blaine pointed out through the view port. "We could at least pull some of the smaller pieces into one of the cargo bays."

"Those sections could still be crawling with god knows what. I'm not about to roll out the red carpet for them."

"The signal from Reeva is coming back online, the squad must be moving closer towards the hull."

"Do they have the generator?"

"Bear with me sir, the transmission is still very faint."

"Blaine, fire her up, be ready."

"Aye sir."

"The transmission's clearing up sir. Miller has the generator and…" Clarke stopped.

"What is it?"

"One of the squad is down sir. The big man is dragging

him."

"Where are they?"

"They're about six hundred yards from the breach."

"Blaine."

"On it sir." Blaine started to move the Dark Star into position.

"There's something else sir, Reeva's sensors are going ballistic."

"What is it?"

"Hold on. Reeva, identify movement ahead." The picture on Clarke's overhead monitor started to zoom in as Reeva altered her view. Her optical sensors adjusted allowing him to see what she was detecting further along the corridor. "Jesus."

"What is it?"

"There's a whole group of machines waiting by the breach."

"Could they be some kind of repair drones?"

"They're not repairing the breach sir, they're just stood waiting." Clarke looked at Hawkins. "The personal sensor devices that the squad carry are little more than biological sensors and motion trackers. If the machines don't move they won't be able to detect them."

"Smart, very fucking smart." Hawkins thought for a moment. "Can we clear them out with the Laser Cannons?"

"There's no time sir, the squad's almost there."

"Open me a channel."

"Aye sir, but I don't think they're close enough to the breach to receive it."

"Hawkins to Miller. Miller, come in. Miller, come in god damn it."

Miller and the squad continued to follow Reeva along the corridor. Unable to receive the transmission from Hawkins they sped along blindly towards their doom.

"Are you sure Zeus?"

"Certain sir, I'm no longer detecting any movement down here."

"I thought we were being tailed?" Miller engaged his pressure-suit's reverse thrusters. "Hold on, something isn't right here." The squad halted. "Stone, your rifle please." Stone was the squad's best marksman. His rifle was equipped with a long range targeting scope for sniping. Miller looked through the scope and zoomed in along the corridor. "Dirty metal bastards."

"What is it Sarge?"

"There are about twelve machines standing around near the hull breach. The sneaky bastards were just waiting for us to fly into them."

"What now sir?"

"Now Deac', I'm gonna give this rifle back to Stone, and smile while he clears us a path." Miller handed Stone the rifle.

"They look like big spiders or something." Stone described what he was seeing through his scope. "They must be five feet tall."

"Can you hit 'em from here?"

"No problem." Stone took aim on the closest machine and pulled the trigger. The blue tint of the plasma bolt disappeared out of Miller's view as it flew down the corridor. "Damn."

"What?"

"Just a second sir." Stone knelt down on one knee to steady his aim before firing off multiple shots towards the machines. He watched through the rifle's scope as the bolts of plasma hit the machines and dispersed.

"Well?"

"No effect sir, I didn't even scratch 'em. It's like shooting at a tank."

"OK, everybody aim along the corridor." The squad obeyed. "Fire at will." Shot after shot the squad sent speeding balls of super-hot plasma crashing into the machines. Stone watched through his scope as he fired. "Hold your fire. Did we get 'em Stone?"

"We hit 'em, but all we did is piss 'em off." Stone looked up at Miller. "They're coming this way sir."

"Deacon, are there any other ways off this ship?"

"Not unless you want to take a three mile trek to the closest cargo bay."

"God damn it!"

"Which way?"

"Straight down below us."

"Fuck me!"

"Sarge, I'm detecting movement closing from behind us."

"How far?"

"Maybe two thousand yards." Miller looked back down the corridor towards the now, barely visible machines.

"We're gonna have to go for it."

"Sarge?"

"Let's find out how fast you can dodge in a spacesuit."

"Sarge, this is crazy."

"Do you have a better idea?" Miller shouted. "Now come on, everybody behind me. Zeus get the generator."

"What about Frost sir?"

"Leave him Zeus."

"But sir."

"You're not slowing yourself down for a body Zeus, now get the fucking generator." With a look of shame on his face Zeus released his grip on Frost's body. He watched as it slowly drifted away from him.

"I'm sorry Frost."

"OK let's move." Miller held down the buttons for his suit's thrusters and accelerated towards the approaching machines. "Spread out. No matter what happens, get that generator out of here. Do you all hear me?"

"Yes sir." Reeva sped off in front of the squad along the floor and smashed into the foremost machine. Miller watched as the surrounding machines closed in and tore her apart.

"Come on." The machine attacked by Reeva was drifting around, thrashing its limbs wildly. Miller saw his opening as it drifted upside down, partially shielding an area from the other machines. He couldn't help but tense up as he reached the blade-covered arachnids.

"Don't stop!" shouted Deacon as one of the machines stopped him in his tracks. Stone could hear nothing but the sound of motors and blades slicing through the air.

"Bring it on!" shouted Zeus as he watched his gap through the machines disappear. He pushed the generator as hard as he could and sent it flying clear as he smashed into the moving barrier. He grabbed the flailing mandibles of the machine looming over Deacon and wrestled with it, muscle against motor.

"Deac', get outta here."

"Come on."

"I can't hold this thing for…" Zeus exhaled heavily as another of the drones forced a limb through his torso. Still he held the machine off Deacon.

"Zeus, no!" Deacon discharged his rifle at the machine. Another set of bladed limbs cut Zeus down from his right hand side, sending the machine he was trying to hold, crashing down on top of his friend. After placing the generator by the hull breach, Miller went back for his team. He grabbed the strap of Stone's chest rig and pulled him off of the blade that had passed through his shoulder. Stone fired at the attackers as Miller dragged him away.

"Miller to Hawkins, come in." Miller looked out through the breach, trying to locate the ship. "Come in damn it."

"Hawkins here, hold on we're coming."

"Sarge!" Miller turned to see the machines almost upon them again. He took a couple of deep breaths and dragged Stone and the generator out into open space.

"Captain, I could use a little help here." His suit's thrusters out of fuel, Miller could do nothing but drift and wait.

Hawkins and Kane rushed into the cargo bay. Stone and Miller had removed their helmets and were lying on their backs panting.

"Are you two OK?" Miller looked up at Hawkins.

"No Captain, I'm pretty fucking far from OK."

"Kane, get Stone to the medical bay."

"Aye sir." Kane picked Stone up off the floor and walked him out of the cargo bay. Miller stood up and started to remove his pressure-suit.

"I'm sorry about your squad Miller. They were all brave men."

"They were the bravest men I've ever met." Hawkins nodded solemnly.

"Hawkins to Clarke, get in touch with the Sanctuary, I want a ship up here to search through the fighter wreckage."

"Aye sir."

"Blaine, lay in a course back home."

"No problem Captain."

"Oh yeah, and Clarke?"

"Yes sir."

"Finish off that fucking mother-ship."

"My pleasure sir. Clarke out." Hawkins turned his gaze back to Miller.

"Let's make sure they didn't die for nothing."

CHAPTER: 14

Hawkins sat in his office with the lights out. His ashtray was full now and the bottom of his whisky bottle was within reach. Even as he stared out into the blackness of the uninviting ocean, he couldn't help but think that they had been lucky. Sure he was sitting in the only quiet place in the Sanctuary and yes, due to the overcrowding he slept here too. The constant daily struggle to hold the water out of the fast constructed domes had been the mental end for two engineers already. In his inebriated state it amused him when he thought that these people were, technically, the lucky ones.

"Clarke to Hawkins."

"Yes Clarke."

"The jump-drive generator's reinstalled in the Star Captain. The crew of the Polaris managed to salvage two more from the wrecked AI fighters."

"Any casualties?"

"Three dead sir, Captain Sykes, his first mate Swan and one of the engineers. I think they said his name was Barrows."

"Any families or loved ones?"

"No sir."

"Log them into the casualties register. Reassign their quarters to someone who needs them."

"I think they all lived on the Polaris sir."

"Then find Captain Fletcher, he's been without a ship for months. Have him move onto the Polaris and reassign his quarters."

"Aye sir."

"Make sure he picks his two crew replacements from sector eight. God knows those people could use somewhere comfortable to sleep."

"Consider it done sir." Hawkins gulped down the last of the

whisky and placed the bottle clumsily on the desk. He sat for a few seconds pondering on an idea that had been troubling him for some hours now.

"In fact Clarke, get someone else to sort that out. I want you to find Miller and the boys and bring them all up here as soon as possible."

"Err, OK sir. Sir?"

"Yes."

"Is everything OK?"

"You can draw your own conclusion when you've heard what I have to say."

"Yes sir. Sorry sir."

"Don't worry about it. Oh yeah, make sure Kane brings a supply inventory with him. I need a list of every spare component we have."

"No problem sir."

"Thanks Clarke, Hawkins out."

Three weeks later Hawkins called a meeting of the entire colony. Every man, woman and child was ordered to attend. A gathering such as this had not taken place since the abandonment of the Peru Sanctuary. No one knew why the meeting had been called but everyone knew something was terribly wrong.

"Quieten down everyone!" Clarke shouted down from the gantry above the crowd, where he and his shipmates stood. "I want order, now." Sure enough the chattering roar of the crowd gradually subsided. Hawkins stepped forward and leant on the cold metal safety rail that surrounded the platform. He took a slow sweeping glance around the packed storage chamber and began to speak.

"Good evening, thank you all for coming." Hawkins paused and took a deep breath. "As you all probably know by now, Sergeant Miller and his squad managed to obtain a wealth of information during the attack on the orbiting AI mother-ship." Hawkins held up his hand to silence the crowd as they began to clap. "What most of you probably don't know is that the information had with it a set of co-ordinates. Co-ordinates that we believe could be the location of the AI System." The room filled with the sound of chattering and once again Hawkins raised a quieting hand. "Tonight an attack force will be launched to those co-ordinates to determine whether or not the AI System is there."

"What if it is?" came a voice from the crowd.

"Then we send it straight to hell." Kane pushed a button on a small pad he was holding and a large three-dimensional picture appeared in the air above the crowd. The looming cylindrical projection twisted and turned to provide a full view from anywhere in the room. "What you are seeing!" Hawkins shouted to be heard above the ever-increasing din. "Is the design schematic for a crystalline explosive device. Kane and Sergeant Miller have been developing it over the last three weeks. It's basically a large crystalline reactor that's been hooked upto the Sonic Pulse Generator from the Dark Star. In theory, creating a power feedback loop through the crystals should cause an explosion. Doing this whilst the crystals are under the influence of the Sonic Pulse Generator should increase that energy release a hundred fold."

"How do you know that will be enough?" came another question from somewhere in the crowd. Hawkins smiled.

"My friend, we'll be lucky if this explosion doesn't wake the gods." The crowd was divided now between faces displaying excitement and faces that displayed an obvious look of worry. This made Hawkins' next statement even more difficult. "The AI mother-ship had plenty of time to send a distress call when we attacked it, as such, the AI System probably knows that we are now able to launch an attack. Taking into account that it's probably expecting us, I feel that a large-scale attack will have been anticipated and would fail. Using our Sub-fighters as a diversion, the Dark Star and the Polaris alone will attempt this assault. With only two ships, we'll be able to exit the anomaly gate much faster without risking collisions. Both ships will be equipped with a crystalline explosive device to ensure that at least one ship completes the mission."

"Who will be commanding the Dark Star Captain?" Hawkins scanned the crowd for the familiar female voice.

"Ah Commander Redmond." Hawkins smiled. "The only person that leads my ship into battle is me." The crowd's mood turned to one of chaos.

"But surely someone else should take command of the

ship?"

"Your place is here." Hawkins raised his hand again and the crowd slowly quietened down.

"Let's not kid ourselves, this mission is more than likely a one way trip. I will not and cannot allow anyone to take my chair just in the interest of saving my own ass. However, I realise that a commander's place is here with the colony." Hawkins paused for a moment. "I would therefore like to name First Officer Eugene Clarke of the Dark Star as my successor." Clarke's face dropped as Hawkins turned to face him and gave a salute. The crowd looked almost as shocked as he did and stood in total silence.

"What the hell are you doing?" Clarke whispered as he tried to keep his composure.

"Eugene Clarke, your bravery and strength of character has been proven time and time again whilst serving at my side. I have no doubt that you are more than worthy to serve this colony as leader and protector." Hawkins smirked, still holding his salute.

"Oh, you dirty bastard!"

"Do you except the responsibility that has been charged to you and promise to defend this colony and its people with your very life?" Hawkins leaned a little closer to Clarke and whispered. "You'd better say something, they're not going to stand there forever."

"But I'm not, I mean…"

"Stop babbling Clarke, if I didn't think you could handle it I wouldn't be offering you the position. You said you'd like your own command."

"I meant a starship not the whole colony!"

"In at the deep end as they say." Hawkins took a deep breath and shouted. "Do you accept?"

"On my honour and my life, I accept." The sound of thousands of boots hitting the floor made Clarke jump as the entire room saluted. He looked out over the sea of faces and smiled. "Thank you Captain, thank you all. Well we have a lot of work to do so I suppose we'd better get moving." Clarke looked at Hawkins who smiled and nodded his head. Clarke shook his head and grinned in disbelief as he turned back to the crowd and shouted. "Dismissed!"

The preparations for the launch kept most of the colony busy for the rest of the day. The sudden change in leadership lead to many mixed opinions but everybody that knew Clarke had no doubt that he was worthy of his new position.

"So the explosive devices can be activated with these remotes?"

"They can only be activated with those remotes. I thought it would be safer to have only one triggering mechanism for these things."

"Yeah, probably a good idea. So once I press this button, how long do we have before it blows?"

"There is no time delay sir. I didn't want to give the AI System the chance to break the encryption code before it blows."

"So the second I press this button..."

"Goodbye everything that isn't out of range." Hawkins nodded.

"Fair enough. Did you explain this to Captain Fletcher?"

"Captain Fletcher and the entire crew of the Polaris have been informed how to use their device."

"Well done Kane."

"No problem Captain."

"Blaine, how's she look?"

"Ready to rock sir."

"Hawkins to Polaris, are you ready to fly?"

"Fletcher here, lead the way."

"Miller, give me a gateway."

"Jump-drive generator engaged Captain, anomaly forming two thousand metres below the ship."

"Launch the fighters."

"Miller to Davidson, launch when ready."

"I'm always ready Sarge." A great roar of thrusters echoed through the ship as Davidson's two fighter wings rocketed out of the cargo bay.

"Fighters entering the gateway now Captain."

"OK Blaine, let's do it."

"Engines to full burn, here we go." Hawkins watched through the view port as the ships descended into the whirlpool-like vortex beneath them. As always the forces exerted on them by the gravity well disorientated the crew. Momentarily distorting reality, as they perceived it. The immense gravitational forces bent the very timeline around them as they passed through.

"Returning to normal space sir." Hawkins shook off the disorientation quickly and returned his attention to the view port.

"Jesus." For a moment he froze as he stared out at what appeared to be a large asteroid. Dozens of AI fighter ships tore through the space around them, engaging Davidson's totally overwhelmed Sub-fighters. Upon a second look at the spinning asteroid, Hawkins noticed several large structures embedded in its surface. "This is it. Blaine, head for that rock."

"Aye sir."

"Miller, see what you can do about those fighters."

"Way ahead of you Captain." The Dark Star's Laser Cannons began to fire as Blaine began to manoeuvre through the enemy fighters.

"Davidson to Hawkins, we're getting…" Davidson's transmission turned to static.

"Miller to Davidson. Davidson, Davidson come in."

"He's gone Miller."

"Davidson, come in."

"Miller, concentrate damn it or we're all dead."

"Captain look." Blaine drew Hawkin's attention to a section of the asteroid as it revolved into view. An enormous skeletal framework crawling with repair drones was protruding from one of the structures on the mammoth rock.

"It's a mother-ship! It's building another mother-ship!"

"Jesus, look at all those drones crawling on it. No wonder it can replace the ships we destroy so fast." Hawkins gripped the armrests on his seat as a large shock wave shook the ship.

"Report."

"The Polaris has been hit sir, she's no longer registering on my screen."

"Fuck. It's down to us Blaine, keep us in one piece."

"No problem Captain. These arseholes couldn't hit the side of a barn with…" Blaine's boasting ceased as the Dark Star bolted violently. Shaking the crew like rag dolls in their safety harnesses.

"We're hit! We're hit!"

"Propulsion is down. Kane, I got no control."

"Kane, any hull breaches?"

"We took a direct hit. The ventral stern on the starboard side is gone. The lower seventeen decks are open to space. Energy seals are holding."

"Blaine, slow her down. Retro rockets, thrusters, anything!"

"I got nothing sir." Blaine looked out through the forward view port towards the rapidly closing asteroid. "The helm is dead." Hawkins looked out through the view port where Blaine's eyes were fixed. The asteroid appeared to be spinning due to the Dark Star's erratic, uncontrolled approach.

"Vacate the bridge."

"Sir?"

"Get outta here!" he shouted as he rushed to remove his harness. The crew followed his example and headed for the bridge's rear access door. Hawkins watched the surface of the asteroid closing in on the view port as the doors hissed shut.

"Get down on the floor, brace your feet against something that faces the bow. This is gonna be bad." The lights of the corridor were replaced with deafening noise and darkness as the ship collided with the asteroid's surface. Miller cried out into the darkness as he felt a tremendous pressure against his stomach. He didn't know what it was but he could not move.

Hawkins regained consciousness and slowly sat up. He wrestled to free himself from whatever it was that had him pinned to the ground. From the pain he was in, his arm was obviously broken. The corridor was totally black and he had no idea where his crewmates were. He couldn't even see his own hand as he blindly felt around the walls for the emergency support locker.

"Who's that?" he whispered into the darkness as he heard someone cough.

"It's Miller, that you Captain." Hawkins finally managed to find the flush locker door in the corridor wall. He fumbled around inside it and managed to find what felt like a torch. Miller frowned in disbelief as the new light source illuminated the large support strut that passed straight through his gut. Hawkins closed his eyes and looked away, unable to handle the sight as the torchlight hit upon his pinned and skewered crew. Large shards of collapsed bulkhead and tarnished lengths of metal that had speared the bridge's door now ran red with the flowing blood of his friends. Hawkins gathered his strength and moved over to help Miller.

"It's no good," he sighed as he failed to free Miller. Miller coughed and shook his head, a trickle of blood running from the side of his mouth.

"It doesn't matter now." Miller coughed again, spraying blood across Hawkins. "Strange, but it doesn't hurt." Miller grinned and dropped his head back against the bridge's door. "That can't be a good sign."

"I'll go and fetch a laser torch to cut you free." The whole corridor rocked as something impacted with the ship. Hawkins quickly grabbed one of the fallen pieces of metal as the air began to rush out of the corridor. "The section's breached." Hawkins clumsily rushed along the corridor to the closest internal pressure door. He opened the emergency panel on the wall beside it and began to pump the manual priming lever. When he was sure that the air pressure in the pistons was sufficient, he pushed the button beside the door and it hissed closed.

"What was that?"

"Not sure, it couldn't have been from an energy weapon or we wouldn't be having this conversation." Hawkins winced as he knocked his broken arm on a section of the fallen roof.

"What then?" Miller coughed another load of blood from his lungs. Hawkins turned to face the pressure door, as the sound of movement became apparent beyond it.

"Breaching-pods." The smooth flat surface of the door buckled inwards as something smashed into it. Hawkins stood calmly in defiance.

"Any ideas Captain?" A sudden eerie look of calmness spread across Hawkins' face as he turned to look at Miller. He reached into his pocket and took out the remote detonator for the crystalline explosive device, looked at Miller and began to speak.

"Yea, though I walk through the valley of the shadow of death I will fear no evil." Miller nodded at Hawkins, spat one last mouthful of blood and replied with a grin. "For I carry a big stick, and I'm the meanest mother-fucker in the valley."